PENGUIN

EVERYTHING WAS GOOD-BYE

GURJINDER BASRAN's debut novel, *Everything Was Good-bye,* was the winner of the Search for the Great B.C. Novel Contest in 2010 and was awarded the 2011 Ethel Wilson Fiction Prize for the most outstanding work of fiction by a B.C. author. As a manuscript, *Everything Was Good-bye* was a semifinalist for Amazon.com's 2008 Breakthrough Novel Award and earned Basran a place in *The Vancouver Sun's* annual speculative arts and culture article, "Ones to Watch." Basran studied creative writing at Simon Fraser University and the Banff Centre, and currently lives in Delta, British Columbia, with her husband and two sons.

Gurjinder Basran

EVERYTHING *was* GOOD-BYE

PENGUIN

an imprint of Penguin Canada

First published by Mother Tongue Publishing Limited, 290 Fulford-Ganges Road, Salt Spring Island, B.C.,
V8K 2K6, 2010
Published in this edition, 2012

5 6 7 8 9 10 (WEB)

Manufactured in Canada.

Book design by Mark Hand

LIBRARY AND ARCHIVES CANADA CATALOGUING IN PUBLICATION

Basran, Gurjinder
     Everything was good-bye : a novel / Gurjinder Basran.

ISBN 978-0-14-318257-3

     I. Title.

PS8603.A789E93 2012   C813'.6   C2011-907810-4

www.penguinrandomhouse.ca

 Penguin
Random House
PENGUIN CANADA

For my mother and my sisters,
who taught me that love and strength have many forms

ACKNOWLEDGEMENTS

Sat, Amit and Arun for their love and understanding in this and all things.

My publisher, Mona Fertig, for her kind partnership when it came to all aspects of the publication of this book. My editor, Cheryl Cohen, for her commitment to the writing and rewriting—the pursuit of perfection in both story and style. Betsy Warland for giving me my start in writing and guiding me every step of the way since. Pasha Malla and Wayde Compton for their fine mentorship at very different stages in my writing. Elee Kraljii Gardiner, my steadfast first reader, for her feedback and friendship that have spanned countless revisions and just as many years. Melinda Fabbro and Kulbinder Bains for their infinite faith in me. Caroline Adderson for her thoughtful insights on an early draft. Chris Labonté for his encouragement and good counsel. Ayelet Tsabari for telling me about the Search for the Great BC Novel. Jack Hodgins, Kathy Page, Karen X. Tulchinsky and all of those involved in the Search for the Great BC Novel. Shauna Singh Baldwin for sharing her thoughts on transliteration. The Wired Writing Studio at the Banff Centre for the Arts and The Writer's Studio at Simon Fraser University for including me in such wonderful writing communities.

My friends and family for loving me always. May we all become stories.

CONTENTS

ONE FOR LOSS

1.1

The smell of chai—fennel, cloves and cinnamon—tucked me into my blanket like a seed in a cardamom pod. I steeped myself into the warmth of waking, listening to the sounds of Sunday morning. My mother was in the kitchen scrubbing the sink, her steel kara clinking against the basin—keeping time with the shabad on the radio. When I was fifteen, I'd told her I didn't want to wear my kara anymore; I didn't like the idea of being handcuffed to God. My mother, to my surprise, hadn't argued with me but simply said that the kara was a symbol of the restraint I would learn to show whether I wore the bangle or not.

"Is Meena not awake?" my mother asked, her voice cracking through intermittent radio static.

"Get up, Meninder. It's eleven o' clock." My sister Tej was the only one who used my real name; she knew how much I hated it.

I heard her footsteps in the hallway and pulled the blanket over my head.

"Just five minutes."

"No, not five minutes. Mom wants you up now. I don't know why you think you get to sleep in while I get stuck with all the chores. You're such a brat." Tej yanked the blanket off and looked at me with disgust. I was sleeping in a tank top and panties instead of the old-lady nightgowns that Masi had sewn for us from scraps salvaged from the textile mill.

"Fuck off, Tejinder." I shut my eyes against the light and pulled the blanket over my shoulders.

"Why can't you wear proper pyjamas like everyone else, or at the very least a bra?"

"You're just jealous."

Tej crossed her arms over her flat chest and stared me down, silent and saintly, until I felt the familiar beginnings of guilt harden in my stomach and take root in my toes.

She reached across the bed, drew the blinds and slid the window open, filling my room with the sounds of barking dogs, sprinkler jets and crows. When I turned my back on Tej, she shook my shoulder, stood over me, arms crossed, mouth zipped. She seemed unhinged.

"What?"

Tej stormed out of the room, muttering complaints to my mother, who yelled louder for me to wake up.

I kicked the covers off, stretching and collapsing my limbs before relaxing into my waking self. I lingered in my own touch, daring a quiet and quick exploration, cupping my breasts, running fingertips over flesh and folds. I wasn't sure exactly when my body had changed but it seemed to have done so in secret. I'd woken up one day the previous summer with Bollywood breasts, curvy hips and long legs. My dreams realized were just the continuation of my mother's nightmare. Like my sisters, I was no longer allowed to play sports or wear shorts. Our sex was meant to be hidden, even from one another. We dressed modestly, hiding our flesh, living somewhere deep inside our skins—chaste and quiet.

My mother was seated at the kitchen table, the Sunday paper splayed in front of her, sliced and dissected to the weekly flyer section. She flipped through ads for laundry detergent and dog food while talking on the phone to my sister Serena, scrunching her face, pushing her oversized glasses up ever so slightly to magnify portions of the page. I sat next to her, drinking a cup of stale tea, wondering why she bothered with reading glasses when she could not read.

"Eighty-nine cents," I told her impatiently. "Limit six."

She stared curiously at the picture of canned beans before licking the tip of her middle finger and turning the page.

"Achcha, achcha... it's expensive yes, but if you buy them in the case... When you were kids we used cloth diapers; it was so much work... Well you have to be disciplined, put him on the potty every few hours, he will get used to it... None of my children wore a diaper at his age... Tonight, the party... Who is it?... achcha achcha, his cousin's wedding."

Her voice skipped and jumped, picking up threads from the previous day–a patchwork of words. She flipped to the next flyer, told Serena that Similac Infant Formula was on sale at London Drugs, then sat squinting at the fine print.

"One case per household," I read for her.

My mother nodded as though she expected as much; she probably did. She knew which stores had the freshest vegetables, which had the cheapest; she knew the weekly sale cycle of all the local shops and had a well-stocked wallet of coupons grouped by date and commodity. She could figure out the price of toilet paper by the square, never fooled by the ever-changing sheet count per roll. She took her flyers and coupons to stores, looking for price matches and bulk buys. She knew the clerks and cashiers by face and at times attempted some small talk about the weather, but none of them ever returned the kindness. This only motivated her to count her change more closely, enumerating each penny on a rung of her finger the same way she counted minutes, hours and days. Once a cashier accused my mother of stealing a chocolate bar. The pimply faced security guard took her to the back office and went through her purse and pockets. After finding nothing, he sent her on her way with a warning. She came home upset and confused, much the same way I did when I was teased at school. When she told me what had happened I drove her back to the store and demanded to speak to the manager. He was apologetic about it and every time he'd seen her since, he was sure to ask her how she was doing, whether she needed anything. He even helped take her groceries to the car. My mother told everyone about it. "You should have seen how Meena talked to them. They even gave us a store gift certificate."

"Get dressed," my mother said, glancing at my jeans.

"I *am* dressed."

"Don't argue. Not now. We are expecting guests."

Phone still wedged between her ear and shoulder, she stood, moving like a pecking bird, as though in a hurry yet somehow unsure of her destination.

She put the dishes in the sink and stared out the window, her marionette frame bent in at the shoulders, her head lowered. The window looked out over the neighbours' manicured lawn, the perfectly pruned boxwood hedge and the grapes that wound along the fence. As usual on a Sunday, the neighbours were out on the lawn playing bocce. Their loud Italian voices and exuberance for life kept my mother curious and she watched them through the broken slit in the blind, as though trying to decipher their happiness. Sometimes they saw her standing at the window and waved "hello" or beckoned "come over." Today, as always, she turned away seeming both embarrassed and shy—feelings that for her and me were interchangeable.

"Why are you still standing there?" she said, turning on me. "I told you to change your clothes."

In my room I pulled out a plain salwar kameez from the bottom dresser drawer. The satin made me sweat and the smell lingered into the next wear, reminding me that I hated wearing Indian suits almost as much as I hated this ritual of belated mourning. Even though my father had been dead for sixteen years there were still enough relatives to fill every Sunday with pity. It was always the same. We would get up, clean the house, do the laundry, mourn the past and go to sleep. We existed between past dreams and present realities, never able to do anything but wait. For what, I didn't know.

When I was five, I'd thought we were waiting for my father to return. I had no memory of him but attempted to stitch his life together from the remnants that were everywhere. The house was full of black-and-white photographs of him from when we lived in England. Pictures of him standing next to the guards at Buckingham Palace and of the family in front of a tiny brick row house on Warwick Road still graced the mantel. Even my mother's closet was full of him. His starched cotton dress shirts hung neatly alongside sports jackets that smelled like yesterday's rain. His brown-and-black leather shoes were lined up beneath the shirts and jackets, next to a locked suitcase that I pulled out to stand on in order to reach the top of the closet.

Buried on the top shelf, I found an attaché case full of documents, which I could not yet read, and behind it a photo album and shoe polish kit. Resisting the urge to shine my father's shoes, I sat cross-legged beneath the empty embrace of hollow-armed suit jackets and opened the album. The yellowing photos made every face look familiar. They were the usual assortment of pictures—birthdays, weddings, picnics—except for four photos on the last page that were turned over.

I sat for a moment, wondering what was on the other side, before pulling back the plastic protector and peeling one of the photos off the sticky surface. It was a picture of my father in a pink satin-lined coffin. A long garland of spring flowers like the ones I'd seen worn by newlyweds was draped around his neck. His eyes were closed and weighted, his shoulders rigid, chest tight as though he were holding his breath.

My heart skipped and fell. The descending beats echoed in my chest, palpitated in my breath. I put the photo back in the album and the album back on the top shelf, preserving my father's death just as my mother had so carefully preserved the details of his life. Just as my father's mother—my dadi—had when she'd come to Canada to mourn her son five years after his death.

"How we remember," my dadi told me and my sisters, "this is how we exist."

"The past is the only thing that matters," she said, shaking her head like a slow pendulum between bitter glances at our braids. "It is the only thing we know."

"We cannot make something out of nothing. That is for God to do."

This is what we were told. This is who we were.

After dressing, I returned to the kitchen to finish my breakfast. I was always a slow eater. My mother had to force-feed me as a child, every spoonful of curry followed by a gulp of water to wash it down; I hated the bitter subzi, soft and chunky mounds of potatoes and cauliflower. "Shit"— that's what the white kids at school had said my leftover lunches looked like. "Meena eats shit."

Tej shuffled by me, pushing the vacuum with one hand while balancing a laundry basket of wet clothes on her hip like a baby. She leaned against the table and pushed the basket towards me. "Your turn to put these on the line to dry. And you have to vacuum. Mom and I are going to the Indian store to get groceries."

She held up a list of chores that I would need to complete by the time they returned. I took the list from her, crumpling it in my free hand as I opened the porch door to hang the laundry out. I closed the door on her curse words.

Our porch backed onto a fenced-in grid of suburban yards dotted with broken-down garden sheds and vegetable plots that were a haven for squirrels and other rodents. No matter how quickly we picked up and composted the rotten apples and spoiled cherries, the critters would come up from the nearby bog, skulking along the top of our rickety fence in search of a meal. Once, one of the kids at school saw me chasing a raccoon off our garbage bins with a broom handle and looked disgusted, as though having raccoons in our neighbourhood were somehow my fault. We lived in one of the older grids in North Delta, a suburb just outside of Vancouver, where the large evergreens and pines were dying a slow death, mostly by crowding and years of various untreated seasonal diseases that caused the bark to peel away in long, ragged strips.

The houses on our street had been bought and sold several times and were victim to shoddy renovations, like the slanted sunroom addition next door. New neighbourhoods were devoid of such things; the ones built on flattened forests above the ravine had courts, boulevards and crescents that wound around one another to panoramic views of Boundary Bay. Each new cedar house there looked onto both a dogwood tree planted in the sidewalk meridian and a carefully manicured postage stamp-sized front yard filled with some variation of tulips, daffodils and rhododendrons. Behind the cedar fences draped in clematis were the popular girls who spent their weekends sunbathing, sometimes topless (so the boys at school said), listening to Casey Kasem's *American Top 40*. On a clear day I could hear them splashing in their pools and singing along with Madonna. None of them had to chase away raccoons or spend their Sundays hanging their knickers on a clothesline for the world to see.

I snapped the mismatched sheets in the air and pegged them onto the line. In the distance a squall of cloud was rising and I wondered how long it would be before the rain set in. The clouds were jagged at the ends, torn sheets of grey sky, not the kind of drifting childhood pictures that my sister Harj and I had imbued with meaning. "A boat! A car! A plane!" I'd yell. "How unoriginal," she'd laugh. Of a cirrus cloud, I once said, "Whipped air and angel hair." Harj was lying in the grass at the time, picking at a scab on her elbow. "Only white people can be angels," she said, without looking up.

Halfway through my wash-load hanging, Liam appeared, walking towards the house, his long afternoon shadow turning corners before he did. As always, he was wearing his headphones, and I wondered if he was listening to the mixed tape I'd made him for his birthday.

I'd met him at the beginning of Grade 12. He'd transferred from Holy Trinity and at first didn't go to class, preferring to wander the hallways and occasionally kick a locker door as he passed. He was rumoured to have been expelled from the Catholic school, but no one knew why. Some kids suspected he'd been kicked out for drug use and others had heard that he'd been in one too many fights, but what everyone agreed on was that he was best left a loner. Whenever he walked by, people veered out of his way, and in the crowded hallways he stood apart from the others in what seemed like contented arrogance.

Moments before our first meeting, I was rushing across the field, my face tucked into an armload of books to avoid the sun's glare. As I approached the school's main entrance, I saw him scaling the face of the building as if he were Spiderman. Just as I was about to walk by, he jumped down, falling at my feet. Startled, I dropped my books. The bell rang. I was late. I knelt down and began collecting the books, occasionally grasping at my papers as they fluttered in the breeze, threatening to take flight. Liam handed me a stack of papers and a few books.

"History, don't want to lose that one."

"Actually, I would. But thanks." I looked up to take them from him. The sun should have been in my eyes, but he had eclipsed everything.

Later that same day, I'd found myself sitting in front of him in history. The teacher hadn't arrived and the class was on the verge of the usual anarchy. Liam slumped over his desk, ducking under a paper airplane as he tapped my back with his pen. "Meninder, right?"

"Meena," I corrected, wondering how he knew my full name.

He squinted and nodded his head as if to say "All right, yeah." He had a face that was older than his age, a square jawline and blue eyes that changed colour depending on the light.

"You live in the beige house, the one with the fucked-up trees?"

I hesitated not wanting to encourage a conversation. "Yeah, why?"

He leaned back into his chair until the front legs lifted off the ground. "So, you want to get out of here?"

"And go where?"

"Does it matter?"

When I said it did, he smirked as if I had missed something obvious, and left the classroom, leaving me alone and surrounded by kids who acted like I didn't exist.

After class, he was waiting outside and asked if he could walk home with me. After working up the courage, I asked him where he ended up going and he told me, "You know, just around."

He always said "you know" as though I did know. Somehow it made me think I did.

I pegged the last of the wash on the line and cranked it out towards the remaining patch of sun. Liam stood beneath the porch and looked up at me.

"What's up?" I asked.

"Nothing. I was going downtown, thought you might want to come."

"I can't." I looked to see if my mother had seen us talking. "We're expecting company and I have some stuff to do around here."

"Like laundry," he said, picking up a few of the pegs that I'd dropped. When he started up the steps to hand them to me, I rushed down the stairs, carrying the basket in front of me so he wouldn't see me in my Indian clothes, though I suspected he would've seen beyond them. He never seemed to notice when my hair smelled like curry or when I wore the same clothes two days in a row.

I took the pegs from him.

He was smiling or smirking at me. I couldn't tell which; his slight underbite made everything seem like a flirtation or dare.

I stood there in Liam's silence. He was often like this; he didn't feel the need to speak, to fill in the blanks, to use up air. Talking with him was always a relief.

"Maybe we could do something tomorrow?" I suggested.

"That'd be cool," he said.

"Meena!" my mother yelled from the window, in a tone that matched the glare she shot at Liam.

"Look, I have to go. See you tomorrow."

I rushed back up the stairs and took the empty basket inside, walking by Tej and my mother, who were on their way out.

"Gora? A white boy?" my mother snapped.

"He said hi. What was I supposed to do, not talk to him?" I pushed the vacuum into the living room and flicked it on, drowning out any hope my mother had of lecturing me about talking to white boys.

White was the colour of death and mourning; it was the only colour my mother wore apart from grey. In the kitchen, while ironing her chunni, she reminded us how to behave when the guests arrived. Tej listened and replied dutifully in her pitiful Punjabi. Although we'd attended Punjabi summer school when we were kids, her accent was still terrible—she couldn't say the hard "t's" the way I could but I couldn't be bothered to make the effort, and answered my mother's Punjabi in English. I wondered how much was lost in this routine, which forced us to follow along a word at a time, or a word behind, interpreting what was said even when, for some expressions, there was no translation. My mother would often get frustrated and remind me that when I started preschool the only English word I knew was good-bye. As we walked home from school that first day, I waved good-bye to the bus stop, the lamppost, the trees... My mother yanked my hand, pulling me along, tired of my valediction. "Everything was good-bye," she told my sisters later.

Steam rose to her face as she pressed the wrinkles from her chunni, the heat forcing her to look up. "Tie up your hair," and then with one motion of her hand dismissed me to the basement washroom. She didn't want us to use the upstairs washroom; she'd emptied the garbage and removed the diaper box-sized packs of Kotex that proved this was a house full of women. I'd been mortified when she stuffed our shopping cart full of those discounted maxi-pads at Zellers. I wanted to use tampons like the girls at school but my mother regarded the insertion of such an object as impure. I bought a box anyway and stashed it under my bed, along with the birth control pills Serena bought for me. I was only eleven when I got my first period and since my mother hadn't let me watch the sex ed. films at school, I was sure I was bleeding to death—I thought kissing made you pregnant. After a day of enduring excruciating cramps and hiding my soiled panties in the corner of my bedroom, I confided to Serena that I was dying. When Serena told my mother that I'd started to menstruate, my mother didn't speak to me for a week. My becoming a woman so early was a shameful reminder of our sex, of the burdens she bore.

My cramps were awful and I spent the first two days of each month at home, curled on the floor throwing up. After three years of this, my mother finally agreed to let Serena take me to the "woman doctor." The gynecologist prescribed birth control pills to regulate my cycles and ease my cramps. Serena knew my mother would not approve and made me swear to hide the pills and never tell anyone. I agreed, wondering why anyone would admit to being a virgin who used birth control. It just sounded stupid.

The guests were arriving. I heard the scurry of footsteps above as my mother took her place on the sofa and Tej rushed to get the door. I wondered how many people had come this time. Harj and I had always guessed, making a game of it. It was the only variable part of the ritual and even then it hardly varied. I waited until I heard them go upstairs before peeking into the entrance hall to survey the shoes. I thought that the sensible shoes with the evenly worn soles indicated that one of our guests was an old lady shuffling through life to the end. The gold strapless sandals probably belonged to a new bride still happy to clip-clop through life, and the two sets of men's dress shoes creased only at the toe belonged to young men whose gait was restrained by entitlement. I slipped my foot into the bride's sandal and pointed my toes, disappointed that there was nothing Cinderella about it.

I walked up the stairs, avoiding the creaky third step, and slipped into the kitchen unnoticed. There I sat at the table, staring at the faded green butterfly wallpaper, counting wings. When my mother called for me, I lowered my head and walked into the room with a tray of water glasses, which I set on the table. My mother cleared her throat, looked at the tray and back at me. I picked it up, offering water to the men first, then to the young woman wearing wedding bracelets and lastly to the elderly woman, the matriarch whose loose caramel skin hung from her jaw. She refused and I set the tray down, waiting to be excused. Harj used to bring the tray in after she'd spat into each glass. But now that she was gone it was my job to offer the water and though I thought of her brazen act each time, I could never repeat it.

"This is the baby?" the elderly woman asked my mother, without taking her coal eyes off me.

"Yes, this is the youngest, Meninder." My mother gestured towards me in a way that made me feel like I was a parting gift in a game show, something off *The Price is Right*. "She'll be eighteen soon."

The woman feigned a sympathetic smile as I joined my hands in greeting to the group. "Sat Sri Akal." I offered her an obligatory half-hug. Just like my dadi, she reeked of mustard oil and mothballs.

"You wouldn't even remember your father, would you?" the woman asked.

I shook my head, pretending that it was some kind of compliment. She inspected me for a moment, pushing my cheeks from side to side, tilting my chin up and down, before touching my head in blessing. I stood there long after she'd sat down, waiting to be excused.

My mother sat on the sofa, head tilted, eyes weepy and withdrawn. I wondered if she were acting or if her grief after so many years could be this real. I'd never seen her cry without an audience; her tears were of little use when there was so much to be done, so many to care for. She never even mentioned my father other than to say how different our lives were when he was alive, how different it would have been had he not died. I always waited on the edge of those sentences, hoping for more. But my mother never spoke of what preceded his absence and I was too frightened to ask. Until I'd discovered it for myself, I didn't even know his name.

After learning to read, I'd returned to the closet and found, typeset on a half-empty container of penicillin: "Akal." Years later, while reciting the morning prayer in Punjabi school, I paused on his name:

Ik Onkar
Satnam
Karta purukh
Nirbhau
Nirvair
Akal moorat
Ajuni saibhang
Gurparshad
Jap.

That was the only prayer I learned, and I repeated it several times before asking my Punjabi teacher what "Akal" meant. She told me that it meant "not subject to time or death."

I whispered it sometimes—at night as I fell into the quiet possibility of dreams, and even at times like these when I needed something to mute the staid condolences that made loss less than what it was.

"So unfair... such a tragedy... he was so young, such a good man..."

As always, my mother's face fell, the distance of events blurring behind warm eyes. Her voice cracked, her tone dropping into soft gulps of lapsed grief. "They said it was an accident...there was an investigation...they were sorry...some of them even said it was his fault, but I know he was careful." She spoke of it in fragments, allowing everyone else to complete her sentences with sympathy.

My father had fallen from the twentieth floor of a luxury high-rise apartment building where he'd been framing the walls. He was proud of his work and boasted about the complex's amenities: air-conditioned units, an in-ground pool, a private park. It seems strange to me that this building existed somewhere outside our mention of it. That somewhere people were living in these air-conditioned units, pushing their blond, blue-eyed babies in strollers along the very sidewalk where my father lay dead; he'd died instantly. Sometimes I dreamed I was him. Sometimes I dreamed I was the fall. Either way I woke with a screamless breath escaping, my gut twitching into knots. I would lie back loosening them with thoughts of something, and then nothing.

But no matter how many times I dreamed of his death, I could not conceive of it; he was a myth and my mother was a martyr.

"If only he had a son... what can we do... it is kismet."

I listened to them explain our entire lives away with one word. Apparently, it was my mother's fate to be a widow with six daughters and our fate to become casualties of fractured lives. Though I struggled against such a predetermined existence, I knew that my sisters and I were all carved out of this same misery, existing only for others, like forgotten monuments that had been erected to commemorate events that had come and gone.

"No one knows why these things happen. Only God knows. *Satnam Vaheguruji*," said the matriarch. She joined her hands in prayer towards the lithograph of Guru Nanak that hung above the brick fireplace, before falling silent, nodding to the beat of the grandfather clock that clicked like a metronome. Serena had given it to my mother for her birthday several years ago and since it was too large and cumbersome to fit in the hallway, it was left standing in the living room like a watchman. At the end of each month the pendulum stopped and the clock fell silent until it was wound again—a small reprieve.

Twisting a handkerchief in her fingers, my mother echoed prayer in whispers. I half expected an origami animal to appear out of the cloth. But all that appeared was a distant look on her face that dissolved only when her chunni slipped off her head. She quickly readjusted the fabric and wiped her eyes with the palms of her hands. "Meena will get the chai." She hurried after me into the kitchen.

"Use the good dishes—the cottage rose china," she whispered, and ushered Tej in the direction of the silver tray, reminding her not to forget the coasters. "Make sure you let the tea boil after you add the milk," she instructed, as though we'd never made chai before. But the chai had to be perfect. Something had to be.

My mother returned to our guests composed: the perfect widow in perpetual mourning. I listened to the guests' dutiful sighs, knowing that they would go back to their homes full of sons thinking *Better her than us*, and congratulate themselves on their happy lives. After they left, others would take their place. It was a modern version of sati; instead of being burned on her husband's funeral pyre, my mother was repeatedly singed by their reminders, cremating her life inside herself.

1.2

The furnace hummed over the sounds of the house settling. I pulled the blinds up. The sun was absent; the sky, a morose canvas of smudged graphite and charcoal. Streams of water trickled down the glass, puddling along the windowsill before settling into the veins of cracked paint. I wrote my name in the condensation and after a moment wiped it away.

I didn't mind walking to school in weather like this. I hated carrying umbrellas or wearing hats, and submitted to the steady stream of rain. I pulled my Walkman from my coat pocket, put the headphones on and trudged through the puddles and potholes, water seeping into the cracked soles of my shoes. I was listening to Joy Division's *Unknown Pleasures*. Harj had said that they were the pioneers of post-punk. She said it was real music, not like the superficial sound bites from rappers that were all MC or DJ somebody.

By the time I arrived at school I was soaked and my hair fell in dripping black waves around my face. As I walked down the hallway towards my locker, my shoes squeaking against the shiny linoleum floors, the janitor shot me a disapproving look. I curled my shoulders into my chest, shivering a passive apology.

I dropped my bag into my locker, shook my hair and combed out the knots with my fingers. Warm, dry white kids, driven to school by their parents, paraded past. Girls with syrupy laughs recounted their weekends in giggles that dropped into accusatory laughter when they saw me watching them.

"What are you looking at?"

I clamped my jaw and turned away, pretending I hadn't heard.

Harpreet was walking down the hall towards me, spinning a basketball on his finger, performing for the popular girls who had only noticed him since he'd stopped wearing a turban and become the captain of the basketball team. He seemed to have forgotten that the kids who befriended him now were the same ones who had taunted him in elementary school— "Paki! Hindu! Turban twister!" Harpreet had been new back then, and didn't speak English; he smiled at their insults. He didn't know enough to be angry, but I did. I'd witnessed my mother's anger when cars squealed by our house as voices yelled "Paki, go home!" and eggs hit our windows.

One night when my mother's brother, Mamaji, was visiting, it wasn't eggs. The window exploded and a firecracker rolled towards me through shards of broken glass. I sat stunned; it looked like a sparkler. Mamaji leaped forward, picked it up and hurled it back out the window. It howled down the street, nipping at the heels of dark figures. Mamaji called to my mother to get the baseball bat that sat by the front door, and together they ran into the night. I wanted to watch from the window but Serena shut the drapes. She tucked us into our mother's bed, assuring us that nothing had ever been thrown through that window. When they came back later that night, Mamaji was asking my mother why she hadn't taught the sala kutta gora a lesson when she had the chance. My mother told him that she had taught the boys a lesson, one in compassion. When a dozen eggs hit the window the next night, I knew she wished she'd taught them a lesson in retribution.

Once I'd tried to protect Harpreet from the kids and yelled at them to leave him alone. Two of them cornered me and pushed me down onto the gravel field. I picked up a handful of rocks and stood up slowly, my knees raw. I threw the stones at them until they ran away. When I asked Harpreet if he was all right, he kicked me in the shin.

I waved across the hall to Carrie. She was with Todd. He was good-looking in a *Miami Vice* kind of way. Carrie was wearing leggings and a miniskirt; several hoops looped their way up her ears, which, I'd told her, was the exact look I would have worn were I allowed to get my ears pierced more than once. We had been best friends in junior high school, but she'd since traded me for the fame that came with being runner-up in the Miss Teen Canada pageant. I envied her popularity and adopted a new group of friends to replace her: the Smart Ethnics. They weren't FOBS, or fresh off the boat, as we referred to the immigrants who smelled like onions and had body odour that was thicker than their accents. Nor were they DIPS—the Dumb Indian Punjabs who clustered together like jalebies, driving around after school in their Firebird Trans Ams. They were the ethnics who took all the advanced classes in algebra, thinking this would somehow help them in life just like the French-immersion kids thought that their piss-poor French would land them dream jobs.

My locker was next to my least favourite Smart Ethnic, Tina, with her incessant cheeriness and bullshit stories. In PE she had brought in an autographed picture of Arthur Ashe; her dad had played tennis with him. In history she brought in pictures of Idi Amin, who had been their neighbour in Uganda, and in law she did a presentation on Clifford Olson, a family friend before he was a serial killer.

"Hi, Meena," Tina said, putting her pink lipstick on. She smacked her lips together and smiled at herself in the tiny locker mirror. She always wore blue eyeshadow and frosted Revlon lipstick caked over her chapped lips. By the end of the day the lipstick would have settled into cracks and adhered to flakes of dry skin, her mouth a pout of pink scales that she would pick at when she thought no one was looking. She pulled at her leopard-print leggings and adjusted her leather anti-apartheid medallion, which hung between her ample breasts in a display of social outrage despite her name-brand Ralph Lauren shirt. I wondered who she thought she was kidding. This display of ethnicity was all purchased from the African store in the mall where everything was made in Hong Kong. There was nothing authentic about her. She was part melting pot, part multicultural and part privileged, the kind of person who would get exactly what she wanted from life with very little effort, not realizing that for the rest of us, life was not that easy.

"Hey," I mumbled back, wishing that she would stop being so nice to me so I wouldn't feel so bad about hating her. I slammed the locker door without looking at her. "See you in class."

I sat in the middle of the classroom, not close enough to the front to be seen as eager but not far back enough to be a slacker. As the other students took their seats, conversations shifted into whispers and note-passing. I wondered what the notes said and wished that one would come my way. Carrie and I used to pass notes, and when we weren't in class together we would write long letters to each other. Her writing was always entertaining, full of inside jokes that made me laugh out loud until I saw that everyone was looking at me wondering what was so funny. The teacher would then say, "Would you like to share the joke with the rest of the class?" To which I would reply, "No," and slip the note in my textbook until she wasn't looking.

I kept all the notes and letters that Carrie had ever written to me. I reread them last summer, embarrassed that I'd preserved the details of junior high school crushes in folded sheets of loose-leaf paper. I worried that someone would find them, and burned them all except for the one that said: "James totally wants to jump your bones. He's invited us over after school." I didn't want to forget that someone had wanted me; I wasn't the type of girl that boys were interested in. I wasn't unattractive, but I wasn't beautiful like the white girls whose hair smelled like green apples. I had features that on their own were not pretty: my lips were thin, my nose was long and my wide brown eyes belonged on a fawn. I was the "could be" pretty girl; with some makeup and a great haircut, one day I *could* be pretty.

James was Carrie's cousin. He came to our Valentine's Day dance in Grade 10 with Carrie's then boyfriend, Brian. When he walked into the gymnasium everyone stopped and stared. I told him there weren't any black kids in Delta and maybe they expected him to do the moonwalk or something. He laughed, saying that they should be able to tell from his acid-wash jeans that he was only half-black and not at all the Michael Jackson type.

After Carrie lost her virginity to Brian, it seemed logical, in a sixteen-year-old way, that I should lose mine to James and agreed to go to his house. Carrie explained that the sex would hurt and would probably only last about five minutes but the kissing after was nice. I nodded like I knew this, like the one time Carrie had sex with Brian made her an expert.

When we got there, Carrie sat on the couch watching *Oprah* while James and I made out on the loveseat across from her. I kept opening my eyes to make sure she wasn't watching. After half an hour, we went to his room, which was the entire unfinished basement of his house, lay on his king-sized waterbed and kissed. Our hands moved under clothes, undoing zippers, buttons and clasps. I wished I'd been wearing a nicer bra, but I didn't have anything other than plain white cotton Smart soft-cup bras. I was wondering why a brand of bras would be named Smart when James slipped mine off, and lay on top of me. I sank into the bed beneath him; every time he moved the water beneath us shifted and we struggled to regain hold of each other. I hadn't seen him naked. I'd felt his nakedness but wondered if I should look. I closed my eyes and tried to imagine that we were on a yacht and that this moment was romantic, like the ocean. But each time I opened my eyes, the partly framed basement walls, cement floors and single light bulb dangling from the ceiling shattered the fantasy. James did all the things that my sister's *Glamour* magazine said he should, but I wasn't responding the way they said I would. I stopped his hands as they slid between my legs. "I can't do this. Not like this." He rolled over onto his back and asked me if I'd at least give him a blow job. I got dressed and left.

"So," Carrie nudged me in the ribs as we walked down the street afterwards. "How was it?" When I told her that we hadn't done it, she seemed disappointed, like I hadn't kept my end of a weird bargain or something.

The class quieted as Mr. Ellis blustered into the room, clearing his throat. "Turn to page 86." He shuffled papers on his desk and organized his pencils in a neat row before reaching for a menthol cough candy from the top desk drawer. Just as he was about to start the lesson, Liam slid in the door, drenched from the rain, his black hair clinging to the frozen angles of his face. Droplets of water trailed down his neck, charting pathways.

"Late again, Liam. Time is money. Let that be your first lesson in economics today," said Mr. Ellis.

Liam took off his jacket and slumped into his seat at the back of the class. "So does that mean I get paid for being here?"

"Your payment is an education." Mr. Ellis adjusted his glasses and pulled at the too-short sleeves of his tweed jacket. I wondered if he had cats, if he lived with his mother, how he felt about Freud.

"Today we will continue with our discussions on labour practices in the emerging economies of the Third World."

I hated the term "Third World" and its arrogant implications of a modern-day caste system not unlike the one that existed within the G7. Nations built on the backs of immigrants who worked more and earned less in hopes of building a better life that only left their children to ask: "Better than what?" In India my father had been a respected engineer; in the West he was considered unskilled labour. Eventually, it killed him. After he died, my mother cleaned motels at the end of twelve-hour shifts on the farm where she picked whatever was in season for little pay and no benefits other than the spoiled vegetables that were not good enough to be sold but would be just fine in subzi. "We were not poor when we came to Canada," my mother once said, pausing as she mashed overripe berries into jam. "But this country tells us we are."

Mr. Ellis smoothed his scanty comb-over. "Specifically, let's talk about the labour practices we read about in Chapter 11 as they relate to corporate responsibility."

Hands went up in the front rows: the Smart Ethnics jockeyed. Mr. Ellis looked past them, past me, to the dumb, popular girls who put out.

"Crystal, how about you?"

She shrugged and walked to the podium. Amid an elaborate array of eye rolls, sighs and gum chewing, she spoke in rapid iambs, each syllable straining into the next. "I don't really think the corporations should be blamed. They're just following the laws of *those* countries." She twirled teased strands of hair between her fingers, examining the ends until her eyes seemed to cross.

Her hair was as platinum as that of the Barbie dolls that we used to play with at recess. Once in Grade 3 she'd invited me over to her house to play with her Malibu Barbie pool and cabana set. I didn't know what a cabana was but was eager to find out. I accepted the invitation and raced home, picked up my banana seat bike and rode to her house, listening to my "Tiger" Williams hockey card clipping in the spokes as I pedalled faster and faster. Barbie in hand, I knocked on the door of her new cedar split-level home. When her mother opened the door I told her I was there to see Crystal. She seemed annoyed and said, "Crystal has gone to her friend's house to play. She must have forgotten you, dear." When I didn't reply, she raised her voice and repeated herself in the slow, mannered way that the cashier at the drugstore used when my mother spoke in broken English. I turned away and rode my bike around the neighbourhood for two hours so I wouldn't have to explain to my mother why I was home so soon. She had warned me about white people and I didn't want her to think that she was right.

The next day at recess Crystal and Amanda showed off their matching friendship bracelets and strawberry Bonne Bell Lip Smackers. They became best friends, the popular girls, living out a Barbie life, long after I had stopped playing with dolls.

Crystal continued: "I mean who are we to question the laws of those countries anyways? At least the factories provide them a job that they probably wouldn't otherwise have."

Bafflingly, the rest of the class nodded their heads and applauded her mediocre effort.

"Who would like to take an opposing position?" Mr. Ellis scanned the room, again bypassing the ethnics. "Liam, how about you?"

"L-l-l... - iam," Craig mocked as Liam got up to the podium. There was collective laughter at the memory of his apparent grade school stutter. I wanted to tell them to shut up, but I was a coward and glad that the attention wasn't on me. Mr. Ellis quieted the room with a stern look. I sat up, attentive. Liam always had something interesting to say; he paid attention to the world, read *Maclean's* and *The New York Times* and watched *The Nature of Things*. He knew more about Gorbachev, the Berlin Wall and the Cold War than the history teacher did and I suspected he knew more about economics than Mr. Ellis.

Liam leaned against the podium. "Those are expensive runners you're wearing, Crystal. Must have cost, what, eighty, ninety dollars?"

"Try one hundred and twenty."

"Do you know that the cost to make those shoes is less than ten dollars?"

She didn't answer.

"Did you know that children work eighteen hours a day in sweatshop conditions and earn less than fifty cents so you can have those shoes? So some fat, bald, middle-aged man can deliver soaring stock prices to shareholders and buy his son a pony?"

He detailed the intolerable conditions and the multiple infractions to human rights throughout the world and called Western consumerism the single largest enabler of these injustices. After a few minutes, I stopped listening, fixed my attention on Crystal's face and watched her smug expression fade. I knew he had defeated her when she shuffled her feet, trying to hide the swoosh on her shoes. The Smart Ethnics led the applause as Liam took his seat.

Liam casually shoved Craig, knocking his books off the desk as he walked by. "Did I stutter?" he asked as he slid into his seat.

I waited for Liam under the magnolia tree. Although we never actually hung out at school, we did walk home together. He would talk about life and I would listen. I loved his grand ideas of socialism, his romantic notion of communism and the sweeping hand gestures he used to express himself. He was symphonic.

He was still reeling from his victorious debate in economics, making exclamation marks in the air as he spoke, kicking a rock along ahead of us as he walked.

"You could be an opera," I told him.

"No, you've got it all wrong. An opera needs tragedy. And that's your department. You're tragic through and through. Depeche Mode must have written 'Dressed in Black' for you." He sang the first verse, his voice dramatizing the depressing lyrics. He kicked the rock ahead a few paces. "I bet you own Fluevogs."

"I don't wear them anymore," I said, and kicked the rock across the street.

I didn't want to admit that in Grade 9 I'd saved all my birthday, Christmas and rakhi money to buy those shoes. But by the time I had bought them, everyone was wearing Doc Martens or Chuck Taylors.

"What's wrong with dressing in black?" I asked.

"Nothing—as long as you don't see the world that way."

"I wear brown, too."

"Yeah, I noticed that you've got the free spirit gypsy vibe happening lately. I've been trying to get my head around the contradiction."

"What contradiction?"

"You. Will you be angry or will you be free?" Liam ran ahead, jumped up and grabbed the branch of a large, blossoming cherry tree, swinging himself forward. The tree dropped its soft petals and the wind picked them up, scattering them around us, and for just a moment it seemed like we were encapsulated in a snow globe. When all the blossoms had dispersed, I was still covered in them. As I began tussling them from my hair Liam reached for my hand. "Leave them, they look nice."

Liam took off before we reached the amputated fir trees that flanked my driveway. He always made an excuse to speed ahead, though I knew he did it to spare me my mother's wrath. I had never said anything to him about her but somehow he knew just the same way he seemed to know everything.

I looked up at the trees apologetically. My mother had disliked the mess they made in the winter when their branches sagged and needles dropped, littering the asphalt with spikes and sprigs. When she wasn't complaining about that, she worried that a strong wind might knock them onto our house, killing us as we slept. To avert the mess and potential tragedy, she had called her brother and asked him to come by on a Sunday to trim them to a manageable size. All Sunday morning Mamaji had stood on his rickety ladder, sawing the lower branches into stubby amputations. When he'd climbed down to admire his work, my mother handed him a frothy almond milkshake, just like the ones she'd made him in India. He took it from her without averting his eyes from the tree, wiped the sweat from his brow, gulped it down, handed her the glass, adjusted his ladder and climbed higher. His upper body disappeared into the crown of the tree in search of a place to set the chainsaw's grinding teeth. My mother, my sisters and I stood in the driveway, mesmerized by the buzzing sound of this battle above. It only took a moment for the tree's elegant neck to snap. I watched the crown teeter and fall like a bird from the sky, expecting it to make a thud as it hit the ground. But it didn't. It surrendered softly to the lush grass below. Mamaji emerged a hero. My mother applauded and I stood stunned, staring at the tree's orange wounds, feeling phantom pains.

Liam assured me that the tree would grow back. "Everything does," he explained.

Then he took me for a walk through the nearby ravine, past the stumped old growth that lay like fallen monuments beneath a spindly canopy of fir trees. To me they all looked like Douglas firs, but he could tell which was a Sitka spruce, a hemlock or a Western red cedar and he called them by name. Twigs and branches cracked beneath our feet, and small birds scuttled about in the lush undergrowth, scurrying along their own path to avoid ours.

We headed down into the ravine, grabbing exposed roots to keep from slipping down the moist earth. "Be careful," Liam said. At the bottom, he dropped his backpack at the foot of a tree and began to climb. "You coming?" he called from a few branches up.

I shook my head and pulled at the hem of my gypsy skirt. He jumped out of the tree and took hold of my hand. "Come on, it's worth it. I'll help you." His half smile nudged me on as he pointed out which hollows to place my foot in, hoisting me up when I faltered. My legs scraped against bony branches. My skin felt as raw as the peeling bark it pushed against.

"It's okay, I've got you, you're fine… you're fine." He motioned for me to cross in front of him. I teetered on the branch and grabbed his arm. He pulled me closer, anchoring my body, telling me I was okay. His breath fell on my neck, pulling my skin into tight rows of goosebumps. He smelled like cumin, like home.

As I opened the back door, I was overwhelmed by the smell of mud and stale tea. My mother was home. Her grey lunch box, once black, was soaking in the laundry basin. Her filthy boots lay on the painted green concrete floor that was meant to be cheery. Her dirty 1960s' thrift-store clothes were resting on the laundry machine that was never used; my mother said it was too expensive to run more than once a month and insisted we wash the farm clothes by hand. But no matter how hard we scrubbed, they still smelled like the newly dead or the almost dying: manure and mushrooms, dirt, bitter gourds rotted by rain, bruised fruit teeming with flies, all embedded in the polyester plaid she wore with pride.

I took my shoes off and hung my jacket in the closet beside my mother's fake fur coat. As a child I'd been terrified to open the closet for fear that this lion of a coat—with its massive fur collar, soft beige leopard pile and leatherette belt studded with topaz stones—would pounce on me. My father had bought her that coat while on a short trip to Paris in 1958, along with a tiny bottle of perfume that was still in the pocket where he'd placed it.

As I often did, I dipped my hand into the pocket of the coat. My fingers fumbled in search of the heart-shaped glass bottle. I held it in my palm for a second. Somehow, it seemed an important thing to do.

I always wondered why my mother had left the perfume in the pocket, the coat in the closet: all this beauty locked away. Poor beast. She'd never worn the coat since his death.

"Meena? Is that you?" my mother called out.

"Yeah, coming!" I shut the closet door, picked up the pieces of mail that were on the floor, and riffled through them as I walked up the stairs into the kitchen. I handed my father's Workers' Compensation Board cheque to my mother along with a stack of flyers. This simple, unapologetic envelope that arrived once a month was our patriarch, its contents meant to replace the sum of a man.

My mother was holding the phone between her shoulder and ear, and walking around the kitchen in square sweeps like a trapped housefly as she complained to Masi in random and regular patterns that the rain had spoiled the fields, forcing her to come home early, and that she would likely have to take Tej with her to make up the time on Saturday. Unlike my older sisters, who spent their summers toiling in the fields with my mother, I hadn't gone since I was eight years old.

That last time we'd loaded into the contractor's VW van at five in the morning, shoulder to shoulder along the wooden benches that replaced seats, trying not to slide into each other as the van turned corners. I sat on the end of the bench clutching the side to keep myself from falling into the cracked window held together with duct tape. By six the van was full of mothers, grandmothers, daughters and granddaughters. All were silent, except the toddler who shuffled in her mother's arms and the contractor man who sang Hindi songs that I whispered along to under my breath.

That day I could not keep up with my mother; the piece rate of pay distanced even her shouts for me to hurry. When my sisters came to look for me, I was playing hide-and-seek in the rows of bushes by the ditch with the other children. They scolded me, reminding me of the three boys, no older than me, who had drowned in a gravel pit on a farm in Langley the week before. I thought of the news, the protesters demanding safe working conditions, the people marching and yelling "Zindabad workers' rights!" under a unionized banner. As I picked up my half-eaten bucket of blueberries, I turned to my sisters and repeated what I heard on the TV, that this was no place for children. I knew I would never go back.

My mother narrowed her eyes as I opened and closed the fridge looking for something to eat.

"If you are so hungry, why don't you finish your lunch?" she said, interrupting her phone conversation to throw my lunch bag at me. I hated the way she juggled two conversations at once. It made everything she said sound frustrated and disjointed. I never knew if her anger was meant for me or if it reflected the other half of the conversation she was carrying on. I sat at the table and pulled out the half-eaten peanut butter sandwich. My mother placed tea in front of me and I dipped the sandwich in, trying to make the filling taste like something other than peanut butter.

She put the phone down and looked out the window. "You were walking with that boy again." She still sounded angry, but the very nature of the Punjabi language was terse.

"Relax, Mom, he's just a friend."

"Speak in Punjabi, Meena! Friend shmend," she mocked before retreating back to Punjabi. "He is a boy, a white boy! What will people think when they see you walking with a boy? They will think that he is a boyfriend. The last thing you need is to hurt your reputation, hurt your chances of making a good match, or worse, your sister's. I won't have you wandering the streets like a dog.

"Mom, I don't wander the streets like a dog; I was just walking home."

She uttered a prayer, the same prayer she used for everything, but this time I was sure she meant for God to bring us all suitable husbands and to free her of her maternal obligations. It calmed her only momentarily. "You do not need friends," she continued. "You have sisters to be your friends. I do not send you to school to make friends. You should go to school, study and come home. None of this friends business. Now tie up your hair!" She attempted to pull it back, to tame it furiously in one orderly braid. "What is this?" she asked, picking at the blossoms between strands. I pushed her away. She released the half braid and sat next to me, her frustration wedged between us. I sat still, gazing into my tea, wishing it hadn't rained, wishing she hadn't come home early.

The back door opened and slammed shut. The china that had never seen a happy occasion quivered in the glass cabinet, reverberating an entrance through the wood-panelled walls.

"Hello!" came a voice, as footsteps ran up the stairs towards us.

It was Serena, my oldest, smartest, married sister. She had spiral permed hair and had given birth to a healthy baby boy, ending the daughter curse that had plagued my mother for twenty-eight years. Serena, who wore inexpensive drugstore perfume and bought my mother candied ginger and pastel-coloured chocolate mints, saved me from my mother's lecture.

"Hi," I muttered, breezing by her on the way to my room. I suppressed the urge to slam my bedroom door; my mother hadn't allowed closed doors since Harj left. 'Families do not need privacy," she insisted. "In India a family of ten can live in one room and never argue." I flopped onto my bed and stared at the ceiling, searching for patterns in the stucco as I listened to my sister and mother's conversation float down the hall from the kitchen.

"What's wrong with her?" Serena asked my mother.

"I knew we should never have let her go to high school dances."

I heard my mother get up from the chair, to make chai no doubt; tea companioned all events, soothed every emotion.

"Mom, a dance never hurt anyone."

"She's never happy; she mopes around all day, her head in silly books and now I just saw her walking home with *that* white boy. Is that what it takes to make her smile?" I flinched at the hostility in her voice. "She is too much like Harjinder."

"Mom, just because Harj left doesn't mean she will. Give Meena some space. It's been hard for her."

"Hard for her? What about me? I am the one who cries for Harjinder, I am the one who wonders where my daughter is, what she is doing, who she is with. She is out there, somewhere, living like a gora, pretending that she is one of them. I don't want that for Meena." I sat up, listening more attentively when I heard Harj's name mentioned alongside mine. "Sometimes I think I should send her back to England to live with her sister, or maybe

India this time? She could learn to cook, learn some respect and usefulness. Indian girls in England are still Indian. She could learn something."

"Mom, you can't send her away again. It won't do any good."

"Why not? It did her some good the first time. When she came back she was respectful, even spoke Punjabi."

"Yes, you're right, she was different, she is different; she's not Harj and you can't keep treating her like she's the one who ran away. Look, I'll go talk to her."

I put my headphones on and opened up a notebook, scribbling in the side margins when I heard Serena walk down the hall towards my room.

She sat on the edge of my bed, pulled my headphones off and held them to her ear. "What are you listening to?"

"New Order."

Serena got up, walking around my room, studying the walls covered in *Rolling Stone*, *Vogue* and *Elle* magazine covers. "Wow. Mom never let me put anything like this up in my room. But then again, I never thought to ask."

The only thing that Serena had on her bedroom walls when she was my age was some pictures of ducks that she'd painted. I thought she was an artist until I realized they were from a paint-by-numbers kit. She sat down again, picking up my Walkman, turning it around in her hands. "Harj was so excited when I bought this for her. She wore it everywhere. You remember that time she even wore it to the gurdwara, with the headphones hidden under her chunni?"

I nodded, half laughing. "That was classic."

"I was so worried that Mom would find out that I sat so she couldn't see Harj." Serena looked away, negotiating the silence. "What are you writing?"

I put the notebook down. "Stuff."

"New poems?"

"Yeah. I've been reading a lot of Neruda lately and—"

"That's good. It's important to have a hobby."

"It's more than a hobby." I pulled a university application out of my backpack, showing her the creative writing program in Toronto that I wanted to apply for.

"Oh Meena... You know how Mom feels about that. It's been hard for her since Harj left. Don't make things harder for her."

"I'm not."

"I know. I know you're not. But she worries and, well, with Harj gone..." She paused. "Things are *different*... I know it's hard, we all miss her, but she made her choices and we're all living with them. For you part of that is doing what Mom wants you to—unless you want to go back to England?"

I pulled my knees into my chest. "And when do I get to do what I want?"

"When you get married."

"When I'm married? Then I'll just be someone else's daughter and someone's wife. When will I get to be who *I* am?"

"This is who you are." She touched my shoulder in an attempt at affection before leaving to answer our mother's call to tea.

I lay on my bed thinking about Harj. Two years ago I'd come home from school to find Tej crying. When I'd asked her what was wrong, she handed me the note that she'd found on the coffee table. I'd said good-bye to Harj before I left for school; she told me to have a good day. I tried to think if she'd said it differently than she usually did. Should I have known by her tone that I wasn't going to see her again? But I wasn't paying attention. It was just another day that I was wishing away. At times, I thought it would have been easier for my mother if Harj were dead. There was no betrayal in that type of loss; it was acceptable, even manageable.

The year that Harj left, my mother sent me to England for the summer to stay with my sister Parm and her new husband. After a week, I realized my vacation was an intervention; I was sent there to learn how to be good. I spent that summer vacation wearing a salwar kameez, mouthing prayers from the *Guru Granth Sahib* and learning how to make roti. I passed my days with chores and between tea time and supper would retreat to the solarium while Parm sat in the front room, tuned into the much-loved Australian soap opera *Neighbours*. Oddly, it was during an episode of *Neighbours* that I met Ranjit, who lived next door in an identical red brick house. His mother had sent him over to get some spinach from our garden so she could make fresh saag paneer for dinner.

He was two years older than me and, despite a very religious and traditional Sikh appearance, turned out to be pretty cool. He wore Pepe jeans and khakis before they were common and had a CD player even though stores were still selling records. He was passionate about the hybrid of hip hop and house music, claiming that it gave the world a sound to match the technological revolution. He was sure that Macintosh and MS-DOS would change how we experienced life, so he studied computer programming while living within the confines of our cultural programming. We were a lot alike. He wore a turban to please his mother and I was trying to learn how to make a round roti to please mine. On the days that Parm and her husband were at work, Ranjit and I would sneak away and take the Underground into London to explore the world that we were not supposed to be part of.

Two days before I was to return to Canada we were on the train, on our way back home, when he suddenly asked me if I would ever marry someone with a turban. His eyes were as intense as the silence that followed. I didn't want to tell him no; I didn't want to tell him yes. I sat for a moment, wavering between reason and emotion, swaying with the movements of the train.

"No, I could never marry someone who was so religious and traditional," I told him.

"Yeah, but you can look the part and not be, you know?"

"No, I don't know."

That was the last time we spoke.

1.3

Mr. Peters looked up from the blackboard just as I was attempting to slip into English class undetected. He put his chalk down and wiped the dust on his denim pants before adjusting the waistband. He was the kind of man who apparently didn't realize that over the years his stocky build had turned to fat rolls that were slopping over his belt, pushing his jeans to new lows, causing shirt buttons to pull and seams to show their toothy grimace.

"To be in class or not to be in class, Meena? That is the question."

I caved into the desk in front of Liam's. "To be."

"And?"

"But I was only a minute late."

I sighed and waited for him to hand me my poetic punishment.

Liam leaned forward, his breath in my ear, and whispered, "How about Lord Byron?" Mr. Peters slapped his ruler on the desk. He was a former rugby player who often used his class as a captive audience for the stories of his glory days. Worse were his poetic indiscretions; at the end of Grade 11 he had written in almost every girl's annual: "She walks in beauty like the night, of cloudless climbs and starry skies, And all that's best of light and dark meet in her aspect and her eyes." Although I thought his licence in messing with genious was perverse, I felt slighted when he scrawled only "Have a good summer" in mine. Shortly after, I decided that there was nothing he could teach me that I couldn't learn on my own so I began skipping every other class and had continued to do so this year. Whenever I actually showed up, Mr. Peters went to great lengths to single me out with his condescending tones and Shakespearean theatrics.

"To be, or not to be," he repeated, handing me my essay on Hamlet, frowning despite the A+ that was scrawled and circled at the top. I wasn't sure whether it was my lack of participation and attendance that offended him or whether it was the fact that despite the lack of either, I still had the best mark in the class. "We're waiting," he said, returning to the front of the classroom.

"To be, or not to be." My voice snagged.

"Louder please," he said, leaning against his desk. "And stand up."

I stood up, clearing my throat above the rush of laughter behind me:

"To be, or not to be: that is the question
Whether 'tis nobler in the mind to suffer
The slings and arrows of outrageous fortune,
Or to take arms against a sea of troubles."

Mr. Peters motioned for me to sit down and asked Tina to finish the soliloquy. She stood, without having to be asked, and offered a performance that was almost as bad as her portrayal of Annie in the school musical.

Liam passed a note over my shoulder: "The correct answer is 'Not to be in class'... meet me out front in five minutes." A few minutes after Liam snuck out the back of the classroom, I followed; he was waiting for me in the parking lot.

"Where to?" I asked, tossing my books into the back of his '67 powder-blue Mustang.

"The beach."

"Are you sure your car will make it this time?" I asked, recalling the last time we'd skipped school together and ended up walking three miles to get to a pay phone. We'd waited inside that cramped phone booth for his friend to pick us up, safe from the steady rain that caused my hair to fall in dripping curls as we watched our breath settle onto the glass. Occasionally

Liam would reach over my shoulder and wipe the condensation with his palm, laughing nervously as we bumped up against each other; our laughter would suddenly turn quiet, our voices to whispers that made the glass fog with the heaviness of anticipation.

Liam started the car, a grin across his face as he looked over at me. I wondered if he too was remembering the last time we'd been so close and yet no closer. I popped the cassette from my Walkman into the deck—The Smiths' "How Soon is Now?" blasting.

"Don't worry," he shouted over Morrissey's drone. "We can make it. I just took it in to shop class this morning." Mr. Conner, who spent most of his time flipping through *Playboy* magazines that were not so discreetly hidden within his curriculum text, never even noticed that Liam wasn't one of his students. After half a semester, Liam had learned what he needed to and stopped attending, occasionally sneaking his car back in for tune-ups. It was during one of those visits that he found Mr. Conner's collection of porn stuffed into a red tool box. He decided that he wanted to expose his classmates to the subject matter that absorbed all of Mr. Conner's time and placed the collection of pornographic tapes among the hundreds of documentaries that were housed in the audiovisual room. The tapes became legendary and were well guarded by the scores of boys suddenly volunteering to be AV monitors. When Liam told me what he'd done, I asked him if he'd kept any of the video tapes for himself and was glad when he replied, "No, I'm not into that shit." I was relieved even if it was a lie.

At the beach I gazed over the edge of the pier, holding the railing with both hands. The water was calm, except for the speedboats that swept the greys into greens and the greens into browns. I imagined climbing over the railing and jumping into the water, sinking into the shadowy depths; kelp forests entangling my body, pirate ghosts capturing me for an eternity until I was reborn and transformed into a water nymph with threaded wings of seaweed tasselled with golden coins. I would be neither blue nor green, neither fish nor girl, but something magical and intensely beautiful.

Liam jumped behind me, pushing my shoulders. I tensed. "Scared you'll fall in?"

My body tightened, resisting his hands. "Liam, don't." I shoved him away, swatting him with my backpack.

"Come on, I can teach you," he said, already abandoning the pier and walking towards the bend in the beach that was bordered by tall grass and driftwood.

I trailed behind. "I don't have a swimsuit."

"Neither do I." He walked towards the water, removing his clothing layer by layer until he was naked. The sun struck his body at an angle that reduced him to a thin black shadow lined in molten gold and yet when he looked back at me I could make out his smile. It was electric. He motioned for me to follow, but I refused, preferring to sit on a nearby rock, the tide splashing against me as he rushed into the surf. Watching him disappear and reappear in the water, I squinted against the twinkling light that reflected off the water until my sight was infrared. I closed my eyes and leaned back into the breeze, listening to the sound of his strokes, the waves. I'd been too frightened to go into the water since last semester's phys. ed. class. The boys had hooted and hollered at the white string-bikini girls who slipped into the pool. I'd sat on the edge of the pool with my arms crossed over my black maillot and watched the boys dive in, grab the girls beneath the water, and playfully tug at their strings. The girls feigned shock and outrage in giggles and wet back slaps.

When Ms. Richards saw me loitering along the side, she yelled at me to get in. I edged into the pool slowly, feeling for the bottom, fighting against the water's attempts to swallow me. I bobbed along until there was no bottom for me to push against. My heart began to race as my legs flailed beneath me. I told myself not to panic, and in between mouthfuls of water, I told myself that I was fine. I felt like I was inside a wave: a hollow hum passed through my ears and over my head, until all sound was a dampened echo. The water above me punctured, a surge of pressure came towards me, and Liam's hand reached for mine. "It's okay, I've got you, you're fine... you're fine."

Now Liam walked out of the water, silver and clean, his shadow falling over me. He flopped onto his back in the sand, sun-drying, eyes closed. I looked over at him, watching the heat radiate off his skin until I felt its flush on my own skin, felt my own pulse deepen. I tried to stop looking but couldn't. I'd never seen a naked man except for the ones in the *Playgirl* magazine at a 7-Eleven that Carrie had dared me to look at. All the men were oiled and erect; their expression, wanting and contrived. None of them were as beautiful and vulnerable as Liam.

"You should have come. The water was great." I didn't answer and quickly looked away as he got up and pulled on his jeans. I handed him his shirt; sand fell from his flesh onto mine like brown sugar. "You would have liked it," he said pulling his shirt over his head. Patches of sand on his skin shimmered, the hairs on his body lit up like gold filigree.

I looked over his head into the sun. "Another time," I said, and walked back along the shore, combing through the tidal debris with my toes. Liam came and stood next to me, skipping rocks along the water.

"Teach me to do that?"

"Sure." He pulled a rock from his pocket and handed it to me, explaining that the rock had to hit the water at just the right angle and speed to skip. This was all about physics.

He stood behind me, rock in my hand, his hand on mine, imitating the motion a few times before pulling my hand back with his and freeing the stone. I counted the ripples as it skipped across the surface.

"See. Now you try it." He handed me another rock and I held it in my palm for a moment before I lobbed it towards the horizon. I looked back at him quizzically when it plopped into the water.

"It takes practice." He picked up a pebble to demonstrate. "You just have to snap your wrist faster."

The breeze twisted my hair into ribbons. "Show-off!"

A rush of whitewater chased me from the shore and I retreated to a nearby log while Liam walked into the waves. He knelt down, etched something in the sand with a stick and watched the water take it away. I pulled my journal out of my bag and as I read my thoughts, hoped the tide would pull them out to sea. Liam wiped his hands on his jeans and sat next to me. "What are you writing?"

I closed the book. "Nothing."

"Can I see it then?"

I hugged the leather journal close to me. "No. It's private."

"Come on." He reached over again, placed his hand on mine, tilted his head and looked up at me with a smile that curled on one side like the crest of a wave. "Come on, let me see."

"Okay. But promise you won't laugh."

"Yeah, promise." He pried the book from me and opened it to the dog-eared page. Sand from his fingers sprinkled across the page and settled in the crease as he began to read: "The smell of chai—fennel, cloves and cinnamon tucked me into my blanket like a seed in a cardamom pod... ."

"Liam, don't read it out loud!"

"Okay, but I can't read silently, never could. I can't comprehend anything that way. Some weird learning disability... so I'll whisper it, okay?"

I agreed, but before he continued, I took the book back. "I changed my mind."

He reached into the sand and picked up a piece of paper that had fallen out of the book. "What's this?"

I tried to grab it. "Give it here."

He unfolded it and held it out of reach, mumbling the words as he skimmed the contents, announcing the highlights. "Your personal essay 'The Have Nots'... has been awarded second place in our Young Writers of Canada contest... invited to Toronto to accept your scholarship prize... ."

I grabbed it from him and crumpled it into my bag with the journal.

"What's the matter? This is amazing. Why aren't you happy about it?"

I shook my head and pitched my toes in the sand. "Because my mom won't let me go."

"Why?"

"It's complicated." I watched the tide roll over itself.

"Well, then, explain it to me," he said, scrawling my name into the sand with the sharp end of a stone.

"Because Toronto is too far from home and because she thinks that writing is a waste of time and wants me to do something more *productive.*"

"Like what?"

"I don't know. She wants me to go to university, be a lawyer or a doctor, some shit like that."

"You can't let her tell you what to do. You've got to go. It's what you want, what you've always talked about."

"I wish it were that simple." I scooped a fistful of sand, sifting it through my fingers like an hourglass. "Sometimes I just want to run away, you know. Figure things out on my own."

"So why don't you?" he asked.

I thought about Harj. I had almost admired her for running away, for doing what no other Punjabi girl before her had done, until I experienced the consequences of her leaving, felt the rawness of my mother's tears, the ripples that her absence had created in all of us. Her choice to leave seemed to leave me with one less choice. "I don't think I could ever outrun myself." I picked up a rock and tossed it into the water, surprised that it skipped.

"You know, a lot of things that don't make sense are done because people don't question things enough."

"Huh?"

"I'll show you." Liam got up and walked towards the railway track. I followed, stepping on the cross ties as he balanced on the edge. "The distance between these rails is 56 ½ inches, not because it's the best-engineered width but because of the cultural engineering surrounding the gauge."

"What are you talking about? What does a railway track have to do with me?"

"Well, the width of a railway track is based on the width of the wheel spacing on a horse-drawn wagon, *which* was actually designed based on the width of a Roman chariot, *which* was designed to accommodate the width of two horses' asses. Technically, the tracks should have been wider; the trains would have been more stable and there'd be a lot less derailments. But no one ever even thought to make it differently. No one questioned anything."

"So what you're saying is that if we don't question anything we'll make asses of ourselves?" I laughed and shoved him from the rail. He got up smiling, dusted the sand off his jeans and chased me along the dormant tracks towards the abandoned house that was the scene of many drunken teenage parties.

The house reminded me of home. Of the house my father had bought when he came to Canada, how abandoned it looked on the day that we moved away with the last of our belongings piled into the trunk of Mamaji's Chevrolet Impala. When my mother locked the door and stood in front of the freshly sprayed graffiti that marred our leaving, I realized that in the face of such unyielding realities we had vacated my father's dreams, taking only the emptiness that remained.

I ran up the porch steps and looked through the dirty glass that had been cracked and sparingly boarded. Liam tried the door. It shook but didn't open.

"There's got to be a way in."

I followed him to the back of the house. "Liam, we shouldn't."

He pulled a loose board off the window and climbed in. "Go around to the front. I'll open the door."

As I entered, I covered my mouth with my hand. The house smelled like cat piss and weed. "Home sweet home," I muttered. My voice resonated through the graffiti-covered walls and the only inhabitants of the house—a few pieces of decrepit furniture, that lingered in rooms like ghosts. "I wonder why whoever lived here would leave their stuff."

Liam shrugged. He had taken a camera out of his backpack and was taking pictures. It was the newest of the old cameras he'd found at the thrift store the last time we'd ditched class. We always cruised the Sally Ann aisles and loitered in the furniture section, where we sat on settees with split upholstery, reading five-cent romance paperbacks, before checking out the antiquated electronic sections for yet another camera for his collection.

"Maybe it was easier," he mused between frames. "You know, leave the past in its place... Hey, do you have a felt pen?"

I took my backpack off, pulled a felt marker out and handed it to Liam, who had put down his camera to read the writing on the wall—love, hate and lust all tumbling over each other towards the white space where he scrawled "Liam and Meena were here May, 1990." Then he took a picture of it.

When I got home, Serena and my mother were in the bedroom talking in hushed voices. I pressed my ear against the door, trying to hear without being heard. Serena seemed upset; her tone rose and fell in broken words that I couldn't make out. I wondered if she and Dev were fighting again and if she would really leave him this time. Just after A.J. was born, she moved back home for a month and lay on the couch in my mother's housecoat watching reruns of *Dallas*, drinking countless cups of tea, her bruised ribs mending. "It hurts to breathe," she'd told me. I nodded as though I understood, and in a way I did. Life was asphyxiating. Once Serena was well enough, my mother had called her mother-in-law and brokered her return. They came to collect her, drinking their tea in measured apology, and in return we all became good at avoiding asking her how she was; we learned to look away when we talked to her and pretended not to notice her vacant eyes and dramatic weight loss. Her body was pulled in on itself, flesh wrapped tight, calling attention to protruding bones and joints. Sometimes I'd reach for her hand and pluck bones like guitar strings.

Cupping my hand around my ear, I pressed my body close to the door just like Harj had taught me to. "Be strong," my mother said. "Think of your son. He needs his father." Serena did not seem to answer. I wondered why she still sought my mother's counsel—the advice never changed. Perhaps that was what she wanted: Affirmation. Validation. Acceptance. How easily we confused these things with love.

I rushed into my room when I heard their voices draw closer. A moment later Serena was in my doorway, her face pale as she looked in on me. She was transparent, barely a fraction of her former self. I waited for her to say something, but she just stood there in a daze, eyelids drooping, leaning against the wall as if she were holding the house up. Hollow-eyed, she stared out at nothing just as we all did—with blindness and longing.

1.4

Just before third period, I grabbed my Walkman and backpack and hurried across the parking lot, squinting through intermittent raindrops. I turned the music up, matching my steps to the rhythm of "Personal Jesus," navigating past the smoke pit and huddled fringe groups who hung out by the portables. "Feeling unknown... ." I replayed it until I was off school grounds and on my way to Liam's house. He had missed school before, but never for this long. Last time it had been a week, but even then he'd dropped a postcard in my locker—his way of saying "see you soon." Liam was always buying old photographs and postcards from thrift stores and he occasionally passed some on to me. Once when we were reading the back of 1960s' vacation postcards, I told him that it was sad to buy other people's memories; he reminded me that he was the only person who wanted them. He made collages out of them, adding in new pictures that he had taken, until you couldn't tell new from old. My favourite was simply a collection of postmarks pasted and overlapped on photographs of corner stores, stoplights, park benches, street corners and empty beaches. He called it "Wish You Were Here."

I trampled through his overgrown front lawn, past the unkempt flower beds that hinted at better days, and up the steps to the front door. The stoop was littered with local newspapers, junk mail and cigarette butts that hadn't made it to the tinfoil ashtray on the railing. I knocked and knelt down to pick up the mail and was sorting it into a neat stack when Liam answered.

He pulled my headphones off. "Miss me?"

"Just curious where you've been." I handed him the pile of junk mail, trying not to bite my lip on the lie. By now he knew all my tells.

The house smelled like stale smoke and wet dogs, like the cheap motels my mother cleaned. I followed him up a few stairs and down a dingy, green-carpeted hallway adorned with a "Jesus loves you" embroidered wall hanging and fading family photos. I stared into the placid smiles and solemn eyes, pausing at a photo of a four-year-old Liam blowing out birthday candles, his mother smiling at his side.

"Do you miss her?" I asked.

"What's to miss? I barely knew her." He went quiet for a minute and stared at the pictures. I reached for his hand but he moved away before I could hold it. "She lives in Saskatchewan with a guy named Chuck." He laughed that painful laugh that I had initially misinterpreted as satisfaction. "Can you believe that? Chuck, what a name... Chuck rhymes with *fuck.*" He walked farther down the hallway. "This is my room," he said, pushing the door open. The walls were covered in vintage art and rock 'n' roll posters tacked and taped in place, one overlapping the next. His photographs were thumbtacked all over his closet door. There was even one of me. I had my hands up in a don't-take-my-picture way, but you could still see I was smiling. His bed was unmade and showed no signs of ever having been made, his mahogany dresser and nightstand were missing handles and he had a milk crate full of records beside a 1970s' sideboard-style stereo. Books were balanced in piles on the threadbare carpet, and between the Prousts and Emersons were mounds of clothing. His room was like a flea market—a crowded thrift store at best.

I picked up one of his cameras and looked at him through the lens. "So... where have you been lately? Are you sick?"

"Yeah," he said and reached for the camera to show me where the shutter release was. I clicked off a few frames." Well, I mean, no. Not really."

He sighed and pushed his hair away from his eyes, only to have it slip back. "You know, I'm just sick of school, so I'm taking a break. A sabbatical, so to speak."

"What does your dad think about that?" I asked.

"He's hardly around." He picked up another camera and took my picture taking his picture. "That'll be a neat one," he said, taking another.

"Aren't you worried that he'll find out?"

"No, not really. Besides, he wouldn't even care."

I nodded. Part of me wanted to ask him why, but our relationship was built on not knowing.

I put the camera down and walked across the room to look out the window at the backyard. It was littered with rubbish: car parts, rusty bicycles, a dilapidated 1970s' swing set, a Mr. Turtle pool filled with rainwater and leaves, and an old German shepherd who appeared equally defeated. I looked away, not wanting to see my reflection in the neglect. Liam was sitting with legs outstretched on the bed, flipping through an encyclopedia. A stack of them teetered on the floor nearby.

"Did you rob the library or something?"

"Funny," he said flatly. "I picked them up from the Sally Ann; this is my education in lieu of school. I'm already on *D.*"

"Wow," I said, matching his tone.

"Did you know that dinosaurs only get a few pages? Millions of years ruling the earth and they get a few measly pages."

I picked up the newspaper that was on his bed and unfolded it to the crossword. "Well, I guess humans should only get a paragraph then."

"I was thinking a footnote, if we're lucky."

He picked up volume *E*, opened it and started reading. His lips mouthed the words like tiny breaths. I sat down next to him, pulled out the pencil that I'd used to tie up my hair, and shook the knot loose just like the girls on all the shampoo commercials did.

I worked away at the puzzle for an hour, aware of how close we were sitting to each other, aware that he had looked up from his encyclopedia several times and traced the line of my leg to the hem of my "Blondie" miniskirt. I was sure I had seen a picture of Debbie Harry wearing a similar black-and-white-striped skirt, or maybe I'd seen it on TV. I couldn't remember; I was just a kid when my sisters had huddled around the TV set watching her sing "Heart of Glass" on *American Bandstand*. We always watched *AB* on Saturday mornings and *Solid Gold* in the evenings. When other kids were going to piano, ballet or soccer practice on Saturday mornings, I was taking the bus downtown to A&B Sound, Zulu Records and Odyssey Imports.

I walked over to Liam's stereo and pulled a record from the yellow Dairyland crate. *"Platinum Blonde?"*

"I just liked the one song."

"Doesn't Really Matter?" I asked, as I put the album back and picked up Simple Minds.

"What's wrong with that?"

"Nothing. I have the record too, only mine is autographed."

"No way."

"Yes way. They were signing records at A&B. My sister and I lined up for three hours to meet them."

"So what were they like?"

"Short."

"I guess that's why they have big hair," he said, smiling. "Napoleon complex meets Vidal Sassoon."

I laughed as I pulled the Simple Minds record from its sleeve, placed it on the turntable and lowered the needle on "Don't You Forget About Me."

"She should have ended up with Bender?"

"Huh?"

"In *The Breakfast Club*—Molly Ringwald, she should have stayed with Bender."

"*The Breakfast Club?* Was that the one with the quintessential dweeb named Duckie?"

"No, that was *Pretty in Pink*."

"Seen one John Hughes movie, seen them all."

"That's not true. They're kind of different."

"How? They're all about white suburban kids with no real problems, except for that Ally Sheedy character in *The Breakfast Club*. She's morbid, a bit like you."

"I'm not morbid," I said, flopping down next to him on the bed.

He picked up the paper and handed it to me. "I saw you reading the obituaries."

"I glanced at them… what's wrong with that? The paper is filled with stories about life and death. I was just reading the abbreviated versions."

"So, Miss Morbid, have you spent time on what you want your obit to say?"

I folded the paper. "No—but I know what I *don't* want it to say."

"What's that?"

"Well, I don't want it to use the phrase 'survived by.' It's such a euphemism. Why not just list the people who were left behind rather than say that the deceased was *survived by*. I can't imagine you actually survive the loss of a love, you just bear it, and you just go on until you become someone else so you can forget who you were … how you were."

"Do you think that's what your mom did?" Liam turned towards me, propping himself on his elbow. He waited in my silence, both of us staring at each other as if we were playing a game of chicken, waiting to see which of us would give in. Me. Always me. I tossed the newspaper onto the floor and walked back to the window. "What's your dog's name?"

"Darwin," he answered.

"Seriously?"

"Yeah, my grandmother got him for me when I was in Grade 10 as some kind of compensation for making me go to Holy Trinity."

"I can't believe you ever went there."

"Tell me about it. That's why I named the dog Darwin. It was my first attempt at religious rebellion."

"There were more?"

"Yeah, I did whatever I could to get them to kick me out of school."

"Like?"

He sat up straight and put his encyclopedia down. "Well, for starters I quoted Nietzsche and questioned everything. In religious studies, I pointed out that if Mary Magdalene was a prostitute it was likely that Jesus was a john. In English I wrote an essay called "Jesus, Portrait of a Coloured Man," arguing that, based on anthropology, Jesus could not have been white."

"How long before they kicked you out?"

"A whole year. They wanted to save me, that is until they caught me making out with Jennifer Milton in a confession booth... her dad donated tons of money to the school. Needless to say, I was expelled the following week."

I laughed even though I felt a pang of jealousy in my stomach. "So this Jennifer person, was she your girlfriend?" I sat down next to him, my thigh brushing his.

"No, I've never had a steady girlfriend. But there is this girl I like." His palm grazed my leg. I stared at it, half expecting it to have left a mark.

My voice caught in my throat and rattled out, "Really?" I tried to seem disinterested and flung my legs over the side of the bed, my back to him as I picked up an encyclopedia and flipped through the pages for a few minutes. "You should tell her."

"I've thought about it. But if I told her that I like her then everything may change. I may lose her—I don't think I could survive that."

I stopped flipping pages, tentative and almost frightened as I turned towards him. "Yeah, but if you never tell her, you won't know if she feels the same way."

He stared at me until the slightest smile formed on his lips. "She'll know it by what I don't say."

I picked up an encyclopedia and lay down on my stomach next to him, both of us quietly flipping through pages, not reading a word.

As I walked home I wondered if the aunties on the street had seen me leave Liam's house, and if they did, whether they would report back to my mother. My sisters and I referred to them as the Indian Intelligence Association. As members of the IIA they were induced by their morals to spend their afternoons looking out windows, gathering gossip and delicious details that they spread through a game of broken telephone. They were a blend of town crier and gossip columnist who spun stories like webs, occasionally devouring victims like my sister Harj.

Two years before, she'd been walking home from the bus stop when a group of DIPs in a yellow Trans Am followed her home. They'd been following her every day for a week and every day she'd come home in tears, too ashamed to repeat the things they had said. She knew not to turn around, not to pay them any attention, but the sound of their car rolling over the gravel made her skin prick with fear and like animals, they sensed it. It was the only encouragement they needed that day.

They pulled their car up beside her and one of the boys jumped out, grabbing the back of her arm, pulling her against his body, laughing as she begged for him to let her go. The aunties must have watched from behind their sheer living-room draperies, they must have heard her cries, they must have seen the trail of dirt and stones as the car careened away, because when she came home my mother had already been told that my sister had gotten in a car with a group of boys.

Harj tried to explain what had happened, that she had been grabbed, driven to an empty lot... Her words fell back, swallowed in open-mouthed sobs. My mother slapped her. "Stop it! Stop it! Not another word!" she'd yelled. Serena rushed to Harj's side to save her from more injury. My mother dropped her hand, her eyes full of the questions she saved for God.

Harj, who had studied sociology in university, once told me that we were a natural target for judgments: a family already wounded was easy prey for a community that often turned on itself. She ran away a few months later. Despite my mother's attempts at reconciliation, she would not return home. Tej and I visited her once, and though we were appalled by the squalor of her Eastside apartment—the mousetraps in the corner, the red-bricked views, the black mildew on thin-paned windows—we said nothing of it. Her roommate, who I later realized was her boyfriend, was sitting on a plastic patio chair by the window, chain-smoking cigarettes. Harj didn't introduce us; she acted like he wasn't even there and made us jasmine tea from small green packets she had taken from the Chinese restaurant she worked in. "So how is Mom... Serena... A.J.?" She asked after everyone, the way we were taught to do, and we summed up family health in small reassuring statements that opened to truthful sighs.

"What will you do?" Tej asked. "Where will you go?"

"I don't know," she said. Perhaps admitting it out loud frightened her, because for the rest of the visit she stared out the dirt-streaked window without saying a word. When we came home, my mother called us into the kitchen where she was making roti. I couldn't tell if she was angry or if the dry heat off the cast iron tava had simply settled onto her cheeks. "Goapy Auntie called. She said she saw you in the city today."

"She's wrong." I glanced at Tej. "I was at school and Tej was... " Before I could finish my sentence my mother lifted her hands from the tava and hit me. "Liar!" I fell back and reached for the counter to steady myself, but only managed to grab hold of the stack of plates piled on it, pulling them down with me.

My mother turned the stove off and walked to her room, where she stayed barricaded for the next two weeks. She ignored our knocks, our pleas at the door, our tear-soaked apologies. The only person she would speak to was her brother. Mamaji came by once a day, and each time he emerged from her bedside I looked into the room to see my mother lying in the near-dark, discarded tissues piled on the nightstand next to empty teacups. Once she saw me peeking in, and told me in a small voice to come inside. I hesitated, my steps short and heavy, approaching with the trepidation of a child looking upon the old and infirm. I sat on the edge of her bed, saying nothing as I listened to her breath fall into a sedated sleep—slow and rhythmic, perfectly prescribed. As I rose to leave, she startled and clasped my hand, looking at me as if I were a stranger, the edges of her reality softening into the mercies of sleep. I sat in the dark watching the little light there was play on her face like a language of dreams. I lay next to her and slept there for the next year.

Occasionally Harj sent me a card. Any time one arrived, my mother stared at it for a long time before asking me to read it to her, and then was disappointed that all it ever said was: "Missing you. xoxo Harj." Sometimes my mother would buy a box of ladoos and send it to the return address. I told her that Canada Post would not deliver ladoos to a po box, but she insisted on sending them. They were Harj's favourite. My mother was always saddened when the crumpled box of sweets was returned stamped "Address Unknown." She took the contents—broken bits, sugary yellow crumbs—and scattered them on the front lawn. "For the crows," she'd say.

I stopped in front of our home, looked around, and through the front window of the house across the street saw an auntie standing in her living room. I wondered if she was clocking me or whether she was wondering, as was I, why there were so many cars in our driveway. I rushed inside to find out. The house smelled like an Indian sweet shop; the intense aroma of ghee filled the spaces between chatter and smiling voices. I hadn't heard such bright voices since Harj had left.

"What's going on?" I asked Serena, who was standing in the kitchen with Masi. Masi smiled and took off her glasses. She handed me a large, folded aerogram. I opened the knifed edge and pulled out a 4x6 studio portrait of a young Indian man. The constipated expression on his face belied the seemingly thoughtful posture he had assumed, with his arms folded across his chest. The edges of the photo were softened and air-brushed, not at all like the edgy and candid portraits Liam liked to take.

"He is handsome, isn't he!" she said, clapping her hands.

"Yeah, I guess—who is he?"

She grabbed my shoulder, shaking and hugging me with a force that was greater than her five-foot frame. "This is Kishor Auntie's nephew. He is here from England looking for a bride."

"Kishor Auntie?" I had always thought it strange to call every Indian woman, related or not, "Auntie." Harj had told me that she thought giving strangers titles was a way to rebuild our villages outside of India; adopting the appearances of community was easier than creating a real one.

"Yes, you know the lady that I carpool with. When I heard about her nephew I showed her a picture of Tej and she asked if they could come over for tea and meet her."

"When?" I hadn't taken my eyes off the photograph. The suitor looked typically Indian: lentil eyes, a pakora nose and thin lips. His shortcomings were made somehow handsome by a mall glamour shot.

"Tonight. They will be here tonight." Masi's smile grew wider as she clasped her hands to her chest and looked behind me. "Oh, Tejinder, look at you, you almost look pretty!" I turned around. The perpetual scowl that stretched across Tej's face, wrinkling her forehead and pinching her nose, had disappeared; her face had softened, as if someone had smoothed out her fleshed disappointment. "Maybe a little powder, heh?" Masi suggested, reaching into her purse for a compact. "Even out your complexion a little more. I think you have been getting too much sun."

My mother came rushing into the room, her hands busily knotting her hair into a bun, her mouth holding the pins that would keep it in place. She stopped as she looked at me, and unclenched the pins from her frown.

"Meninder, change your clothes, you know you should not be wearing such things," she said, pointing at my skirt.

"What's the big deal? I'm not the one they're coming to see."

She poked the pins into her hair. "He has a twenty-year-old brother; God willing, he may be perfect for you."

Masi clapped her hands. She was always clapping her hands, as if she were aware of a rhythm to life that we could not hear. "Oh, what an idea! Two brothers marry two sisters. Just like a Hindi movie."

"Those movies always end badly," I said. "Someone either dies or kills for true love."

My mother offered a tight-lipped smile. "Love shmov! That is best left to movies. Now, go change your clothes."

That afternoon we rolled gulab jamun in coconut flakes, scattered pistachio crumbs on burfi and prepared the dough for samosas. Masi rammed her fist into the dough and tunnelled her fingers through, reaching out the other side, folding the dough in on itself while singing "Mere Jeevan Saathi"—My Life Partner. She batted her eyes and teased Tej with the hip-twitching choreography of a Bollywood sequence, dancing around the kitchen with a jug of water balanced on her head, until we all collapsed into laughter. Even my mother grinned. We sat end-to-end, filling the dough cones with potatoes and sealing them with milk, Masi's chatter filling the space between tasks. "When I was your age, girls did not meet their husband... until the wedding night," she said, wheezing with laughter.

My mother elbowed Masi, recalling that when Masi's betrothed had come to see her, she'd hidden in a tree. "I had to climb up the tree to get her and by the time we came back to the house, they had left," my mother said.

"Well, no one was as lucky as your mother in marriage," Masi said. "Your father: so kind and handsome... The village girls swooned any time he came around. He looked like he was from a Bollywood film, a young Dharmendra riding around on his motorcycle, hoping to get a look at your mother. You know, he had come to see our cousin, but when he saw your mother he asked for her hand instead."

"Mom, you never told us that," Tej said.

"Oy, oy, enough of this. We are falling behind," my mother said, heating the frying oil, a flustered embarrassment about her.

It was two hours of assembly-line work that was full of gossip, the occasional giggle fit and my mother's momentary culinary concerns turning to full-scale cooking catastrophes when she lamented the loss of one over-stuffed samosa that had burst at the seams and tainted the frying oil with bits of potatoes. "Oh, ho, now look what has happened," she said over and over, slapping her forehead.

"No matter," Masi said, fishing the remains out with a ladle. She wrapped her arm around my mother's shoulder. "Everything will be fine. Everything will work out."

I watched from the kitchen as Masi led our guests into the living room, where my mother greeted them. Kishor Auntie waddled to the couch like a fat duck struggling to get to water. She dabbed at the sprays of sweat on her temples with her chunni. The young man, whose name was Mandip, was shorter and darker than he'd looked in his picture. He sat down and examined the shag carpet, not looking at anything but his mismatched sport socks while Kishor Auntie verified our ancestry.

"Pind kera?" she asked, removing the chenille cardigan that had been stretched over her massive bosoms. I thought of the Indian woman who had sat next to me on a bus the previous week. She'd stared at me even though I was staring straight ahead, and as I shuffled in the discomfort of her glare she asked me, "Pind kera?"

I wanted to yell at her and say "Who cares? You're in Canada now? What difference does it make what village my father was from or what caste I am." But instead I lowered my head and answered respectfully just as my mother did.

"Patial."

"Kishor Auntie smiled and leaned forward, her breasts resting on her distended abdomen. "We have relatives not far from there."

"Well then, we are practically family!" Masi exclaimed. Everyone nodded and laughed nervously.

I listened until the laughter hummed into loose sighs. Our house was full of this sound each time one of my sisters got married. For days before the wedding, the house was a festival brimming with family, food and ritual happiness. Uncles, aunts, cousins—the real, the distant, the removed and the pretend—descended on our home from cities near and far to sleep on rolled-out blankets in whatever space there was. It was like a three-day carnival that, upon completion, left us with a shag carpet full of confetti. When my sister Parveen got married and moved away to Edmonton, her father-in-law assured my mother that she would be treated as his daughter. He told her that daughters are not born into their true families, and must marry into them. Though my mother knew his intentions were good, I could tell by the glaze in her eyes that she was wondering, as was I, why such good intentions reduced us to less than ourselves.

I snuck into Tej's room, where she was pacing back and forth, flattening the shag carpet while muttering, "Sat Sri Akal Auntie" in various pitches trying to find the most pleasing tone. "Is it time?" she asked.

"For you to serve tea? No, not yet."

She paced the length of the room again before sitting me down on the bed. "Tell me then, what are they like?"

I told her that Kishor Auntie was fat and smelled like patchouli, but had kind eyes and that Mandip seemed sincere. Sincere—that was the nicest way I could describe his hunched shoulders and insecure gaze.

"Do you think that we would look good together?"

I smiled. "Yeah, I think you'd make a really nice couple." She looked relieved and threw her arms around me. I was taken aback by her uncharacteristic affection, but steadied myself to her embrace. "So, is this what you want?" I asked.

"I know what you're thinking. You're thinking that I should want to fall in love, right?"

"Well, yeah. Don't you want to choose who you love?"

She turned away. I knew she must be thinking of Preet. Although they'd just been friends, everyone had hoped it would amount to something more. I remember her crying his name on the phone, demanding to know how he could go to India to marry someone he didn't know, someone he didn't love. I wondered if he'd answered her between her gulping sobs. I wondered if he'd had the courage to tell her the truth that we all suspected—that since Harj's departure we had become an even less suitable family to marry into.

Tej turned back to me and put her hands on my shoulders, her eyes locked squarely on mine. "Meena, love is never a choice. You don't get to choose who you fall in love with. You love who is chosen for you."

1.5

I sat cross-legged on the floor of the gurdwara, drawing crop circles in the carpet pile the way Harj and I used to. Behind me, most of the old ladies—the bibis who sat lining the walled perimeter—kept their eyes closed and pretended to listen to the scriptures when they were actually half asleep, pins and needles in their feet occasionally jolting them awake. The aunties sat in front of them, whispering to one another out of the sides of their mouths while their buttery-faced pre-adolescent daughters twirled about, their stiff crinoline frocks opening and closing like lace parasols. Occasionally one of the aunties would reach over and slap her daughter on the leg, forcing the girl to sit down, while little boys dashed around, sliding into imaginary bases unfettered and unchecked.

When I was these girls' age I was allowed to play outside with the boys after the prayers. We played Simon Says in the empty parking lot and frozen tag between parked cars, and sometimes we climbed the balconies of the temple, pressing our fleshy cheeks against the windows to see inside. I'd wave at my sisters, who sat like ducklings on the carpet next to my mother, and wait for their stern disapproval before skipping off to join a game of tag. Once I darted into the parking lot so quickly that a car struck me. The driver was a woman my mother's age; she emerged panicked and flustered, yelling at me that I should have been more careful. Adults gathered around me in a circle, protecting and scolding me, treating me almost the same way they did the woman who'd hit me. After that, God and temple were no longer things to play at and I joined my sisters inside, learning how to be quiet and well behaved.

Fortunately my mother made us go to the temple only when we were invited. Though she believed in God, she didn't believe in lengthy prayers. She said they never helped. The only time I'd seen her pray was after Harj left, when for days she'd flipped through the *Guru Granth Sahib*, mouthing words and stopping only for food and water. Illiterate in two languages, she turned the pages too quickly and came to the end before her prayer recitation was complete. Like everything else, she knew God only by memory.

Serena's mother-in-law was standing before the *Guru Granth Sahib* throne, which was canopied in silk fabric and tinsel garland reminiscent of Christmas decor. She had put her money in the trough and stood with her eyes closed and hands clasped in prayer. After a minute she knelt, touched her head to the floor, rose and repeated the action—a theatrical display of faith that Tej and I snickered about. Serena kicked me in the back with her foot and when I turned around she raised her index finger to her mouth. Her mother-in-law made her way over and sat down next to us, forcing us into silence. She glanced my way and smiled until her eyes disappeared into slits. She smiled so hard I thought her gums would bleed. When I turned away, I could sense her kohl-lined eyes sizing me up and looking me over in the same measured beats as the tabla, until the music finally stopped.

"Vaheguruji Ka Khalsa, Vaheguruji Ki Fateh."

The turbaned giani took his place at the podium and tapped the microphone. "Testing." He smoothed his horsetail of a beard and cleared his throat before unleashing a prayer—a blessing for Tej's engagement to Mandip and a wish for happiness, for sons. I nudged Tej. It was enough to make her blush.

The giani continued, monotone and serious, his prayer mutating into a sermon on the danger of Western morals encroaching on Indian culture. He held his kirpan in his hand as if he were about to draw the sword on us, as if he were going to engage in battle. "Our children are lost. Vaheguru. They have no time for family. Vaheguru. They drink and smoke. Vaheguru.

They disobey their parents. Vaheguru. We must save them. Gurbani says: "Why O son, do you quarrel with your father? It is a sin to quarrel with him who begot you and brought you up." The aunties nodded in a silent but evangelical way. "Vaheguruji."

Tej and I muffled our laughter behind our chunnies. Masi had told us that she'd heard this giani had been caught in the act with his brother's wife; I couldn't help but wonder if he fucked with his turban on or off. When I asked Tej what she thought, she smacked me for being so crude.

I fidgeted, uncrossed my legs and crossed them again. Half of my ass was asleep and I was attempting to wake it up slowly. When my mother saw me rubbing my buttocks she slapped my hand, and I dropped my head in false obedience, I didn't want to upset her any more than I already had this morning when we'd argued about Liam. One of the aunties on our street had called to tell her that she'd seen us together. When my mother asked me about it, I turned my stereo up, pretending I couldn't hear her. The more she asked me, the louder the music got. "Michael Jackson is ruining you!" she yelled, pulling the needle off Depeche Mode's new album. The record screeched to a halt. "It's not Michael Jackson!" I pulled it off the turntable, examining the scratch that would render it useless. "Fuck!" I threw the record on the floor. "I don't even like Michael Jackson! Harj liked Michael Jackson. I fucking hate that shit. I hate this shit!" I ran out of the house, slamming the door so hard that the windows shook.

When I saw Liam he could tell I was upset so we skipped first period and took the SkyTrain into the city. At the first tunnel he told me to scream. I nudged him away, telling him he was crazy.

"Come on, it's as close to a primal scream as you can get. People say it feels like being born. On a count of three. One... Two... Three!" We stared into each other and screamed with our eyes open, laughing, oblivious to those around us. We got off the train still smiling hard, ribbing each other with private jokes that reduced the world to the two of us. I stared into his eyes. His pupils, dilating in the light, held me.

"What?" he asked.

"Nothing, it's nothing," I said, searching for myself in his eyes.

As I scratched his name into the gurdwara carpet, I wondered how he saw me.

"Satnam Vaheguruji," the giani concluded. The aunties began singing their tuneless warbling like a chorus of injured cats. "Vaheguru. Vaheguru." I ran my fingers across carpet, adding my name to Liam's, trying out hearts and arrows. My mother glanced my way. I straightened up, pressing my shoulder blades together, and looked up at the glass dome in the ceiling that was covered in bird shit, then down at our names, and with the haste of the unenlightened I brushed his name away.

After the prayers, we waited in line at the langar hall with our empty steel trays. The bibis jostled to get to the front, cutting off the young women and children who had no choice but to yield their hunger to them. By the time I bit into my food, the subzi was cold, the daal was swampy and the rotis were dry and brittle. I pushed my food around while my mother scraped her tin compartments clean.

"Spicy," my mother said, motioning to the kitchen helpers to bring her another glass of water, spit and daal collecting in the corners of her mouth. "Are you finished?" she asked, wiping the spittle with her hand. She reached into her cardigan sleeve and pulled out a crumpled tissue, wiped the daal from her fingers, and then tucked the dirty tissue back into her sleeve. I nodded and she scolded me for wasting so much food. She took the tray from me and poured the remains into her tray, shovelling spoonfuls of food into her mouth. An auntie stopped at our table to congratulate my mother on Tej's engagement. Tej looked up smiling.

My mother pushed the food in her mouth to one side and got up to thank her. They hugged in a one-armed embrace, my mother's smile lopsided.

The auntie smiled at me. "The youngest one?" My mother nodded. "You are so grown up now." She spoke with the blunt consonants and round vowels characteristic of ESL. "I think you and Pinky are the same age." She pointed across the room to where her daughter was standing against a cement pillar talking to her cousins, snapping bubble gum between words. Harj had always said they chewed like cows. "The two of you should get together some time, heh? Just like old times." I nodded, even though I had no intention of hanging out with her daughter. When we were little, Pinky used to bite my Barbie's feet until they looked like fins, and then she'd pull their heads off. Once when she'd come over, I waited until she left the room and pulled off her Ken doll's clothes. When she came in and saw me running my hands over his bumped crotch, she told my mom and I got in trouble.

Pinky saw us talking and waved me over. She thought she was cool now that she'd had a nose job. "So what's with you and Liam?" she asked. The other girls tucked their heads into their skinny shoulders and giggled.

"Nothing."

"I've seen you guys at school. You're with him all the time."

"No, I'm not."

"Yeah, you are, and everyone knows it." She blew a bubble, popped it, and tore at the piece with her tongue. "So do you like totally like him or something?" She pulled the gum again, this time with her fingers.

"No. I barely know him. He's not even my type." I clamped my hands across my chest, though I knew my face had flushed with the lie.

The other girls laughed louder this time. One even snorted and said, "What a freak," like I wasn't even there.

"Go fuck yourselves." I turned around and walked away, my face ripening with shame, their laughter turning my stomach.

1.6

Clouds rushed across the sky, ragged strips of blue appeared and disappeared, and when it burned through, the dime-sized sun stung my eyes. Head down, I walked to school.

"Meena!" Liam pulled his car up beside me, motioning for me to get in. I tossed my bag behind him and slid into the passenger seat.

"Where have you been? You missed the history final. You can't keep doing this or you won't graduate. What the fuck is going on with you?" I clipped my questions when I saw a hint of his sleeping bag lying crumpled under the seat.

Liam saw me eye it and with the heel of his foot tucked it farther out of sight. "I-I-I'm not going back."

I had never actually heard him stutter before. He looked away. His confident facade disappeared into a spittle of syllables.

"Y-you want to come w-with?" Though he wouldn't look at me, I saw his face was red, the flush spreading across his cheeks and creeping down his neck.

I let my silence answer him. I didn't ask him what had happened, and he didn't volunteer the information. It seemed that the longer I knew him, the less I knew of him, yet the closer I felt to him. I wondered if that was what it meant to know someone by heart.

Liam reached into the glove compartment for the mixed tape I'd made him. His hands were red with cold. I took the tape from him and fed it into the deck, forwarding it to "Never Let Me Down Again," his favourite Depeche Mode song.

"Are you hungry?" I asked, offering him an apple from my bag.

He shook his head. "I ate. I'm okay."

I took off my jacket and flung it into the back. The floor mats were covered in empty soda cans, Tim Hortons to-go cups and McDonalds cheeseburger wrappers. I added them up, trying to calculate how much time he had passed in his car. The week before, when his dad had kicked him out, he'd pawned his cameras for money and lived in his car for days before I'd found out. He would park in the school lot after dark, and wake up early so that no one would realize that he had been there all night. But one morning, for whatever reason, he didn't wake up early, and instead was jarred from sleep by the taunts of the cool kids thumping their fists on the roof, their pink faces pressed against the window as they pointed and laughed at him, calling him "white trash." By the time I arrived at school, one of them had tipped over a garbage can and was kicking the contents at him. When I saw what was happening I rushed over and jumped into the driver's side and, without looking at Liam, demanded the keys. As I started the car, I caught his frigid stare in the rear-view mirror. Still in his sleeping bag, he slumped into the corner, leaned his head against the window and closed his eyes. I drove for an hour without a clear destination, and when Liam woke again I took him to my house so he could get cleaned up. Any awkwardness I felt about him being there was cancelled out by his own. He walked through the house, looking at our cheaply framed photos and budget artwork with tentative interest. He reached for the ballerina music box that sat among the dusty knick-knacks above the stairwell, and examined it from every angle. He wound it, and held it to his ear as it twisted out the broken melody of "Raindrops Keep Falling on my Head." He smiled, and though I didn't know why, so did I. He placed the twirling ballerina back where he'd found her and as he started down the hallway, peeking in rooms asking me which one was mine, I rushed after him, rearranging everything he touched, erasing any trace of him in the present, hoping that no one would ever know that he'd been here. He stood in front of my mother's open bedroom door, pulling the contents in with one long look before walking in. He picked up a photo of my parents, glancing at the picture and then me. I had inherited my mother's sad eyes and my father's gentle mouth. The combination made me look wounded, withdrawn.

"You must miss him."

"I don't remember... I was too young."

He put the picture frame down. "I miss things I don't remember."

I straightened the picture frame before joining him in my room. He asked me when my mother would be home. I told him, "Late." He dropped his backpack onto the bed, and began to undress, asking if he could throw his clothes in the washing machine. My answer, a feeble yes. I looked up and around, trying not to notice his naked torso. But unlike that one day at the beach, I was unable to stop myself from stealing glances. He was more athletic than I remembered. My eyes traced the thread of hair from his chest to his belt. I swallowed hard, feeling the flush on my cheeks spread deep inside me.

While he was in the bathroom, I caught snatches of him through the open door and steam-covered glass; he looked like a shadow made real. I closed my eyes, and imagined water running off his body like fingers trailing skin. Sound became touch. I undressed, slid the shower door open and stepped inside, leaving only a steady stream of water between us. We kissed with our eyes open.

After, while we waited for his clothes to dry, he sat on the living-room sofa in nothing but my pink robe, eating the peanut butter and jelly sandwiches I'd made for him, watching *The Young and the Restless*, both of us pretending that this was normal.

Liam parked the car at Prospect Point. We watched boats travel through the morning light, crossing the Burrard Inlet towards the north-shore mountains, while tourists bought postcards and took pictures. "Smile and click," Liam said in no general direction, his hands in front of his face, squared off like a camera. Next to us was a Japanese couple, struggling to take a self-portrait.

"Newlyweds," I told Liam.

"How can you tell?"

"Just look." The man had his arm slung over the woman's shoulder, loose but possessive. Her hand slipped into his back pocket, fingers digging into flesh, the same way she probably did when they made love. I imagined alabaster limbs wrapped and lengthened, folded and contorted, the push of each other, her red lipstick smeared. The man took his wife's picture. He said something in Japanese that made me blush. When they kissed each other, I felt it.

Liam offered to take their picture. After, when I asked him why he'd bothered, he said, "Because one day they'll need something to remember they were happy."

I didn't know what to say and wandered away towards the jewellery carts that lined the parking lot. A man with dreadlocks tried to sell me a hemp bracelet, a fat woman in a tie-dye T-shirt was hawking jade and moonstones to unsuspecting tourists, and behind them a Chinese man was drawing charcoal portraits.

He saw me looking. "I draw your picture? Twenty dollars."

I turned out my empty pockets. "Sorry."

"Ten dollars? Special price," he said to Liam. "I make your girlfriend's picture."

Liam looked at the man, his pictures. "She's not my girlfriend," he said and walked off towards the seawall. I didn't hurry to catch up.

We spent the next hour in silence, walking around the park's marine path, stopping only to look at Siwash Rock.

"Do you know the story behind it?" I asked, looking down as water rushed around the sea stack.

Liam shook his head.

"The Squamish legend says that the rock was once a brave warrior who was turned to stone as a reward for unselfish acts and his devotion to his family."

Liam snickered. "How is that a reward?"

"It was a gift of immortality."

Liam didn't say anything and continued walking down the path. After a few other feeble attempts to engage him, I stopped trying.

It was late that afternoon by the time he began speaking in complete sentences again. I was sitting on the seawall steps, eating my bagged lunch, while he stood on the beach below watching seagulls swoop in and peck at the remains of a crow tangled in tidal debris.

"I've got to get out of here. I can't stay. I can't take it anymore." He turned towards me. I tossed the crusts of my sandwich in the air, hoping the gulls would prefer it to the crow.

"I won't end up like him, drinking at the pub, talking about the fucking good old days like there were any." As he detailed the how and when of departures, I wasn't surprised—he always had a plan. Unlike me, he knew what he was doing, where he was going. He was sure of the only thing that mattered. Himself. I almost hated him for it. The longer he talked the less I heard, the emptier I felt. He was leaving and I would be alone with all of my inevitabilities, my life plodding at a steady and predictable pace. I looked up at the sweep of blue sky over Stanley Park and watched the cars drive over the Lions Gate Bridge, listening to the constant hum of back and forth: everyone was going somewhere except me. I hung my head, cursing myself for having thought that he and I were something.

"Maybe up north I could go work the oil rigs, or maybe I could hitch a ride east," he said.

"Yeah, maybe you could. What's stopping you?"

He looked at me and then looked away into the wind. He leaned over the dead bird, looking into the small sockets where black eyes should have been. He grabbed a stick and turned it over. "Meena, check this out," he said, nudging it with his foot, pushing it towards the gulls.

"It's already dead—you don't need to kick it!" I got up and walked away, tears spilling from the corners of my eyes. Liam followed a few steps behind, his voice drifting on the wind, cancelling out the things that memory would eventually devour. I imagined that in time we would look back and recall only the details that framed the beginnings of good-byes. We would remember the sandy remains of a dead crow, the cry of gulls overhead, the dense odour of the trapped inlet and the sound of the world passing us by.

On the way home, we stopped at the Carnegie Centre. Liam wanted to give his sleeping bag to one of the homeless people by the dumpsters behind the building; once he'd given a man there his shoes and driven home barefoot. As we continued walking along the streets and alleyways, he nodded as though he were tipping his hat, sometimes addressing the locals by name: "Pete, Jane, Mary..."

"Like Mary Magdalene! Remember?" a woman said, howling with laughter.

"Remember what?" I asked him. He didn't answer. I walked with my hand tightly knitted in his, rigid by his side, leaning into him when anyone spoke to me or came so close that I could smell their liquored breath and see into their cavernous mouths. Black tongues. Missing teeth. I avoided eye contact. Liam gave his sleeping bag to a man called Joe who went into a tirade any time his name was spoken out loud. He was sure the government was after him. "They're everywhere," Joe said, his eyes wide and frantic. He smelled like piss, like rotten fruit—acidic. I held Liam's hand tighter and when we got back to the car he scolded me for triple-checking the locks and harbouring bourgeoisie values. As we drove home in silence, I wondered if Liam would end up like these people—shoeless and crazy, fighting with their own paranoia, numbing their senses with tourniquets. Liam confessed that he felt sorry for them. He wanted to save them, even if it was only for a little while. It made me wonder if he felt the same way about me.

1.7

Liam was leaving. It was all I could think about. Days passed. Nights were endured. I lay on my bed, not studying, not writing in my journal, not listening to music, just tossing from side to side, wrestling with the idea of him. Tej walked by my room and glanced in. I grabbed my Walkman and pressed play.

"Are you okay?"

I pretended not to hear. She asked again. I closed my eyes.

"I'm talking to you."

I took my headset off. "What?"

She stood by my bed. "What's going on with you?"

"Nothing, I just want to be alone."

"You know you can talk to me."

"Right. Like I'm going to talk to you," I said, pushing her away. "All you care about is your stupid wedding."

"That's not true and you know it."

"Look, I just want to be alone."

"Meena."

"Fuck, Tej, just leave me alone. Jesus." I grabbed my jacket and ran out the front door, away from her cries for me to come back. I walked around the neighbourhood for an hour, until the sun met the western sky and began its descent, until I found myself looping back to Liam's house. I stood out front, waiting for him to notice me.

He opened the front door and let me inside, past the dog who was circling me like my own doubt. Liam called the dog off, rubbing the scruff of his neck until his bark subsided into a heavy pant. I smiled only because I didn't know what else to do. All of my words were a jumble of thoughts and all I could manage was silence.

I followed him up the stairs into the living room, which looked like every other dated 1970s' living room—a white brick fireplace stained in soot, a wood-panelled feature wall, velveteen sofas, and a matching set of veneer end tables that anchored each corner of the room. The coffee table was covered in highball glasses, the contents of which had spilled and dribbled, rendering the table surface sticky with opalescent spheres. When he went into the other room, I picked up a half-empty glass and twirled its amber contents; the biting odour made my throat close. It smelled like the old Indian men who loitered in the athletic parks playing cards and chewing paan, muttering village obscenities through their toothy grins as they passed flasks around, each of them drawing a sharp breath after swallowing, exhaling low whistles, small-eyed and mean as they stared at us. I never understood what they were saying, but Harj assured me it was not good. Though Indian women were not permitted to drink, my mother kept a bottle of whisky in the house for her father. Once when he was visiting, Papaji drank to hallucination and grabbed Harj by the hair. Tej rushed into the room, pleading with him to stop as she avoided the blind swats of his cane. I rushed over and yanked the cane from him, the force of which pitched him forwards and rocked him back. He staggered for balance, trying to grab us as we fled from his reach. He fell, bumping his head on the coffee table, and dove into unconsciousness. When he had been still for a minute, Harj walked over and poked him with his cane. He stirred. His breath—long and loose as if he had never exhaled before—made us all laugh into tears. We'd thought we had killed him. Harj gathered his feet and Tej and I each grabbed an arm, hoisting him up onto the couch, arranging him in an afternoon nap. I repositioned his turban, tilting it to the left to hide the bump that had formed. Tej, still sobbing, went to her room. Harj grabbed his glass, and downed the remaining whisky in one gulp.

I put the glass down when Liam came back in the room. "You want some?" he asked, pointing to the bottle. I shook my head. He walked to the mantel and picked up one of the porcelain figurines of Mary holding Jesus, their painted faces faded to silhouettes by years of direct sunlight and hardened dust. "Secret stash," he said, pulling a joint out of the hollow base. He handed it to me.

"No thanks."

"Suit yourself." He tucked the joint in his mouth and managed a flat James Dean smile as he mumbled, "You don't smoke. You don't drink. What do you do for fun?" I turned away from his truth-or-dare tone. I'd never played that game, even though I played out its daily scenarios— calculating risks, collecting perceptions, equalizing my choices down to agnostic indecision.

"Are you a virgin?" he asked, lighting the joint.

Nerves crept up my neck, needling me with insecurities. I picked up his parents' wedding picture from the mantel, brushing the dust from the grooved wooden frame.

"They were really young."

"Eighteen." He took a long drag, exhaled slowly. "He knocked her up."

I nodded and put the picture down, not sure what to say next.

"So are you?" he asked.

"Am I what?"

"A virgin."

"Fuck, Liam. Don't be an ass."

"What? I just want to know." He sat down, waiting.

"Are you?" I asked.

He leaned forward. "I asked you first."

"It's none of your business."

He blew smoke in my face. "Isn't it?" The blue haze hung over him like a halo before disappearing into the sliver of dying light that pushed between the sheer draperies.

I turned away from him, wondering why he was being so cruel. I thought about leaving, but couldn't. That much I knew. I glanced at his half-packed duffle bag by the couch. "Where will you go?" My pent-up curiosity about his leaving seemed to surprise him, though it had been pressing on me since the day he told me he was planning to go. "What about Montreal?" I asked. "Will you go there?"

"Je ne sais pas." He answered with genuine French disinterest. He'd always talked about moving to Quebec. I could imagine him sitting at cafés, scribbling in notebooks, wearing sunglasses even when the weather didn't call for it. Artists would befriend him. He would have lovers. Affairs. I didn't stand a chance.

"Then where, if not Montreal?"

"I'm gonna crash at the house on the beach for a while. Until I can sort things out."

"You can't stay there."

"Why not?"

"Because." I crossed my arms over my chest.

"It's not permanent. Just until I have a place to stay. It'll be like camping."

"Indian people don't camp."

"Serious?"

"Yeah, if they want to rough it they pack a suitcase of cornflakes and toilet paper, and head to India for a month."

"And would you like to go to India to rough it?"

"Maybe one day when I'm not in danger of having suitors sprung on me."

"What, like an arranged marriage?" he asked.

I nodded.

"Would you actually get one?

"I don't know. Probably." I was almost surprised by my truth-telling. Lying was so much easier with everyone but him.

"That's such a cop-out."

"Like running away isn't?"

He returned my truth with a dare and led me to his room.

It wasn't how I imagined it would be or how other girls had told me it would be. He didn't try to kiss me, he didn't tell me he loved me, he didn't ask me if I would; he simply took off his clothes and waited for me to take off mine. There we stood naked in the half-light, featureless and lonely, the push and pull of emotions between us. Our hands mimicked eyes and our mouths mimicked hands. Our shadows tumbled in the room, crowding the walls with shades of ourselves.

After, we stared at the ceiling as if it were sky. Liam's heavy breath filled the room. He reached for my hand. "Are you okay?"

I nodded.

"Did I hurt you?"

"No, it's fine. I'm fine," I said, even though I could still feel him: the fractioned distinction of pleasure and pain. I turned on my side to hide the tears that were welling up. "I should go." I whispered it, lingering on the three words that betrayed me. I wanted to tell him that I loved him.

Liam sat up and offered to drive me home, just as the front door opened. The dog yelped. A man spoke, his gravel tone spinning profanities.

I scrambled out of bed, searching for my clothes in the tangle of sheets. Liam handed me my shirt. "It'll be fine. Just get dressed."

After he left the room I crumpled the bloodstained sheets into a ball and threw them into the corner. The room still smelled like sex, which made me wonder if I did too. I sniffed my skin, then reached for his cologne and doused myself in it. I yanked my clothes on, pushing my arms into sleeves, lining up seams, fumbling with buttons, listening to his father's footsteps trudging up the stairs, then his slurred temper.

"Well, look who decided to come home… I told you a million times to keep your dog outside… Don't just stare at me. Do it."

"Come on, Darwin," Liam replied.

I looked at myself in the mirror. My cheeks were flushed, my neck and breasts covered with broken blood vessels. I pulled my hair up to get a better look, examining the marks with my fingertips, tracing the subtle remains of slow-mouthed bites so different from the hickeys that the girls at school hid with scarves. I stood back, looking at myself once more, wondering if anyone would be able to tell that I'd had sex. I opened Liam's top dresser and routed through his cigar box of junk looking for something I could take—something he wouldn't notice was gone until he needed it—and after sifting through paperclips, postcards and foreign currency, I settled on a roll of undeveloped film.

I heard a slide door open and close, Darwin's paws scratching against a window and then Liam's voice reassuring him, "It's okay. I'm right here."

I walked down the hallway. I waited for Liam, wondering if I should say something to his father, who was slumped on the sofa watching TV without the sound. Liam came back into the room, offering me a sidelong apology.

His father looked up. "Who are you?" His question sounded like an accusation and I wondered how to answer. I found myself searching the row of porcelain nativity figurines on the mantel for an answer, but none came.

"This is my friend, Meena. Meena, this is my dad—Jack." Liam spit out his name like a swear word. His father glared at Liam and then me.

"Meena— that's Indian, right?"

I nodded.

He sat up straight, and looked at me with interest. "You don't look Indian, maybe Italian or Greek but not Indian. You probably get that a lot, huh, on account of the fact that your skin is pretty light."

I didn't answer.

"I bet if you changed your name, no one would even know."

"Jack!" Liam cursed, seemingly embarrassed by such a racist comment. I wasn't bothered by it. People had told me all my life that I didn't look Indian. I used to wonder what an Indian was supposed to look like, and yet became glad that whatever it was, I didn't look it. When I was in Grade 1 I told everyone in school my name was Maria not Meena.

"Don't 'Jack' me. I'm your father. You call me Dad, or nothing at all." Liam folded his arms and waited. A snarl spread from Jack's eyes to his mouth. "So, Meena, that must be short for what? Meenpreet? Meenjeet?" He laughed, muttering the variations of Punjabi names in a rhyming sequence the same way the kids at school used to, and yet I knew his teasing was ignorant not cruel.

"We should go," Liam said, reaching for my hand. We walked down the steps.

"Liam!" his dad shouted.

I waited at the foot of the stairs as Liam ran back up. "What?"

"Stick to your own kind."

Liam ran back down the stairs, taking two at a time. "Let's get out of here."

We drove to my house in silence. It wasn't the comfortable silence I was used to; it was a quiet of good-byes, a measure of distance.

"What your dad said."

"He's a jerk."

"I know, but... "

"But what, Meena?"

"I don't know."

Liam pulled the car over and took the keys out of the ignition. He rested his head against the window. "Look, I never meant for this to happen."

"For what to happen?"

"Meena, I like you. I like you a lot and I j-just... "

"You just... ?" He didn't answer. I waited for a minute, but he didn't try to speak. "Forget it. Don't worry about it." I reached into my bag and handed him the roll of film I'd taken.

"What's this?" he asked.

"It's nothing." I got out of the car and walked down the street, looking back only when I heard him drive away.

When I opened the back door I could tell that my mother had been cooking. The pungent aroma of onions, butter and masala filled the stairwell and clung to my skin.

"You are in so much trouble," Tej said, passing me in the hall on her way to bed.

"Thanks, like I didn't know," I replied. In truth I was almost grateful that my mother was home, that she was angry, that I would be punished. I wanted a reason to not think of Liam.

I stood in the kitchen doorway. My mother was mixing her tarka with a wooden spoon stained in turmeric. Steam rose up into her face, fogging up her bifocals, as the onions sizzled in the melting butter. She looked up long enough for her glasses to clear and saw me standing there. She quickly turned her attention back to the contents of the steel pot.

"You're here?" she asked, stirring harder. "Why come home now? Just stay out."

"Mom, I just…"

"Just what?" She looked up in disgust. Although her glasses were foggy, I could see her exaggerated stare in the magnified portion of the lens and I wondered if she knew. She must have. "Speak in Punjabi!" she said, slamming her hand on the counter. She took her glasses off, wiped her face with the back of her hand and squinted at me with her near-sighted eyes. I wondered if she could even see me.

"No more going out. No staying at school late, no friends. No more… you understand?"

I nodded.

"You'll go to school and come home… understand?" She put her glasses back on and added pepper to the curry mixture.

My eyes began to water. "It's the onions," I told her.

She leaned over the sink and opened the window.

TWO FOR SORROW

2.1

"Hold still." Masi tugged at the drawstring of my petticoat. "Do you have to tie it so tight?" I sucked in my stomach to accommodate the knotty fingers that nipped at my waist.

She took the safety pin from her mouth and pricked it through the layers of silk. "If I don't, it will fall at your feet before the bride even gets to the reception."

I pulled at the sari blouse while she adjusted the pleats of my blue cocoon. "Couldn't you have made the blouse a little longer?" I pleaded, covering my exposed stomach.

Masi smacked my hand away and then tempered her reaction with a wink. "This is a sari, not a burka. Its seduction is in what it hides and what it hints at." She stood back and smiled, clapping once before placing her hands on her round hips. "If I had your figure, I would wear a sari every day."

"You could still wear one."

Masi covered her mouth with her chunni. "Oh no, I couldn't. Even six yards is not enough to wrap around my body," she said, patting her stomach. "You look just like your mother did when she was your age. Isn't that right, pehenji?"

My mother looked up from the chunni she was hemming, and then down again. "No, I was much thinner."

Masi frowned and swatted the air. "Don't listen to her. You are beautiful."

I'd seen pictures of my mother in her sari soon after she'd married my father. She looked like a Bollywood actress from the 1960s, with kohl-etched cat eyes and pomegranate lips.

Masi straightened the end of the sari over my shoulder and asked me to take a few steps so she could see the sweep of the garment. I walked the length of the hallway and back, minding the size of my steps. Most girls tromped about in their saris as if they were wearing jeans. Their movements fought against the delicate wrap they were confined in, but I was used to being bound by things and knew how to move despite the constraint of the coiled fabric. "I don't see why I have to get all dressed up. I'm not the one getting married. In fact, I don't know why I even have to go at all. We barely know the girl."

My mother put her needle and thread down. "It's Mandip's cousin. It doesn't look good on Tej if we don't go."

"She went to SFU, didn't she?" Masi asked as she draped and pinned the embroidered fabric over my shoulder.

"Who?" I flinched from the pin.

"Mandip's cousin, Priya."

"Only for a bit; she transferred to UBC."

"She is a doctor," my mother said, raising her eyebrows above her bifocals.

"Mom, she's not a doctor. She's a pharmacist."

"Same thing."

"No, it's not the same thing," I said.

"And the boy… " Masi added. "He's from a good family and is an accountant."

"He's not an accountant. He's a bank teller."

"Same thing," they said in unison.

"No, trust me, it's not the same thing."

"This from our English professor?" my mother mocked.

"I'm hardly a professor, mother. I wish you'd stop telling people that. It's embarrassing."

"Embarrassing—she is telling me about embarrassing."

Though I'd given up my hopes of becoming a writer and gotten an entry-level communications job, my mother would still have preferred that I'd become a doctor or a lawyer. Those professions had the best bragging rights. "An English major and a job in cummoon-ick-cachuns... how do I explain that? People will think that you talk too much and no one will want to marry you."

"That's fine by me."

"Vaheguru Satnam. Meena, don't say such things. It is bad luck. Of course you want to get married. God willing, you will have a nice match like this boy Priya is marrying—what's his name?" My mother's eyes crossed as she attempted to rethread her needle.

"Jag."

"He's a friend of Kal's, isn't he?"

"Yeah, they went to UBC together."

"Jagtar and Priya. Same caste, good jobs, such a nice match. I hear Nindra Bhullar arranged it."

"I wouldn't exactly call it arranged, Mom."

Everyone at school knew they had spent their tutorials screwing in his Corvette. She was temple trash; she knew her prayers and mouthed them on her knees. While I spent my university years studying, she came to school plain-faced and in modest clothing, then went to the washroom to put on her red lips, black push-up bra, white baby tee and hip-hop hoop earrings. I had never seen a book in her bag.

"Yes, Kishor Auntie told me they found each other themselves," my mother said. She put her sewing aside momentarily. "Times have changed and however the match was made, at least it is a suitable one." She picked up her stitch again, pulling the needle in and out. "You are too picky. Every boy that I have suggested, you have turned down, and soon they will stop considering you."

"One can only hope." I said it just loud enough for her to hear.

"See how she is," my mother said to Masi. "What am I to do?"

Masi paused, her silence pleading and placating. "Meena, you are twenty-four... It is time for you to get married. When I was twenty-five I had three children."

"Times have changed," I said, mimicking my mother's accent.

Masi smacked me playfully. "Tell me again, what was wrong with that nice boy, Harvinder?" she asked.

"Where to begin... he was less than five feet tall and could barely see over the dash of his suv," I said, counting his offences on my fingers. "He didn't have a job, wanted to live in his parents' house forever—oh, and on top of *that*, he had a girlfriend."

"Kishor Auntie tells me he got married to a girl from India last month."

"See, this is the problem—the girls here are so picky that the boys have to go to India to find a bride. And what about Baljit? What was wrong with him?" my mother asked.

"The cricket player from India?" She nodded and resumed her hand stitching. "He didn't even speak English."

"English is not the language of love." Masi winked at me.

"No, but neither is cricket," I added, winking back.

"*See?* See how picky she is?" My mother slapped her forehead in frustration.

"There's nothing wrong with having standards, Mother."

"You spend so much time writing in your silly books that you have forgotten who you are, Meena. That is the problem."

"I haven't forgotten who I am. That's the problem."

"Heh?"

I reached for my necklace. My father had bought it for my mother the day I was born. She'd been sobbing in her hospital bed, cradling her disappointment, apologizing for having given him yet another daughter. He told her to stop crying and presented her with the necklace. Everyone was shocked that a man would buy a woman such a gift after she'd borne him a sixth daughter. The necklace was meant to be a reminder of our value. When he died the necklace was put away, to be worn only when one of us was of marrying age. Our value unassigned until someone chose us as a wife. My mother's value determined by our choosing.

Masi pushed my hair over my shoulder and fastened the necklace clasp. "Are there any boys from school you like? I could have someone inquire." I thought of Liam. I hadn't seen him since the after-grad party at the beach house. He'd been standing in the corner of the living room, boxed into a drunken conversation with girls who when sober would forget his name. He was smoking, even though he didn't smoke, nodding his head and tapping ashes onto the carpet. He was talking to some blonde girl, but staring at me. He put out his cigarette, wove across the room, took my hand and led me outside to the front porch. He held me by the back of my neck and kissed me long and hard, until my mouth parted and I kissed him back. He asked me to run away with him. "We could go to Toronto. You could go to school there, use that writing scholarship, and I'd get a job or something. We could make it work." I told him I couldn't go with him. He said he'd wait.

"So, is there anyone?" Masi asked again. This time her voice was raised, almost hopeful.

"No. No one in particular."

"No matter," she said, adjusting the sari's embroidered border as if it were a ribbon on a gift. "There is still Kal's cousin Sundeep Gill. Kishor Auntie tells me that his mother was asking Kal's mother about you again. There is still hope."

"Lucky me."

"Yes, lucky you! What a prospect—you know people say he's as tall as Amitabh Bachchan, with a face like a young Shashi Kapoor."

"Yeah, but he acts more like Salman Khan." I'd heard girls at school talk of Sunny Gill. Like a Bollywood bad boy, he was on their lists of eligible but likely unattainable husbands. Troubled by alcohol and fuelled by privilege, he had a life of excess—high-speed car wrecks and ruined love affairs. His last girlfriend had tried to kill herself after he broke up with her; his parents didn't approve of his marrying out of caste. When I'd heard about it, I wasn't sure which of them to feel sorry for.

"Yes, I heard he is a little wild, but boys will be boys until marriage makes them men."

"Well, I don't think he wants to get married anyways."

"What does *want* have to do with it? He must do what he is told. We all must do as we are told," Masi said, her eyes close to mine as she placed a bindi on my forehead. She reached for the crumpled shoebox on the table and handed me the gold sandals that she'd brought from India. They were made of wood and covered in glitter glue. I sounded like a horse when I walked in them, clopping about in sparkles. I knelt down, ratcheted the straps around my ankles and stood up, teetering. I glanced in the mirror and wondered what Liam would think of me now. That was how I thought of him, not as a person but as a reference point, a marker, a compass. If only he had waited. By the time I'd returned to the beach he was gone and the house stood abandoned, with only small traces of his leaving left inside. A few months later he'd sent me a letter. No return address. Just the picture that he had taken of me taking his picture. His reflection was caught in the mirror behind me and the flash washed us in light. Each day since Liam had sent me that picture I'd wanted to throw it away, yet I kept it folded inside my journal, its edges worn, its image fading into the creases.

"What do you think?" Masi asked, twirling me towards my mother, who offered a dismissive nod as she reached for the ringing telephone. She hesitated for a full second before saying hello, bracing for whatever news was on the other side. When her expression and manner lightened, I could tell it was Kal on the other end. He was the only one of my friends she liked. "Why can't you speak Punjabi like Kal?" she'd say. "Why don't you take me shopping like Kal takes his mother?" She saw me waiting and shooed me away, cupping her hand over the mouthpiece. "Five minutes." I nodded and went to my room to finish getting ready, listening to the sound of their ritual conversation through the walls.

We had known his family since I was five. Our mothers had worked together, cleaning medical offices. Kal would go along with his mother, Amarjit Auntie, because she didn't have anyone to watch him, and I went with my mother because I begged her to take me. I wanted to be with her and she agreed as long as I promised to stay out of her way. While our mothers scrubbed sinks, emptied ashtrays and mopped the floors with bleach, Kal and I played jacks and marbles in the 1970s' orange-and-brown waiting rooms. Amarjit Auntie would occasionally break from her work to play a round of jacks, muss his silky brown hair and offer us lemon-drop candies from her purse. She didn't even warn us to keep our sticky hands to ourselves. I told Kal that he was lucky to have such a nice mother. He replied that she was not his real mother—he was adopted. I thought it strange that his mother, who was not his own, loved him like her own while mine, who *was* my own, didn't know how to love me at all. I wished I'd been adopted. At least then I could say I didn't belong to anyone.

The best part of going to work with our mothers was the elevator ride into the building's belly, where garbage was devoured by metal bins. Kal and I always raced to the elevator, because whoever got there first would get to press the buttons. I would usually win, but on that day Kal took a head start and I rushed after him yelling "Cheater cheater, pumpkin eater." The elevator doors were open and we raced straight in. Before I could tell him to stop, he'd pressed a button and the doors had shut the two of us in. I arbitrarily pounded on the buttons, trying to make the doors open, and began to cry when I felt the jolt of descent. Kal put his sticky lemon-drop hand in mine and told me not to cry, which only made me cry harder. He squeezed my hand and kissed me just as the elevator doors opened. His mother laughed at the innocent sight, but my mother scolded me for my part in it. I stepped out and looked back at the empty elevator. That was the moment when I knew I liked boys and hated small spaces.

After our mothers stopped working together, we saw Amarjit Auntie and Kal only during their annual holiday visits. Even though none of us celebrated Christmas in a religious way, they would arrive bearing a box of mandarin oranges and a nativity Christmas card. My mother, who had watched *The Sound of Music* too many times, always asked us to stand in a line and sing "Silent Night" to our guests. Kal stopped making the annual visit with his parents and new baby brother when he was thirteen. His parents were apologetic about it. They'd say things like, "You know how kids are these days. They want to be independent—no time for family."

It wasn't until I was in university that I saw him again. I'd taken my mother to visit them after Kal's father had had his second stroke. While my mother and Amarjit Auntie slurped sugary tea, I spent the afternoon sticking to their plastic-encased sofa, tracing the tendrils of a spider plant that had wrapped itself around the room. I was succumbing to a suffocating boredom when Kal rushed past the living room. His mother called after him to take his muddy boots off and come and say hello. He turned around and filled the doorway with his six-foot frame. Amarjit Auntie told us that he had just come from work. I wanted to ask what work he did, but knew it was not my place to ask a question, and was glad when his mother elaborated, telling us that in addition to his studies, he ran a landscaping business.

He lowered his face into his neck and stretched his white T-shirt to wipe his sweaty face, momentarily revealing his torso. Strands of brown hair fell in his face and as he tossed them back, he caught me staring and grinned. The scar on his cheek disappeared into the cleft of his smile. I looked down into my teacup, letting the steam rise to my face to give my flush some legitimacy. We'd been friends ever since, and my mother hardly seemed to mind. "He's like a brother to her," she told everyone.

When we got to the reception hall, we sat in the car with the engine turned off, my mother madly rooting through her purse in search of the wedding card she needed me to address. "There it is." She handed me the oversized card covered in swirly mint-green writing. Beneath a golden crucifix the message read: "Congratulations on your blessed union." I'd tried to explain the inappropriateness to my mother, but she didn't seem to care. "It is only a dollar," she'd said, holding up the receipt. She watched me write their names on the card, then slipped a fifty-dollar note into the envelope and zipped it back into her purse. "Don't forget to say hello to Jaspreet Auntie—she just had her heart surgery. And Shindoo Uncle's son just got married—make sure you say congratulations. Oh, and Kuljit Auntie's daughter had a baby boy. And don't forget to be nice to Kishor Auntie, and Amarjit Auntie of course." My face tightened at the thought of offering so many smiles to people who had been useless to me my entire life—would-be uncles who hugged me too hard, aunties who contained me in a one suspicious glare, snotty second cousins who retreated to their rooms and their Harlequin romances whenever we visited.

Now I watched these same extended families pour out of their cars and file into the hall. The withering bibis moved as if they had no joints, toddling and tender-footed, huffing with each step. The red-eyed, already drunk and tired uncles jingled keys in the pockets of their 1980s' Pierre Cardin sports jackets; the aging aunties stopped every few feet to fuss with their daughters' attire while their sons walked straight ahead to greet their friends. All the newly married and the soon-to-be-married men hung out-side in the parking lot. They laughed too loud. Everything about them exaggerated—from their Boyz ii Men white suits to the symbolic gold khandas that hung from their rear-view mirrors like crucifixes.

As I walked by them, the Acura boys nudged Sunny in the rib cage, whispering. My mother stopped and turned towards them. They hid their cigarettes and folded their hands in an apologetic greeting. As Sunny leaned against the car in a GQ pose, everything about him slow motion, I wondered if he too drove a lowered car, a boom box on wheels that filled your body with bass and left you fuzzy-assed. We stared at each other with half-interest and curiosity, our subtle inquiry weighed down by our mothers' preoccupation with marriage. He looked at me as though he were trying me on and when he dropped his gaze I felt used and discarded. I wanted him to look at me again but he didn't. Turning, I linked arms with my mother and urged her into the hall beyond the reach of the men's muffled laughter, which left me feeling the same kind of nausea that I got when I ate spoiled food or felt the beginnings of love.

The hall was decorated with fuchsia balloon arches and rented silk floral arrangements that were flecked with a coordinating glitter. The music was already blaring. As we walked by the second set of speakers and bass bins that would pound out bhangra beats all night long, I checked my purse for the emergency stash of Tylenol that I'd need to dull the sounds of my mother's complaints about the music. "Over there," I yelled to my mother, pointing out two empty seats close to Tej and Mandip. She nodded and manoeuvred through the intricate maze of tables and chairs, stopping every few feet to say hello to yet another auntie who was wearing too much gold jewellery, too much perfume, too much powder. It was all too much.

It was then that I saw Kal. He was standing in the bar line, which snaked around the hall. As I tried to catch his attention, my friend Aman rushed over, pulling me aside. My mother continued into the crowd.

"So, have you seen anyone yet?" Aman asked.

"Like who? What are you now, part of the IIA?"

"I was just worried I may have missed something because it took so long at the salon," she said, pointing to her updo.

"They did a good job."

"You should have come too. You could have gotten your hair done, maybe even a manicure or pedicure—I mean, look around, there isn't an unmarried girl, other than you, who isn't all done up."

"Thanks," I said, looking down at my feet.

"I didn't mean it like that. It's just that if you want to get married to a guy like Sunny, you have to market yourself to the aunties," she said, referring to a group of middle-aged women clutching their purses. I watched them eyeing young women lustfully, wondering whose hips would bear children easily, whose breasts would produce enough milk to feed their grandsons.

"I'm not the one who wants to get married."

Aman had kept a scrapbook with pictures of saris, wedding cakes, ice sculptures, invitations and honeymoon destinations since she was twelve. Last year she had gone to India and shopped for her wedding clothes; this year she was shopping for a husband. He had to look like a tall version of Shahrukh Khan, have a university degree and some kind of professional designation, and drive either a BMW or a Mercedes. I envied how much and how little she wanted.

She folded her hands as one of the grandmothers of somebody's son looked over. "Sat Sri Akal Auntie."

"Don't you ever get sick of all this?" I asked, ducking from the auntie's darting eyes.

Aman smoothed her crusty, side-swept bangs. "Of what?"

"The hypocrisy." I motioned to the line of young men at the bar. A blonde girl leaned her breasts towards their requests for rum and Cokes. "All of these women looking for suitable girls for their unsuitable boys."

"They're not all bad."

"No, you're right. There is Kal."

"Kal? Oh my God! Who would want to marry someone who shovels manure onto other people's lawns," she said, searching through her clam-shell clutch. "I can't believe that he and Sunny are related."

"Stop being such a snob."

"I'm not a snob," she said, reapplying her signature maroon lipstick. "I just don't understand why you guys are friends."

"Funny, he says the same thing about you." I waved him over.

"What are you doing?" she asked.

"What do you mean?"

She dropped her lipstick back into her gold purse. "What if Sunny's mom sees you with him? People will think you're together."

"Who cares what people think?" I replied. "Besides, everyone knows we're old family friends. No one will think otherwise."

"I figured you could use a drink by now." Kal handed me a tumbler.

Aman yanked it from my hand. "Meena, you can't drink that. What will people think?"

I took it back. "That it's a Coke."

"Until they smell it on your breath."

Kal picked up a nearby wedding favour—mints wrapped in lavender tulle—and passed it to me. I pulled the ribbon off and handed Aman a mint. "In case you want to have a drink."

She popped the candy in her mouth and smiled at someone across the room. "I have to go say hello to my cousin. Try not to get too corrupted while I'm gone," she said, shooting her disapproval at Kal.

"Hi to you, too!" Kal yelled as she walked away, and then, lowering his voice, said: "Remind me again, why are you guys friends?"

"She asks the same about you."

"I called you today, but I got stuck talking to your mom," he said, chewing an ice cube. "She really likes me; she wouldn't stop talking."

"Trust me," I said, interrupting my words with rum. "She wouldn't like you so much if she ever found out." He fell silent like he always did. On the day he told me he'd met someone else, I'd bumped into an old classmate at the mall. We'd stood there, exchanging stilted questions about high school, about what we had done since, until he finally said that he'd recently heard from Liam. I was relieved at the mention of his name. It reminded me that he existed even if it was apart from me, that he was more than a memory and less than a dream. But as I walked away I was reminded that memory was bound by rules of completion. Liam was further from me than the past. My memory could not contain his possibilities; he had moved on, and without any effort, so had I. That was the part I had forgotten. When I'd gone to see Kal that last time, he could tell why I was there. We knew each other's details; we hoarded them and occasionally whored ourselves to them. I remembered his earthy scent, his breath on my neck, quick and hot, his mouth parched on my name until I was just an exhale, and I pulled him to me faster, trying to forget.

2.2

I slid into my cubicle, unnoticed if not for the one Plexiglas wall that reminded me I was working in a fishbowl. I pressed my hand to my temple and propped my elbow on the desk, trying to block out the white noise of mundane chatter and the glow of fluorescent lights. "You're kidding... she said that... and then what did you say... you're kidding... and then what did she say... yeah, yeah... are you serious?" On and on it went. If only my co-workers recognized that we had only the illusion of privacy. I was tired of hearing their personal telephone conversations and of seeing their pin-ups, their postcards, their boyfriends in heart-shaped frames and their bikini-clad vacation pictures tacked around them. I didn't have a candy drawer, colourful Post-it Notes, novelty pens, pithy quotes on plaques, or a Hallmark figurine collection lining the top of my computer monitor. If I was away from my desk, you wouldn't even know that anyone ever sat there.

I already missed the anonymity that university had given me. There I'd learned how to blend in, disappear even, but here I found myself ill-equipped for the small talk, the water-cooler conversation, and in most cases nodded far more than was required or comfortable. "Did you watch *Survivor?*" I would nod, even if I'd only heard the highlights on the *Larry & Willy* morning radio show. "What did you do this weekend?" I never knew how to answer. As my peers recounted the details of their weekend binge drinking and club hopping, I smiled and laughed along, wishing that

I knew what it would be like to have that sense of independent reckless-ness.

When I'd first started working at the PR firm, I'd gone out with them once or twice, but after spending the evenings abandoned at an empty table of coats and purses, watching their coupled silhouettes on the dance floor, I was almost grateful that my mother insisted I be home by eleven. After that I made excuses for why I couldn't go out after work, telling them that I had a headache or other plans—anything was better than telling them the truth, that at twenty-four I still lived at home, arguing with my mother about arranged marriage. I found that avoiding social situations was easiest and tied myself up in extra projects that made me look too busy to talk. While others took their breaks together, I made up false er-rands and wandered around the city. Sometimes I would eat my lunch on the steps of the art gallery like Liam and I used to or sip my coffee from a to-go cup on the park bench in front of the Burrard Street Station watch-ing people, wondering who they were and where they were going as they rushed by in such purposeful madness. Occasionally I'd walk by the stands of postcards and spin through them, wondering if Liam was still a col-lector. Sometimes I bought one.

One day, instead of wandering the city, I'd eaten in my car. Trish from marketing saw me sitting with my bagged lunch, and though I jumped out of the car talking about the "crazy" traffic, I knew she'd told everyone what she'd seen because when I went back to the office they all stared at me with what resembled pity.

Now Liza was peering over the top of my cubicle, the scent of her musk and the jingle of her charm bracelet preceding her. "Geee-off's back today," she said, giggling, purposefully mispronouncing Geoff's name as I had ac-cidentally done when I'd first met him. Even though he'd laughed it off by explaining that his parents were hippies who refused to spell his name the easy way, I felt bad for making a joke of it and apologized to the point of discomfort. "He's in the copy room." She handed me a fax and strained her neck, shooing me along.

The room smelled like ink, warm paper and the spark of overloaded circuits. It was my favourite spot in the office and Geoff and I often loitered there, cracking jokes and catching up in the way I didn't seem to be able to do with anyone else.

"How are you? How was your vacation?" I asked, feeding my paper into the fax machine. He said "Good," without looking up from the photocopier. The fax sound screeched through the awkward silence. He turned around and ran his fingers through his hair, which looked lighter against his fresh tan. It was always a relief and a disappointment to see him. Besides Liza he was the only real friend I had at work, and when he'd asked me out he was surprised that I'd said no—all of my actions, all of our conversations pointed to "yes." But all I could give him was a cryptic "I'm sorry, I can't." Sometimes I wished I could tell him that it wasn't him. That it was me—that I wasn't allowed to date, that I had never had a real boyfriend, that there was no point in going out with any white guy because inevitably I would have to marry an Indian guy like Sunny or end up being disowned. When my cousin wouldn't give in to her family's ultimatums, Mamaji tore his name from hers and never spoke of her again. Every time he came to our house, he would look at me so long that I saw her missing in his eyes, felt his disappointment in his general detachment. I wanted to tell Geoff all of this, but knew that this truth was more hurtful than an enigmatic lie, so when he asked me why, I simply told him that it was complicated. He shook his head and said, "No, it's not… but you are."

I pulled the fax confirmation slip off the tray and as I turned to leave, Trish walked in, sidling up next to him. "I was just telling Michelle about the swim-up bar at the resort. She's thinking of planning a trip as well. Meena, have you been?" I shook my head, feeling like an idiot as I ducked out. I hadn't realized they'd gone to Mexico together.

Liza sat down, holding her questions when she saw me return to my desk a little defeated. I sat in front of my computer, tapping random keys, watching the letters filling a blank Word document. Somehow it made sense.

When I got home, I slipped off my heels, changed my clothes and fell into a frustrated silence that my mother referred to as moodiness. She never understood my need for quiet and filled the space with numb details that coloured in all of our lonely parts. As she told me about her workday, I nodded absent-mindedly, listening only to every other word. I wondered what was being harvested but didn't bother to ask; her withered expression, her stained nail beds and the dirt dotting her tear ducts all cried out that, whatever it was, it was rotten. The fields were being cleared for something new; the seasons had changed, and if not for my mother I might not have noticed.

"I phoned you five times today," she said, buttering the tender side of the stacked rotis. Though it was only the two of us now, she still made enough food for my sisters. She repeated herself, louder this time, trying to be heard over the hood fan that pulled the singed heat from the tava.

"I know. I got the messages," I said, looking up from the journal I was attempting to write in. Words were not coming easily. "What was it that you wanted?" I asked.

"The boy, Sundeep," she began. "He is from a good family..."

"Mom, not this again."

"Yes, this again. You will not get a better offer."

I put my journal down and looked out the window at the tapping of rain and bare-boned trees. "Do we have to talk about this now? I told you I'm not sure."

"Not sure, you are not sure," she said, nodding her head. "I was not sure when I married your father and moved to England, had six children and then moved to Canada. I was not sure what I would do when your father died and I had to raise all of you alone. I was not sure while I emptied ashtrays or picked berries twelve hours a day to put you through school. I was not sure how to make a better life for you and now you tell me that *you* are not sure," she said without taking a breath. "Meena, sometimes in life you must do the things you are unsure of."

"Mom, I just need some time."

"Time," she repeated as if it were a question or a word that she didn't understand. She wrapped a stack of rotis in tinfoil and ladled daal into a plastic container. "I need you to take these to Serena's house for me."

"Now?"

"Yes, now. She's waiting," my mother said, handing them to me.

Serena lived in Stucco Surrey, where all the boxy houses had red-tiled roofs and lawns that were dotted with the typical Sikh flourish of orange, Khalsa-coloured marigolds that were often crushed by parked cars. Parking in the area was a problem. All the houses—or Hinduminiums, as Kal and I called them—had several basement suites and not enough room for their tenants' cars. To alleviate the problem, a growing number of residents had cut all their trees down, pulled up the grass and landscaped their front yards with asphalt. The combination of shortsighted residential planning and a lack of bylaw enforcement had turned the area into a cement slum which its residents called Chandigarh.

My mother was indignant about the way India was creeping through our suburbs, in the same way that she was about the moss that had overtaken our garden. She did nothing but condemn it with a watchful eye. She stood at the kitchen window watching the house across the street being demolished to make way for a new megahome. Each afternoon, instead of watching *All My Children,* she sat by the window and watched the phases of construction the way I usually watched the changing weather. When I came home from work, she would tell me about the workers who had stripped the house for salvage, the excavator's tracks that had flattened the roses, the wrecking ball that had hit the house like a fist and the excavator jaws that had snapped everything like bone. Each stage was relived in such detail that it left me splintered and torn. I didn't understand why my mother was so bothered by it all until we met the owner's wife. She'd come running into our front yard chasing after her barefoot children, who routinely zipped across the road with little care or attention. She apologized to my mother, referring to her as "Auntie." My mother was polite about it, explaining that she had several grandchildren and understood. The woman wrangled her toddlers, hoisting the little boy onto her hip and yanking the girl to her side every time she dared to stray. She smiled the kind of wide smile that masks all other emotions. A toothy muzzle. She asked my mother the usual sort of questions—how long we had lived here, where we were from, how many children we were, how many were married. My mother was matter of fact about it, offering only a few details, already aware that she was being judged. The woman, who was only a few years older than me, looked my way and asked my mother why I was not married. To my surprise my mother did not commiserate with her and told her that I had just finished university and that in Canada a woman's education was more important than her marriage. "How modern," the woman said, glancing at my jeans and T-shirt. She simmered, grinning before calling to her daughter, who had run into the street again.

Her smile was as good as a slap.

Serena was in the kitchen, standing at the stove, looking slightly di-shevelled in her stockinged feet and navy-blue airport uniform. She smiled my way, distracted by the ringing phone and by my niece, who was crawling at her feet, tugging on the hem of her skirt and pulling at the run in her nylons. I picked Simran up, playing peekaboo while Serena answered the phone and abruptly told a telemarketer that she wasn't interested. "They always call at the worst time," she said, hanging the phone back in its wall cradle before reaching for Simran, who was jettisoning herself into the air towards Serena.

"How was work?" I asked. "Anything interesting?"

"Nothing... *except* there was this one Indian guy who'd tried to hide his stash of cocaine in his underpants."

"Did you have to get it?" I teased.

"Vaheguru!" she said, snapping me with a dish towel.

Serena had always wanted to be a flight attendant, but Dev didn't like the idea of her travelling, or of his caring for the children in her absence, so she'd settled for swatting the security paddle across limbs for eight hours a day over the past ten years. She still had the framed map of the world that she'd bought after high school, but instead of being dotted with pinpricks denoting her travels, it reflected the destinations of all those who had gone through the security gates on her shift.

"Do you want tea?" She was rummaging through the kitchen cupboard, looking for Simran's baby cookies. The kitchen was as it always was: dishes stacked haphazardly in the sink, last night's pizza boxes on the counter, plastic toys and Tupperware scattered on the floor.

I rolled up my sleeves and started into the dishes.

"Did you bring the roti?" Serena asked.

I pointed to the bag on the counter. Serena placed her daughter in the nearby high chair with a cookie and opened the bag, pulling out the stack of rotis and the assorted tins of daal and subzi that my mother had packed. She moved robotically, each joint and bone protruding in purpose. Her eyes were socketed in deep circles that made her look old and frail. She had once been beautiful.

"So how are things?" she asked, transferring the contents of each tin into a microwaveable bowl.

"Things?"

"You know, at home. Mom says you still haven't decided about Sunny."

"She's right. I haven't."

"What's there to decide? He's said yes, his family is loaded, he's good-looking, got a great career. What more do you want?"

"Love would be nice," I said sarcastically, tired that the prospect of Sunny always seemed to garner as much excitement as a celestial event or a religious festival. I rinsed the dishes and turned off the water. The steam rose and fogged up the window.

"Look, love will come later," Serena said. "At least you get to meet Sunny. I didn't get to speak to Dev until our wedding night. All I had to make my decision on was a picture and Masi's recommendation."

I turned towards her. "I don't know how you did it."

"I just did what I had to do," she answered. "And love... well, like I said, it came later." She gestured to a picture of their eldest son. "You'll see, it will be the same for you too." She said it with an assuredness that bothered me. I didn't want it to be the same for me. I had never wanted anything to be the same for me, but could never clarify how I wanted it to be different either.

I turned the water back on and rinsed the sink. "What if I don't like him?"

"Well, you won't know until you meet him," she said, putting her arm around me.

"I suppose." I whispered it, practising submission. "But really, what if I *don't* like him—do I get to say no?"

Serena turned around, busying herself with the tea. "Do you want sugar?"

"Mom's already arranged for them to come over, hasn't she?" I stared straight ahead into the window, unable to see my reflection through the steam, and for a moment it felt as if I'd disappeared.

"Yeah... This Sunday—she was going to tell you, but... "

"But—she asked you to do it."

"She thought it would be easier." Serena quieted when her husband came into the room whistling a Hindi tune. He dropped his lunchbox on the counter and asked about dinner.

While Serena finished warming her husband's food, I bathed Simran and helped my nephews A.J. and Akash with their homework. I could hear her in the other room talking with Dev—or rather taking orders from him, refilling his plate, getting him another beer, passing him the remote control. Things she did as easily as breathing. Sometimes I wondered how she even understood anything he said—his speech was so foreign, his village accent so heavy that I had to strain to get the meaning. He had a way of stammering and snapping, the urgent rhythms out of tune with the context of whatever he was saying. His words were like whips. Harj had hated it too. In fact she had hated him and went to great lengths to show it. She was like that; either she liked you or she didn't and when she didn't all she could think of was how much. My mother had often said she was focused to the point of being narrow-minded and stubborn. Once Harj made a list of all the things she hated about Dev. She hated that he wore sneakers with dress pants, that he wore Old Spice, that he had dandruff, that he wore polyester shirts with pit stains, that his belly looked man-pregnant, that he leered at women, that he picked his nose and flicked it, that he'd tried to grab her ass. The list went on. When Serena found it, she slapped Harj and ripped the piece of paper to shreds. Harj didn't flinch, she didn't move. It made me wonder if she was brave or just plain mean.

When Serena had finished serving Dev dinner, she came into the room, loosening the red scarf around her neck, undoing a button on her skirt, exhaling as if this were the first breath she had taken all day. As she sat on the carpet next to me, building a tower of blocks that Simran repeatedly knocked down, she was quiet with fatigue and contemplation. "It's not so bad, you know... being married... He's not so bad, not like you think." Her words caught, hinging on the silence that followed. Before I could concede defeat, she turned the other way. Both of us exposed.

2.3

I watched the light shift from blue to silver, the sunrise washed out by the layers of grey that stretched and collapsed all the days into one. Dark receded to the corners of my room. I hadn't been sleeping well since I'd found out about the upcoming meeting with Sunny. Each night I tossed and turned with the wind, measured my thoughts with the gusts of rain that rattled the windows, and tried to sleep between storms. But even then, nothing. Nothing but the sound of the neighbours' mournful wind chimes and the sound of my mother's sleeplessness. She shuffled around, wandering from room to room, switching on and off lights, locking and unlocking doors. Sometimes I saw her cross the backyard in her shabby housecoat, a shadow among shadows, picking up strewn branches, garbage cans and pieces of newspaper that had been set tumbling through the night. When she returned to her bed, I'd hear her trying for warmth, the sound of her feet scratching against each other like the rustling of autumn leaves. Eventually she would settle and the only sound in the house would be the howl of the wind, the hum of the furnace, the holding of breath.

When I was a girl, I'd crawl into her bed and warm my cold feet against her calves and she'd push me away, telling me to go back to bed, even though I knew she wanted me to stay. Her breath was always heavy and dense with the smell of cloves. It enveloped me and I'd lie awake remembering the stories she had told me when I was frightened by a thunderstorm. "Ik si chidi ik si kaa... ." Once there was a bird, once there was a crow.... I didn't understand the rest, but I liked the sound of all her stories. Sometimes I would stop her midway through and translate for myself. She didn't seem to mind, back then, that we didn't understand each other, and she allowed me my own interpretations—unlike her versions, they ended with everyone living happily ever after. Once she'd fallen asleep, I'd lie on my side staring at the luminous hands of the clock that she and my father had brought from England. I'd reach out and wind the clock, turning the key round and round, hoping that I could make morning come faster. But it didn't and one day when the clock finally stopped, I worried that it was my fault. I thought I had made time stop.

If only.

Those two words have gathered like ghosts. If only my father hadn't died, if only my mother had had sons, if only Harj had stayed, if only I hadn't met Liam, if only he could have loved me... Once when I was lamenting Harj's departure, my mother told me that "If only" was the beginning of new dreams made of old things and that only God could reincarnate our hopes into such a reality.

I tried to picture how my mother's nights might pass when I was gone and married and she was truly alone. My dadi had once told my mother that a woman without a husband was incomplete, but a woman without a husband and children was not a woman at all—she was simply an apparition haunting her own life. At the time she'd said it to comfort my mother—her daughter-in-law—but now it was no comfort at all.

At 5:30 I heard my mother get up. The squeak of her mattress and the patter of footsteps in the kitchen, the running of water for tea and the clearing of pots and pans from the dish rack: I listened to her morning routine, letting an hour pass between us until sleep overtook me.

I dreamed of Harj. I couldn't see her face—it was indistinct, and warped as if I were looking at her through water—yet I knew it was her. I could tell by the way she moved. Her chin was tilted up, her head held high, her walk as light and quick as a ballerina's. We were at the beach. Harj had wandered to the pier where other teenagers were sitting, their legs dangling off the edge like fishing rods. One by one they took their turns diving into the water below, until only Harj was left sitting there. As she stood up, contemplating the water, I saw her eyes. My eyes. Deep and black, reflecting what was below. Fish swam in and out of her pupils. My pupils. She jumped. I watched the ripples soften and dissolve as I waited for her to resurface, but it was only I who woke up gasping for breath.

Serena was standing over me.

"Are you okay?"

I nodded. My throat was too parched to speak. I glanced at the clock radio. It was 10:30.

"You should get up. Aman will be here soon to do your makeup."

I sat up, running my fingers through my hair. "Makeup?"

"Yeah. You can't meet Sunny's family looking like this."

I didn't answer.

"Are you okay?"

"Yeah, just not sleeping well."

"Probably nerves." She reached across the bed, pulled the blinds up and looked out at the sky. "Well, at least it stopped raining," she said.

"Serena?"

"Hmm."

"Do you ever think about Harj?"

She smiled even though her eyes were sad. "All the time," she said, glancing around the room before leaving. "All the time."

After showering I went into the kitchen, where my mother and Masi were taste-testing the rice pudding. Masi thrust the wooden spoon in my face. "More sugar?"

I licked the end of the spoon. "It's fine."

Masi ran her index finger along the spoon's edge, testing it again herself. "Needs more," she said to my mother, who dumped in another half cup.

"What's all this?" I asked, pointing towards the trays of sweets that were lining the counters. "I thought we agreed that this was just going to be a get-to-know-you kind of dinner and that we wouldn't make a big deal about it."

"We aren't making it a big deal," Masi said.

"No? Then what's this?" I asked, opening the porch door for Aman, who had arrived with her infamous black make-up case. The smell of onions wafted in. I peeked into the yard. Tej was outside in the shed, frying onions on a gas burner.

"We can't cook onions in the house; it would smell," Masi said, lighting a stick of dollar-store incense.

"Of course. We wouldn't want them to know we're Indian." I reached for a cup of tea.

Masi nudged me, winking. "Smile, hmm? You're too pretty to frown so much."

I grinned a toothy smile and she pinched my cheeks.

Aman dragged one of the kitchen chairs into my room and told me to sit down. She opened her case and pulled out her wares, plugging in a curling iron, laying out small pots of makeup, and various brushes on a white towel. She assessed my complexion while pulling and tweezing stray eyebrow hairs. She heated up wax and stripped the hair from my arms until my skin looked ripe and sunburned.

"Is this really necessary? They're just coming for dinner."

She put a cold towel over the raw skin. "Aren't you even a little excited?" She ripped another wax strip off.

"Ouch." I bit my lip. "Only for it to be over."

"It's Sunny Gill. How can you be so cavalier about it?" She slathered moisturizer onto my arms until a smooth glow had replaced the redness. My arms felt fuzzy, asleep, as if the skin were floating an inch above where it used to be. She reached onto her tray and grabbed pots of face powder and concealer, blending foundations on a palette, occasionally holding up the brush to my skin to match the tone. "Just think of it. You could be Mrs. Sunny Gill." She paused as if she were imagining it the way everyone else in the house was. Masi and my mother had been talking about the prospect of it with a controlled enthusiasm that was now bordering on hysteria. My mother had invited all of my sisters, their husbands and children over to meet Sunny. She thrived in the cooking and chaos of the day, raising and lowering her voice and expressions to meet it. One moment she was frying the pakoras, another she was showing Masi all the suits she had bought. Her closet was stuffed with her pre-emptive wedding shopping, an array of suits and saris that she had bought on sale at the local cloth house. The shopkeeper, Gyan, a flat-voiced muppet of a man with a rumpled green turban, had helped us with my sisters' wedding shopping; he'd been delighted when he saw us walk in, and remarked that it was about time I got married. "Ju are the last vun!" he said, twisting his wrist in the air as if my marriage were a magic trick. As irritated as I'd felt by his stating the obvious, I burst into laughter at the sound of his voice and the recollection of Harj's many imitations of him—with her chunni piled on her hair like his sloppy turban, she would tilt her head to each side like a see-saw. My laughter collected, cracking the corner of my eyes with small tears. During the drive home, my mother scolded me and told me this was the last time she would ask me to drive her.

Though she'd gotten her driver's licence soon after my father died, she refused to drive on the highway, saying she could not keep up with the on-ramps, the off-ramps, the multiple lanes and the sheer speed of it all. Once, when we were children, she'd tried to drive us to the Nanak Sar Gurdwara in Vancouver but ended up pulling over on the side of the road in clenched tears. We had to walk along the highway, in our salwar kameezes, our chunnies almost blowing off our heads because of the slicing of cars that raced by us, until we came to a gas station. There we called Mamaji, who came to pick us up. Later my mother remarked how lucky she was that he was never angry, how a husband would have been upset about having to pick us all up, but her brother was always there when she needed him, his mood never adding or taking away anything from hers. He was steady and dependable, the kind of man who didn't usually smile with his teeth, but when prompted by enough Black Label would grin kind madness. It was he who'd scoured the streets for Harj when she left and he who'd given my sisters away in their marriages, and now it was he who calmed my mother's nerves about my marriage.

My mother rushed down the hall in a panic, announcing the time like a countdown. "Forty-five minutes, they will be here in forty-five minutes." She poked her head in my bedroom door. "Meena, why are you not dressed yet? They will be here soon." She tapped her wrist even though she wasn't wearing a watch, and continued down the hallway calling out the time for anyone who hadn't heard.

"Almost done," Aman said without looking up. "Meena, would you stop fluttering your eyelids; you're messing up the liner." She retouched it, then smudged it with the edge of her fingertip and stood back to admire her work. "Close your eyes," she said, and blasted my hair with a steady shot of hairspray. "That should do it." She twirled the chair around so I could see myself in the mirror. My sisters and Masi, who had been waiting outside the door, piled in.

"Vah! Vah! Eyes like Hema Malini!" Masi handed me my salwar kameez and they all faced the wall while I suited up. The embroidery clawed at my skin.

"Done," I said, turning to the mirror. I hardly recognized myself. My fuchsia salwar kameez dotted with gold sequined flowers and emerald stones made me look like a transvestite at Mardi Gras. My hair was a mane of glossy curls, my eyes smouldered in three tons of purple eye shadow and my lips had been plumped up in pink gloss. I looked like I'd been plucked from a 1980s' Hindi movie.

Masi clapped and held her hands to her heart. "She needs more lip gloss… more hairspray… one more time with the mascara." After another half-hour of fussing and primping, Aman stood back with her brushes in hand, assessing my angles the way a portrait painter might look at a work in progress.

"Okay, enough. She looks fine," my mother said, rushing in with a box of pink bracelets.

I tried to slide them on. "They're too small." She reached over and collapsed my hand in hers, pushing the bracelets over my knuckles, the force of which pinched my flesh into accordion folds. "It hurts." I bit my lip as she tried again. Tears formed. Aman and my sisters stepped back, moving out of my mother's way.

"Make your hands smaller," she said. Her eyes narrowed with determination.

"How am I supposed to do that?"

She squeezed my hand so hard that I thought all the bones would break. "Serena, pass me the baby oil."

She slathered it over my hands, pushing the bangles over my raw knuckles one at a time. "We will make them fit."

They arrived according to Indian standard time—an hour late—and by then our anxious chatter had turned to silence and channel surfing. My sisters and I were watching a *Seinfeld* rerun when their car pulled up. "It's a Mercedes," Aman reported from her position at the window, where she'd stationed herself more than an hour ago. I watched them get out of the car and brace themselves against the cold wind. There was Sunny, his mother and father, Amarjit Auntie and Kal. From my vantage point all I could see were the tops of their heads. Sunny's father had a bald spot nestled in his salt-and-pepper hair, and I wondered if Sunny would lose his hair too. They all kept their heads down except for Sunny, who looked up and around as if he were lost and orienting himself to his surroundings. I ducked when he glanced up at the window, and then I peered out from the side of the drapes. Aman was right: Sunny was film-star perfection, with a chiselled face and eyes that drew you out and in. A look that was alluring, that made you want sex.

"What are you doing still standing there?" Serena ushered me into my room, reminding me that I wasn't to be seen until summoned. I heard her quickly raking the shag carpet on our steps and placing the garden rake in the hall closet. No other family but ours raked their shag carpet. My mother thought it looked messy if the pile was not all facing the same way. "First impressions count," she said.

The tray of teacups rattled in my hands. I didn't look up even though I was aware that I was being watched and assessed. I put the tray on the table and handed Sunny's mother a cup, which she accepted with a curt nod. Her hair was cut in a pageboy style and dyed an unfortunate shade of auburn that looked burgundy in certain lights. She had a protruding mole on her cheek, the kind that would eventually sprout hair. Unlike my mother, she wore makeup, gobs of it: a face powder shades lighter than her own skin, maroon lipstick and blotches of blush. She reminded me of another auntie my mother used to work with—one who had worn so much makeup that she'd looked like an Indian drag queen. Harj and I nicknamed her Dame Desi. The recollection made me smile. Kal smiled back. My mother frowned, and I looked down.

As I offered the tea to Sunny, my mother began the introduction, announcing my age and listing my accomplishments. Sunny's mother eyed me up and down with what I was sure was admiration and disdain. Eyeliner pooled in the corners of her eyes like dark sleep. According to Aman, I was at least the eighth girl Sunny had been shown in the past three months.

"Does she speak Punjabi?" his mother asked.

"Yes, of course," my mother replied.

"Can she cook?"

"She is learning," my mother lied. I had never made anything but a cup of chai.

"Educated?"

"She has a degree."

"Sit down," she said, patting the empty spot on the sofa between her and Sunny. She put her arm around me, her expensive perfume choking me like her insincere embrace. I didn't look up. "You know I have no daughters," she said to my mother. "You are so lucky to have five daughters." I wanted to correct her and say six daughters, but I knew that Harj was not to be counted—any acknowledgement of her would be an insult to our present good fortune. I wondered how it was that we had gotten used to her absence. How were we able to pretend that she had never even existed. "I always wanted a daughter to shop for," Sunny's mother said, taking a sip of tea. "I telephoned my sister in Bombay and told her to start looking for the latest fashions for when Sunny gets married. Our styles here are a year behind," she added, eyeing my pink kameez with disapproval.

"Is that where your suit is from?" my mother asked, turning her insult of my attire inside out to compliment her.

"Oh yes, I bought this one on my last trip. I try to go to India once a year. It is so changed since we lived there," Sunny's mother said, directing all her comments now to my mother. "It is very progressive. Everyone has a mobile phone, wears Nike and drinks Coca-Cola. It is very Westernized now."

"I thought you did not like the colonization of India," her husband commented, momentarily embarrassing her.

"Of course I want to be modern, but I also like to keep the customs and traditions of Hindustan, of our India, yes? Just because the British have left does not mean we must remove every trace of them. If we did that we would have no railroads, only rickshaws!"

Everyone nodded and laughed between sips of tea, except her husband, who seemed permanently irritated with his wife: his face was as skewed as her opinions. He was a tall, bony man with slackened skin and wire-rimmed glasses that sat on the edge of his nose. He was her opposite in every way. He hardly spoke. His silence, as I discovered, was not a sign of strength—it was a necessity. There was only so much room for conversation and his wife monopolized it with her Bombay British accent that reminded us she was an educated woman. I wondered if all marriages were like that. Did one partner always defer to the other?

Sunny's mother leaned forward. "There is one thing."

My mother waited for her to continue.

"It is her name—the astrologer suggests it be changed."

"Why? What is wrong with it?"

Sunny's mother put her hand on my mother's shoulder as though she were bracing her for some terrible news. "It is inauspicious. If they wed they would be unhappy, childless even. For their happiness' sake, it would need to be changed."

"To what?"

"Surinder."

"Sur-in-der?" My mother repeated it, deciphering it in syllables.

Mamaji, who had been quiet up to now, spoke. "But Meena's father, he named her."

Sunny's mother pulled me close, squishing my body against her bosom. Her husband smiled and said: "A rose by any other name would smell as sweet."

The room was silent except for the tick of the grandfather clock.

"Perhaps it is too early to talk of such things," Amarjit Auntie suggested. "Maybe we should let the kids talk, get to know each other, hmm?"

Masi agreed and stood up, prompting everyone else to stand as well. "This way," she said, leading Sunny and me downstairs to the family room, where my nieces and nephews were watching *Cinderella*. "Come now, children. Let these two talk," Masi said, and filed them out of the room.

I sat down on one end of the sofa and Sunny sat on the other. We still hadn't looked at each other. I reached for the remote control and turned the volume on the television down, aware that though we were alone we were still within eavesdropping distance. For a moment neither of us said anything. The silence was disconcerting and I wondered if Sunny was shy or simply bored with this process.

"So you're a lawyer?" I asked.

"Yes. Corporate, not criminal."

"Not a huge distinction," I joked.

He didn't laugh or smile. His quiet kept me at a tethered distance.

"And you? You're in communications or something?"

"Yeah. I work at a PR firm downtown."

"Did you go to UBC?"

"No, SFU."

He nodded, his head bobbing as if he were keeping time to a techno beat. I didn't say anything. His nervous tendencies left me unsteady—the slight tic and crack of his neck, the bouncing of his knee—or perhaps it was that when he looked at me, it felt like he was looking behind me, as if I were in his way. He reached into his suit jacket pocket and flipped his phone open, checking for missed calls. His phone wasn't at all like the brick ones that my brothers-in-law carried, but nothing about him was like them. Everything about him was expensive and guarded, from his grey suit to his socks, which had "Polo" stitched onto the heels.

Silence, except for the innocent taunts of the children who were playing outside in the yard, snatching glances at us through the window. "Sunny and Meena sitting in a tree, K-I-S-S-I-N-G. First comes love, then comes marriage, then comes the baby in the baby carriage."

He laughed a little. I was relieved.

"Is your mom serious about changing my name?" I asked.

"Most likely. She had our charts made and the astrologer told her that we weren't a good match. He suggested that if your name was different, our future could be different."

"So, essentially, it would be better if I were someone else?"

"It's not like that. It's really no big deal."

"Really? Then why not change your name?"

"I don't know. I don't know how all that stuff works and I really don't care. But my mom, she's really into it, so I just go along with it, you know?"

I smirked. "Yeah, I know."

"I'll still call you Meena when she's not around."

I nodded. More quiet.

We strained to connect, our conversation limited to polite affectations, our eyes drifting in and out of each other's peripheral vision. He asked me about family, but acknowledged all of my responses with only passing interest and dismissive nods. Any mutual attempt at conversation ended up in the tight awkward silences that come with doing what you've been told to do even when you don't want to. We spoke like strangers, revealing nothing but our discomfort, until I confronted all the lies we were leading.

"You don't want to get married, do you?"

He shook his head. "Not really."

"Then why are you even here? Why go through this?"

He sighed an uneven exhale. "Same reason as you. My family."

We stared at the TV, watching the cartoon images without sound for a few minutes until I turned towards him. "Why not just tell them that you don't want to?"

He reached for my hand and strummed my bracelets back and forth before looking up at me. "It's not that easy, is it?" He ran his fingertips over my knuckles, tracing the broken skin. "Does it hurt?"

2.4

I didn't see Sunny until a week before our engagement party. He'd asked permission to take me out and though my mother didn't approve of us seeing each other before the wedding, during a long phone conversation he convinced her otherwise. "All right, as long as there are other people there," she told him.

But when I arrived at the restaurant Sunny was seated alone, talking on his mobile phone. He didn't get up, gestured for me to sit down and continued his telephone conversation, which, from what I could hear, was both quiet and agitated. He pressed his finger to one ear, drowning out the restaurant sounds of cutlery against china and the head-thrown-back laughter of the table of six across from us. I took my shawl off and sank into the red leather club chair, soaking in the dim amber lighting and lounge music of Vancouver's newest hot spot. Sunny turned in his seat and fiddled with his silver cufflinks. He leaned back and crossed his legs casually. Everything about him looked like an advertisement for men's cologne. His shirt collar was undone as if he'd loosened a tie or taken it off after a long day at the office. He had a five o'clock shadow and a half-closed look to his eyes that suggested propositions of sleeplessness and lust.

He clipped the phone shut and popped it into the inside pocket of his blazer. "Sorry about that," he said, and leaned across the table to kiss me on the cheek. He sat back and took a sip of his Scotch, staring at me through the glass. "You look great."

"Thanks," I said, looking away when I saw him glancing at my breasts.

"The Bollywood look was great, but this dress... Wow. It's... Wow."

I smiled and wondered if he was sincere, especially when he grinned at the blush that such a few words could illicit. The compliments I usually got were backhanded. All the Indian people I had met were experts in deviant praise: either they said nice things to get nice things or they phrased their compliment in a way that cheapened it. My mother's sister-in-law was the master of these artful insults. If anything good was happening in our family, she would come right over to offer her dampening support. Of Tej's wedding clothes she'd said, "Modest, plain, not very fashionable, very fitting to your station in life." She'd seen me in a store recently and had stopped to tell me, "How nice you look. You must have finally lost a few pounds. No one wants to marry a chunky girl, especially Sundeep Gill." Whenever I got a compliment, I'd quietly dissect it, looking for angles and ulterior motives. If I found none, it was the kind of phrase I could replay and live on for days, carefully building my self-worth around it, never wondering what besides other people's perceptions was holding me together. But perhaps that was enough. Approval and acceptance were interchangeable in a culture that valued obedience like love.

"This is a really nice place," I said.

"Glad you like it. A friend of mine owns it." He paused, as if he expected me to be impressed, and I sensed that he was used to impressing people the way I was used to pleasing them. "In fact I asked him to make something special for us."

"How nice," I said, fidgeting with the row of silverware that was more extensive than anything I'd ever seen. The only restaurant I ever went to was White Spot and even then my mother scoffed at how much money I threw away when she could just make me dinner.

"I'm glad your mother agreed to let us go out."

"Me too. It seemed strange to get engaged without a first date."

"I know, right? If it wasn't for Kal, I wouldn't know anything about you other than what my mother told me."

"And... so what did Kal tell you about me?"

Sunny smiled. "He said that you're too good for me."

"Did he?"

"And since I only surround myself with the best of everything... " he said, alluding to our posh surroundings.

"You agreed to marry me," I said, adding the words to the end of his sentence like a punchline.

"Exactly." He laughed, lifting his glass to toast the air. "I did ask him why, if he thought so highly of you, he didn't marry you himself."

"And what did he say?"

"He didn't." He took another sip of his Scotch and clenched his teeth as it hit his throat. His smile flattened into a tight grin that he disappeared into momentarily.

"So is Kal joining us for dinner?" I asked, breaking the silence.

"Him, no. Why would he?"

"It's just... Well, you told my mom that there would be a few people."

"Oh. No, I just said that so she would let us have dinner together," he said, snapping his fingers for the waiter. "What? You've never lied to your mother before?"

"No, I mean, yes. I just thought... " The waiter unfolded my napkin into my lap. "How's your mom doing?"

"She's pretty excited. Spends most of her time shopping and planning for the wedding... Can I get you a drink—wine or something?" I nodded and the waiter was quick to bring over a bottle of red, which Sunny discerningly approved.

"You know how it is," I said. "She was beginning to worry that I'd never get married." Sunny sipped the wine placed before him, pausing as it hit his palette. "Yes, this is nice," he said to the waiter, who promptly filled our glasses.

"And how do you feel now that you are, that is... that *we* are getting married?" I asked.

"Relieved... to have made a decision."

"How do you know it's the right one?"

I waited in his contemplation, soaking in the soft music, hoping that he'd say something romantic, disappointed when he said "I don't."

I smiled, feeling foolish for wishing I could make us into something more than a convenience. He reached into his breast pocket for his ringing phone, excusing himself, gesturing that he'd only be a few minutes. Twenty minutes later he was still standing at the bar, talking on the phone, smiling only when the blonde hostess in the low-cut red dress walked by him. Occasionally she would interrupt him and ask if he needed anything, "Another Scotch, Sunny?" As he paused, drinking her in, I felt the beginnings of jealousy. How easily she satisfied him. He watched her for a time, and then, as though he'd gotten bored, turned the other way and smiled at me. I was surprised by the relief I felt at not having been forgotten.

A few minutes later he returned and sat down, pulling his shoulders back until I heard a slight crack. He was quiet, the way people are when they try to remember something or do math equations in their heads.

"Work?"

He shook his head. "No, it's this real estate deal I've been working on."

"Oh. I didn't know you worked in real estate."

He picked up his fork and knife, cutting his salad into bite-sized bits. "There's a lot about me that you don't know." His tone was almost sharp.

"Please, enlighten me then."

"I'm raising capital for a new high-rise development, condos and what not. If all goes well, I stand to make millions."

"Millions? Wow, I can't imagine."

"I know. I just have my fingers crossed that it all goes through. It's a lot of moving parts at this stage."

"How so?"

"Well, you have the city council and local residents to contend with, not to mention managing the various stakeholders' expectations." He looked up from his salad. "It's complicated. You probably wouldn't understand."

"Stakeholders, expectations—sounds a lot like dealing with family."

He smiled. "Dysfunctional at best."

"Tell me, how do you manage it all? With your work and everything?"

"I just do. I don't want to be like my dad. He worked hard, labouring at the mill his entire life."

"What's wrong with working hard?"

"Nothing. Our parents had to because they didn't have a choice, but we do." Sunny sipped his wine. "I guess I don't want to be one of those people who have to wait until they retire to enjoy life."

"Has your dad retired?"

He nodded. "After I came out here to go to law school, my mom made him sell the mill so they could move to Vancouver as well. She hates being alone."

I nodded and thought of my mother. I wondered if she was surfing through the channels right then, looking for a made-for-TV movie to watch even though the large and small meanings were lost on her.

"Are you okay?" asked Sunny. "You got all quiet."

"No, I'm fine. So tell me, do you prefer real estate to law?"

He put his fork down and called the busboy over to clear the dishes, complaining that the dressing was too oily. "My being a lawyer. That was my mom's idea. Her father was one, so naturally she thought that I should be one too."

"Naturally... Well, they must be very proud of you."

"They are." He nodded unnecessarily.

"You make it seem like it's a bad thing."

"It can be."

Before I could ask anything further, the waiter placed our meals in front of us.

Sunny took a sip of his drink, telling the waiter that he hoped the main course was better than the salad. He picked up his cutlery. "I hope you like it rare," he said, cutting into his steak, pulling the flesh from bone, chewing slowly.

I nodded yes even though I didn't, and forced myself to eat the bloody mess.

2.5

Girls with spray-on tans tapped the toes of their chunky-heeled shoes in protest as I walked past them to the front of the long lineup of partygoers waiting to get into the trendy nightclub. They adjusted their glittery tube tops and folded their arms across their sloppy, braless breasts, watching me greet the bouncer with an inside joke that said I was someone. I was Sunny's girl: I didn't have to wait for anything.

Money was the ultimate equalizer and Sunny had been brought up with all the advantages, connections and favours it could buy. Life seemed to hinge on his presence; his arrival started parties and his departure ended them. Everyone loved him and at times I wondered if I did too, or if I just loved being part of the show. When I was with him people knew me. I was someone even if at times I was unrecognizable to myself. I hated those moments when we were alone and there was nothing to say, the silence a reminder that I might have condensed myself to make room for him. Once I caught our reflection in a shop window as we walked by, my stride half a step behind his, my hand in his hand as he hurried me along. I walked beside myself for a half a block, staring at my vacant expression the way a child might search the ancestral faces in family photographs, desperate for similarity, recognition and belonging. "Surinder," I'd reminded myself, and crossed the street—leaving my other self behind, looking at her from a safe distance.

Inside the sweaty club I narrowed my eyes, looking for familiar faces in the hopping darkness. I wove past the usual party princesses, the circle of pretty suburban girls who clutched their purses under their arms as they did the barely dancing dance—a shuffle, a hip sway, an ass twitch.

"Meena!" Aman emerged from the crowd and put her arm around me. The weight of her slight body lurched onto my shoulder and her drink splashed about in its plastic tumbler. "You're late. Where were you? Everyone's here already," she slurred into her straw, snorting when the fizzy drink splashed into her face. "This is some party!" she said. "And you, you are so lucky to be marrying him. He is *soooo* great." I nodded and helped her to a bar stool. She was weepy with envy and drunkenness.

"Have you seen Sunny?" I asked.

Aman motioned to the corner where members of the desi crowd were playing billiards, double-fisting and toasting the air, spilling their intentions on the floor as they clanked glasses. Sunny was talking to a petite girl with long, straight brown hair that spilled over her shoulders. She was what one would consider cute: barely five feet tall, less than a hundred pounds, small hips and all boobs. I imagined that she probably had a high-pitched voice that made everything she said sound like a surprise. She took the pool cue from Sunny, chalked the end and leaned into a shot, leaving him with a perfect shot of ass and stick.

"It's his ex, Jasmine," Aman clarified. "She's such a bitch."

I nodded, my mouth suddenly too dry to speak. I wondered why she was here and wanted to ask but didn't for fear of the answer. One night, when Sunny had been drinking, he'd told me that his parents wanted him to marry me to keep him from her. I pretended that I didn't know about her attempted suicide and that his admission of caring for her still did not shock me. He was quiet about it, skipping the cruel details, but I felt his ache in the silence and recognized it as my own, matching his wounds to mine word for word.

"Will you be okay?" I propped Aman back onto the stool she kept sliding from. "Can you call her a cab?" I asked the bartender.

"No, no." Aman waved her hands in the air. "I'm fine, I'm good—see?" she said, and teetered in an attempt to stand.

"Just take the cab home and call me tomorrow," I said, my words trailing behind me as I made my way to Sunny.

"Happy birthday." I kissed him, trying not to take in any of the whisky on his breath.

I introduced myself to Jasmine, enunciating the word "fiancée" as I extended my hand, quietly examining her wrists for a scar, some sign of her near love and death. I nestled into Sunny's arms, closing the space between them. I couldn't help but wonder what I'd interrupted; there was an enslaved look between them that resembled the intersection of lust and addiction, making me wonder if they were together still or if what haunted them was simply the memory of it. Jasmine noticed me eyeing her scar tissue and pulled her hand away. She folded her arms across her chest before walking away. Sunny reached for his glass, and downed what was left of his drink.

I stared through the shifting crowd. "Is Kal here yet?" I asked.

Sunny pulled me closer. "Why are you always asking about him? I'm not good enough for you or something?" The bite of whisky hit the back of his throat, clipping his words to ultimatums.

"I'm not always asking. I just asked once." Sunny's friends were looking at the floor, trying to listen and not listen to our conversation. I could tell by their downturned stares that they were the ones behind his growing paranoia about my friendship with Kal. Sunny pointed to the bar. "He's right over there, talking to the blonde." He paused at the end of the sentence as if he were making a point or waiting for me to respond. I said nothing, pretending I didn't care.

Sunny smiled, relaxing the hold he had on me when I twisted in his grip, his mood switching from possessive to dismissive in an undefined instant—alcohol intensifying his contradictions. He called one of his friends over and for a time they talked investment speculation while I nodded on the periphery. Sunny never introduced me to his friends. I knew their names and stories only because Kal told me, and they knew me because I was with Sunny and for them that seemed to be enough. None of them engaged me in conversation and any time I asserted an opinion or a thought, Sunny would smile and look at me with a silence in his eyes that was part plea, part reprimand—a chastising and condescending quiet that changed the tone and course of entire evenings. I quickly learned how to disappear and reappear, drifting in and out of conversations on cue, speaking of only those things that mattered to Sunny, surprised that I found some pleasure whenever he was pleased.

When I mentioned some misgivings to Serena, she told me that I just wasn't used to the "give and take" of relationship. "I give and he takes?" I asked thoughtfully. And though I was wary of being his silent partner, it was in my own distillation, my own vanishing act, that I won the approval of everyone I knew. The women at my office salivated over his picture on my desk, reminding me how lucky I was to be with someone like him. Even my mother didn't mind my going out with him anymore. When I was with him, I was almost free.

The rest of the evening passed through a cigarette-smoke haze that cloaked the patrons in a gauzy shroud, obscuring their intoxicated impulses. It reminded me of when Kal and I were first together. He'd think up a way to sneak me out of my house to find the garage-band dives that no other Indians would go to. We'd sit in the darkest corner, listen to music, get drunk enough to talk and not remember later what we'd talked about, and then sit in his truck until sex or the silence after sobered us up. When we sat there, I'd think of Liam, and wonder where he was and who he was with—just like I was doing now. It had been so long that I could hardly remember his face, but occasionally I would see it in the parentheses of a stranger's smile, the blue of their eyes.

"Looks like you need a drink." Kal pulled his bar stool up to mine.

"Can't—I'm driving."

He nodded. "Not so fun being the only sober one at the party, huh?"

"No." I watched a crowd of wannabe-me girls flock around Sunny, singing happy birthday. "No, not so fun." I looked away when I saw Sunny buying yet another round of shots for his friends. He had his arm around Jasmine, his hand dangerously close to her ass.

"Well, if it makes you feel better, I'm pseudo-sober."

"Oh, is that the technical term for it?" I asked.

"Yes, it is. In layman's terms it means that although I'll have a headache in the morning, I'll still remember our conversation."

I laughed. "I'll have to test the theory tomorrow."

"I always remember the things you say, and the things you won't say."

"Pseudo-sober, hmmm?" I squinted. "I don't know about that… you may just be indiscernibly drunk."

"That the technical term for it?" I nodded. "And what do you think is the technical term for that?" he asked, pointing to Sunny, who had just bumped into a waitress, tipping her tray of shots all over her tight T-shirt.

"Last-call liability," he said, as we both rushed over.

Sunny stumbled to the car in a swagger that took up the entire sidewalk. He grabbed my keys and tried the lock, accidentally keying the door and scraping the paint. "Look what you made me do." He ran his finger over the scratch.

"Sunny, just give me the keys."

He turned around and held the keys above his head, beyond my reach. "No. I want to drive. I already told you, I'm okay."

"Sunny, no… remember the last time."

"I said I'm good." His glare quieted my attempts momentarily.

"Please," I said, reaching across him. "Don't be like this."

He pushed me away. "Fuck, would you just stop. I said I'm fine." He walked along the raised curb, touching his finger to his nose. "See, I'm fine."

"No, you're not and neither am I," Kal said, running to catch up with us. "Meena, can you drive us both home?"

Sunny collapsed into the back seat, his whisky madness softening into a sentimental haze. "I'm sorry, babe. Did you hear me, I said I'm sorry. I didn't mean to yell at you." He leaned forward, his head wagging stumbling affections between the two front seats.

"She heard you," Kal said. "Now put your seat belt back on and relax."

"My mom is right about you, Meena…she said that you're a good girl… that you'll be a good wife."

"No one is arguing with you, buddy. She is great, now just put your seat belt on."

I glanced into the rear-view mirror, unable to see Sunny at all if not for the headlights of the occasional oncoming cars. He leaned forward, and ran his finger along the side of my neck, twirling a piece of my hair around his finger with gentle tension. Frightened and intrigued, I sat up, my posture pushing his hand away. He sat back in a hearty sigh, and though I didn't look back again, I felt his eyes and his hand's imprint, his silence hover and shroud. I never knew what to say when he was drunk. Sometimes alcohol induced openness and all his secrets came tumbling out, and at other times he locked himself inside his own mind as if he were protecting me from something dense and angry. I'd seen it in the occasional flicker of his jaw and the flared intersection of veins in his forehead, and always took this as a sign that I should leave him alone.

I was content to drive in silence, the night passing us in dark sheets, streetlights washing over us in waves, but Sunny couldn't sit still, and fiddled with the automatic windows, opening and closing them in short bursts. He leaned out the open window, sang a few lines from "Close to You," and ended with his own line: "I feel love for you, Meena." Then he closed the window, as if he were taking a bow before a curtain call.

"I love you, too."

"You do?" Kal turned towards me. "You love him?"

I bit down on my lip.

"Of course she loves me… Everybody loves me," Sunny said, his head bobbing as his eyes closed. "What's not to love?"

Kal and I helped Sunny into the house, his legs dangling at the knees as we shuffled to his bedroom suite, where Sunny crashed, laughing as he pulled me onto the bed with him. Kal left the room while I diverted Sunny's ill-timed advances, telling him "No, not now" in the moments before he passed out. He only ever touched me when he was drunk, but even then I refused to sleep with him; the idea of being with him before our marriage seemed wrong, as if it didn't fit his version of me. The only real intimacy we had shared was a botched hand job in the back of his BMW. He'd stared straight ahead for a time, his hand pumping mine, setting the pace he could lose himself in. Eyes closed, mouth parted, he didn't make a sound except for the occasional grunt as he groped for my breasts in the dark. After fifteen minutes of dissatisfaction, he shoved me away. "Fuck, you're not even doing it right," he'd said, zipping his pants up. We sat in the pitch dark, hidden by tinted windows, our frustrations mounting.

Now, as I rose to leave, Sunny woke, pulling me closer, telling me not to leave him until he was asleep. I lay beside him with the lights out. His body was hot, almost feverish against mine, and as he spoke, I imagined the small words lingering around his lips like smoke, something to be devoured by.

When he was asleep, I lifted his arm off me and slipped away, carrying my shoes in my hand. Kal was waiting in the living room, standing next to one of the overstuffed couches that flanked each end of the room. All the furniture was pushed against the walls and floating between them was a glass coffee table topped with an obscure sculpture that made the room look like a museum, something for show. "You think he'll be okay?" I slipped my high heels back on.

"Yeah, he'll be fine," Kal said. "He'll have a wicked headache, but he'll be fine."

I put on my jacket. "Do you want a ride home?"

"No, I'm just gonna crash here."

"All right then," I said, digging through my purse for my keys. "I should get going. I don't want to wake anyone."

We stood in the grand foyer, both of us listening to the upstairs sounds of Sunny's mother snoring in her bedroom. Apart from sleeping, she spent several hours of each day there perched on a La-Z-Boy chair, watching *Mahabharat* over and over.

"Wait… Stay, have a drink with me. She sleeps through everything," Kal said.

"I should go." I lowered my voice. "You know how Sunny is."

"What, he's still mad about last week?"

I nodded.

"But he was the one who told us to go to the movie without him."

"We shouldn't have gone together."

"Is that what you believe or is that what he told you?" Kal walked into the adjacent kitchen and opened and closed cupboards.

When Sunny had confronted me about going to the movies without him, I'd reminded him that Kal was his cousin. He'd nodded and smiled, "That's right, he's my cousin not yours, and you—you're with me not him." I didn't know what to do but agree.

I followed Kal into the kitchen. "Was he always jealous like that?"

"Yeah, pretty much. He's used to getting his way, used to getting what he wants. And right now, you happen to be it." He pulled out a bottle of wine. "Jackpot."

As he uncorked the bottle, I wandered into the family room. Unlike the other room, it was a mishmash of old furniture that hinted at his parents' working-class days. I sat down on the leather sectional and fiddled with the elaborate stereo system that Sunny had recently purchased. Kal sat on the sofa across from me and handed me a glass of wine. "Sunny hasn't figured out how to use it yet."

I laughed. "That doesn't surprise me." My smile faded into silence. "The two of you couldn't be more different."

"Well, I am adopted, remember."

"Oh, so you favour nature over nurture do you?"

"I don't know. I'm too drunk to know much right now," he said as he lay down, legs sprawled out over the edge of his sofa. "But even our nurture was different; after all, my parents are the poor relations."

"Stop it. You're hardly poor."

"Compared to Sunny's family we are."

"Were you two close growing up?"

"No, not really. They lived on the island, so we only visited them a few times a year. When we did visit, it was always kind of weird. Our moms don't really get along and Sunny, well, he was always a jerk."

"Ouch. What did he do to you? Steal your girlfriend or something?" I giggled and leaned back into the couch cushions.

"Ha ha," he said, mocking me. "No. I knew better than to introduce them to him, that is until now."

"I wasn't exactly your girlfriend."

"But you weren't exactly *not* my girlfriend either."

I looked away, not knowing quite what to say.

"I guess it's not really his fault, him being the way he is." He took a sip of wine. "I mean his mom, you've met her, she's a piece of work. Always bribing him to get him to do what she wants."

"What do you mean?"

"Oh come on, you know. His life has been bought and paid for by his mommy and daddy. In high school his parents gave him a hundred dollars for every A+ he brought home. When he agreed to go to law school they bought him a BMW, and when he agreed to marry you, they gave him the money for his latest real estate venture as a wedding present."

"Serious?" I leaned forward.

He sat up. "I'm sorry; I thought you knew. I heard him talking to you about the investment so I figured you guys had talked about it."

"No, he neglected to mention that part." I took the last swig of my drink and set the glass down. "But I suppose it doesn't really matter. It doesn't change anything."

"It doesn't?"

I shook my head.

"It's not too late. You could still change your mind."

"It *is* too late. The invitations have been sent out. The caterers have been booked. Everything's arranged. My mom... everyone expects me to do this. Nothing has changed *that*." I walked over to the window and stared out at the room that was reflected in front of me. Kal got up and put his drink on the table. "So that's it? You're really going to go through with it?"

When I didn't answer, he stepped closer until he was standing directly behind me, his hands on my hips. I strained my neck to his breath, anticipating a moment of intimacy where I knew there wouldn't be one.

2.6

I crouched down on the small wooden board that Masi had covered with red silk, my eyes fixed on the intricate and colourful rangoli design she'd created on the ground in front of me. My sisters held a canopied chunni over my head, while my mother knelt by my side and tied a red string around my wrist. She curled and stretched her lips with each twist of a knot until she knew that no one could undo what had been done. Settling into her own satisfied smile, she passed the ball of red yarn to my sisters, who tied a length on all those present.

My mother called to Masi to say that she couldn't remember the words to the old songs. Masi sang in her place and my mother strained to find the tune as she scooped the turmeric paste into her palm and smeared it across my forehead and cheeks, cleansing me in ritual preparation for my wedding. She dipped her hands into a bowl of flour and wiped them over my face, pushing the paste into dough, until it fell away, leaving my skin with a smooth saffron stain. My sisters and cousins joined in and rubbed the paste into my arms and legs. Aman stood by, ready to slap any hands that got too close to my hair.

"Watch the hair, she just had it done," she kept saying. "For God's sake, the hair... it has to stay like this until the wedding," she said, occasionally dousing me in a spray of vo5. "Okay, only a few more minutes. Meena needs to have her bath before the photographer gets here," she pleaded, all the while dispatching my cousins on various errands.

In the months before the wedding, I'd lived by the weekly checklists and colour-coded calendars that she'd created for me, each task a new distraction. Every Sunday she had come over and assessed what was left to do, pacing back and forth like a drill sergeant strategizing about colour schemes or planning the next week's shopping excursion, in which we methodically replaced every item I owned with something new. By now nothing remained of what I had owned or who I had been. Tomorrow I'd leave my mother's home with a new life wrapped in Cellophane, packed into a series of suitcases or stuffed into the Louis Vuitton trunk that Sunny's mother had bought for me. When my mother cleaned my closet of its contents, the last thing to go was my box of journals. I came in to find her sitting on the carpet cross-legged, staring at the stack, fingering the print in each one, her eyes troubled as if she had deciphered the meaning. It was then that I knew I couldn't keep them or leave them behind, so I loaded the box into my car and drove to the beach, where I read each one, flipping and ripping pages, tearing them up until only bits of paper hung from the threaded binding. I placed them into a paper bag and lay them on a float of driftwood, which I carried into the water. As the tide pushed in, I knelt over the bag and lit it on fire. The rising flame singed the ends of my hair before the current and earth pushed the pyre out of reach. I stood still, buried to my knees in dredged silt and seaweed, watching my thoughts bob and capsize until the ocean made me an island.

"Okay, Okay. That's enough," Aman yelled, pushing back the auntie who had elbowed my updo. She stretched her arms out as if she were part of a crowd-control squad and held the others back as I made my way to the washroom. The aunties followed us down the hall, their shrill singing voices penetrating the closed door.

I sat in the tub, and leaned back until only my breasts were above the waterline. I ran my hands over my body, as if I were cataloguing parts of myself. I turned over and lay face down in the water, ears submerged, dampening and drowning the sound of the aunties during their back-and-forth processions in and out of the house, steel pots and jugs of water in hand. They had started arriving this morning at seven, each of them with their barrel-shaped middle-aged bodies and dishwashing hands invading with offers to help with the food and preparations for the party. There was no spot in the house safe from their prying eyes and spiked advice, and at several points I retreated to my mother's walk-in closet, to sit waiting beneath the empty embrace of my father's suits. For what, I wasn't sure.

When I emerged from the bathroom, the aunties were dancing in the family room, swinging their chunnies and singing folk songs that brought forth short bursts of laughter. I smiled when I heard my name inserted into a song, and though I didn't know what they were saying, I blushed. Over and over, they danced short sweeps of a circle while all the other women clapped the ill-timed beat. Aman translated one of the songs for me and I was taken aback that women who appeared so chaste and proper would sing such crude lyrics, but by then I'd learned that nothing was ever what it seemed. This was what I was thinking when the photographer lined us up from tallest to smallest, pulling us into frame and focus. He held his fingers up, counting them down one at a time, all of us smiling except my mother, who had long since forgotten how. Sweating beneath the camera lights, the photographer clicked off rolls of film, telling us all in his Indian accent, "Say cheese. Smile. Everyone happy. Look this way." I knew that when the film was developed, these pictures, like all other wedding pictures, would be placed in a twenty-pound photo album that would only ever be dragged off a bookshelf to be shown to the aunties who came to tea on Sunday afternoons. The aunties would flip through the plastic-covered pages, their oily pakora-eating fingers leaving marks and stains on every moment.

I was relieved when Sunny's family arrived. The attention diverted from me to the small delegation who came bearing gifts that were laid out in the living room for everyone to see. The gold jewellery and heavy silk saris were passed around for all to admire and as the fat aunties judged the weight and value of the gifts, girls jostled to get a better view, some of them giggling when Kal glanced their way. When Masi teased him that it was not appropriate for him to be there, he reminded her that he had been my friend since we were children so in fact was a member of both sides of the family.

My sisters made several passes in and out of the crowded room, carrying trays of soda pop and tea for our guests, who fanned themselves with the ends of their chunnies. The aunties continued to dance, this time with ornate pots of candles balanced on their heads as they sang the same celebratory Jaago song that had been sung for them when they were to be married. Masi held her small pot with one hand, and with the other, strong-armed people into dancing. Even my mother made a short-lived attempt and danced around the room once. Time looped on itself and when the dancing finished, old songs were resung, toddlers fell asleep at their mothers' feet and scores of nameless distant cousins sat in huddled conversation.

Masi opened the window. The room flooded with the sounds of the children who had been sent outside to decorate the cars with plastic pompoms—which they were instead using for a game of dodge ball. Masi leaned out the window, hollering at them to begin the task of attaching the pompoms to the Styrofoam "Just Married" heart. "Fluff them up so they look like roses," she yelled.

After dinner, my nieces and younger cousins sat in a circle drawing henna peace signs and love hearts on their palms and cheeks as if it were face paint. The mehndi artist held my hands in the air, and twisted them to the light. The little girls watched with curiosity. "Sometimes the palm dictates the design," she said, and filled the trenches with fine swirls and paisley budded branches that bloomed in my fingertips. "Your life is a twist of fate," she said, continuing with a pattern of roots and vines that wrapped around my wrists.

"How do you know? Can you read palms?" I asked. "Can you read mine?"

She put her henna pen down and looked at my hand, and for a moment I recognized sadness in her expression. "There is no life but the one at hand," she said.

I shook my head, not wanting to understand, and as I waited for my henna to dry I remained quiet, disappearing into the sound of the house as guests came and went, as dishes clattered and cleared, as the voices of many strangers became the whispers of a few family members.

Serena came into the living room, picking up stray paper plates and cups before collapsing onto the loveseat. The grandfather clock struck midnight.

"Today is the first day of the rest of your life," Aman said, rushing into the room, banging a pot with a wooden spoon as if it were New Year's Eve.

I looked up at her and then down at my hands, flaking off pieces of hardened henna.

She put the pot down and sat beside me. "Aren't you excited? You're getting married today." I nodded, chipping off another piece of henna, letting the green crusty bits fall into the shag carpet.

"Stop that. You're making a mess of it," Aman said, grabbing my hands. She removed a patch to see if the dye had taken. "Sometimes the colour is too orangey, but this looks really nice." She held my hand up and showed Serena, who agreed that it looked good. "You can probably go wash it off if you want."

When I didn't answer, she looked up at me. "Are you okay?"

I got up, my legs cramped from sitting cross-legged for so long. "Yeah… I just need some air. It's too hot in here. I'm going to go outside for a bit."

"Well, wash that off while you're out there," she hollered as I opened the porch door. "Or the stain will get too dark."

I stood in the backyard, rinsing the dried henna off with the garden hose until all that was left on my palms was the blood red pattern of paisleys. I stared at them, tracing the fine swirls with my fingertips over and over again, falling into a frantic trance. Hands shaking from the cold, I turned the tap back on and scrubbed harder in a futile attempt to regain my sense of self.

"Meena?"

I turned around. It was Kal. "I thought you left," I said, quickly drying my hands on the end of my sari and trying for composure.

He nodded and lit his cigarette. "I did, but your mom asked me to come back and drop some stuff off for tomorrow."

"For tomorrow," I whispered. "You mean for today."
He checked the time on his watch, exhaled, and without looking at me, handed me his cigarette.

"I don't smoke."

"I know," he said, still offering.

I took it from him, alternating drags until there was nothing left.

THREE FOR LOVE

3.1

I ran my fingers along the bolts of fabric that lined the walls and watched a mother-in-law type haggle with the turbaned shopkeeper at the sari-covered counter. The shopkeeper's frustration grew in the perspiration stains under his arms and the spittle on his lips as he smiled and replied repeatedly that $895 was his best price. The daughter-in-law folded her arms over her chest and examined her fingernails, cracking the already chipped red polish, thumbing her wedding bracelets in boredom. I wondered how long she had been married, and counted her bangles as if the number meant something.

My mother-in-law had been furious that I'd taken my churah off after the wedding—these bangles, she'd reminded me, were meant to be worn until they broke off. "The longer they last the happier your marriage will be," she'd said while examining my naked wrists. When I told her that they were too tight, she hissed that taking them off was like throwing my marriage away. Sunny assured her that we would be happy, and asked me to put them back on for the reception, for appearance's sake.

Now I looked up at the daughter-in-law's upside-down reflection in the mirrored-tile ceiling. She stood slightly behind her mother-in-law, speaking only when spoken to, as if she existed only for the benefit of others. She could have been me four years ago.

"Surinder?" The shopkeeper was squinting over his bifocals.

"Hello, Uncleji."

He smiled and twisted his head in an elfish nod. "This is Rani's daughter-in-law," he told the mother-in-law type. She smiled and eyed me up and down with some admiration. I stood taller, recouping my pride in being recognized as someone. "Your mother is already here. She is in the showroom looking at our latest collection."

The showroom smelled like incense. Not the kind you got from the Indian store, but the kind that was sold in overpriced tin canisters at trendy import shops—the kind that made being Indian smell like mango peach and gingered spice rather than the aroma of ghee and tarka that I'd grown up with. Even the walls were painted with a Taj Mahal-like mural, complete with marble pillars and frescoes of the Mughal period, lovers sitting on woven carpets, the bejewelled women feeding men whose heads and eyes were reeled back in ecstasy. Not a picture of a guru in sight.

I wiped my feet on the Persian rug and walked across the mahogany floor to where my mother-in-law was seated in a large rattan chair, sipping chai.

"Hi, Mom," I said, kissing her on the cheek.

"You're late."

I looked at my watch. She was early. "Sorry, I was in another shop and lost track of time."

She nodded. "I had them pick out some things for you. I will wait while you try them—Sita, can you get me another cup of chai?" Sita, the salesperson, nodded and asked me if I would like tea and some sweets. My mother-in-law told her "No," before I could answer.

I came out of the change room and stood in front of a three-way mirror, surrounded by myself. My mother-in-law put her chai down, stood up and shook her head.

"Too many gulab jamuns at Aman's wedding, heh?" she said, pointing to the taut fabric across my chest. I caved my shoulders in, trying to hide my curves, which had long since gone out of style. Even Sunny seemed to prefer the waif girls in push-up bras. After he'd bought me a gym membership for my birthday the year before, I'd gone shopping for undergarments with spandex in them: I needed something to hold me in. "How does Aman like living in England?"

"Well enough, I suppose. She's still settling in," I said, turning around, wondering what Aman would think of this outfit if she were here. I'd seldom heard from her since she'd moved away.

My mother-in-law shook her head. "No, I really don't like this. Try the next one—and hurry. We don't have all day." She ushered me back into the change room.

"What time is the party?" I asked.

"Seven-thirty, but come to the house early because I want everything to be ready before Sunny's chachaji gets there."

"Sunny's chacha?" I asked, knowing that Sunny's father did not have a younger brother.

"Mmm," she said, teacup trembling in the saucer. "It is Sunny's grandfather's cousin's son—he is here for the party."

I nodded, shut the change room door and tried to trace the family tree to work out where this new person really fitted. Was he second cousin once removed, or first cousin twice removed, or maybe second cousin twice removed? I could never figure it out, and just went along with the endless string of dinners she asked us to attend.

When we were first married, she'd accepted social invitations on our behalf, considering our requested attendance as a mandatory function of our marriage. These events were the same regardless of who was the host. I wore a ridiculous amount of gold jewellery, applied a radiant moisturizer to replicate the honeymoon glow that had already worn off, and spent the evening pretending that my existence was completely defined by Sunny and that married life was the only life. I complimented the ladies on their outfits, dished out useless advice to the unmarried girls who wanted to be me, and discreetly watched the clock. I wondered if anyone realized that everything I said was disingenuous. I wondered if their asking things of me and accepting of me was as artificial. While I sat in the family room with the ladies, sipping tea sweetened with polite insincerity and watched our wedding video for the one-hundredth time, Sunny sat in the living room with the men drinking whisky in a whirl of testosterone, crude jokes, pats on the back and burst of laughter. I felt like the punchline.

I'd hoped that when we moved out of his parents' home, these social obligations would lessen but they never did. Whenever his mother asked us to attend a party, Sunny insisted we go, saying that was the least we could do considering how our moving out had devastated her.

Initially, when I'd brought up the topic of moving to Yaletown, Sunny refused, reminding me how much money we were saving by living with his parents and how much money his parents had spent on refurnishing the basement suite to suit us. We had a private entrance, our own kitchen, living area and a master bedroom ensuite complete with a Jacuzzi we never used. "What more could you want?" he'd asked. But as he went out night after night with his friends, leaving me behind to watch Hindi movies with his mother, I knew it was his bachelor status that he was not yet ready to part with. He'd often come home smelling like Scotch and cheap perfume, stumble on and off me in a forceful fuck, occasionally leaving me grateful that he could still make me feel something, even if it was my own discomfort. On those rare nights when I felt something close to desire, he'd cover my mouth so his parents wouldn't hear.

"How about this one?" I asked, turning before the mirror so my mother-in-law could inspect me.

"Masi!" a voice said from behind. My mother-in-law turned around to greet Sunny's hook-nosed bitch of a cousin Preetpaul—Pretty for short. I didn't bother turning around; she was used to talking behind my back.

"Are you here to pick up your sari for tonight?" my mother-in-law asked.

"Just the blouse. They had to take it in… It's so nice of you to have this dinner for me, Masi." Pretty stood behind me, circling. "Jasmine was wearing a similar lehnga last month. She looked stunning. She's so thin she can make anything look good. Apparently her secret is not to eat before a party—that way your stomach stays flat," she said, sucking in her already flat abdomen until it caved in beneath her ribs. "Maybe you should try that, hmm?" she said, looking at my midriff. "Unless you're pregnant."

My mother-in-law's eyes widened at the thought of a grandchild. She was more frustrated with my inability to get pregnant than I was and forced me to endure her suffering. She worried I was infertile and had insisted that I go to see her astrologer, who mapped out my stars, suggested that I no longer eat meat on Tuesdays and Thursdays, and encouraged her to hold a paath to bless us in our baby-making. After a year of trying and tests, our doctor informed us that Sunny's sperm count was too low to father a child. Sunny went into a rage at the mere suggestion, calling the doctor a quack and threatening to sue him for a misdiagnosis. I didn't tell anyone about Sunny's infertility and he did nothing to shoulder my monthly blame. "No, I'm not pregnant," I said.

"Well, when are you going to have kids?"

"When the time's right."

"Well, you may not want to wait much longer—you know, tick-tock," she said, laughing. "I can't wait to have kids. I told Raj that I want to have them right away!"

"Lucky for you that right away is only a few months away," I muttered, knowing the truth behind her rushed engagement.

"What?" She stamped her foot in a controlled tantrum.

I turned to face her. "I just mean that your wedding is only a month away."

"I know, isn't it great." She presented her left hand, showing us her ring as if we hadn't seen it a dozen times. "I can't wait to be a wife and a mother. I think giving life is the most important thing a woman can do."

I tried to smile despite the snub. The only life I'd given was my own. I had long stopped trying to conceive of any existence but the one that I had moment to moment. My mother cautioned me that when it came to marriage, it was best not to expect anything. On my wedding day, she'd told me not to smile too much. When I asked why, she stood behind me and gazed at my reflection in the mirror and told me that life was about depth. "The greater your happiness, the deeper your sorrow." I asked her if it worked the other way—if my sorrow was deep, would my happiness be great? As we stood in each other's reflection, looking forward and back, she narrowed her eyes to a squinted stare. For a moment I thought she saw me, and I knew she did when she answered, "Your disappointments dwell with your dreams."

As my mother-in-law and Pretty continued their conversation, I returned to the dressing room to try on more lehngas, acutely aware of their lowered tones, the pentameter in their verse—the sound of gossip.

When I arrived at the house, my mother-in-law was in the kitchen doing the dishes. "Good, you are here," she said, handing me a tea towel. "Dry these... Where is Sunny?"

"He's working late. He'll come by when he's done."

She shook her head. "He works so hard... He didn't work that much when you lived here. Hmmm. You kids didn't know how expensive it was to live on your own." She turned the faucet off and dried her hands. "Independence. All you want is independence."

"Mom, it's not like that. Everything's fine. We're fine."

"Of course it is; my son makes sure it is. But you, what do you do. Hmm, how much money do you make?" I didn't bother with the dialogue. Ever since she'd hit menopause, her hot flashes and mood swings had ruled the household. "Go tell your father to move the cars out of the driveway so our guests can park."

"Where is he?"

"How should I know?"

I stacked the remaining dishes and went off down the grand hallway and up the stairs to look for him, poking my head into the almost empty rooms that served as guest rooms. During and after our wedding, their megahouse with its massive oak doors and columned entry had welcomed out-of-town guests who came to visit us and bask in our post-wedding life. We'd spend the day taking them sightseeing, pointing out the best places to take pictures, posing with them in Stanley Park or on the top of Grouse Mountain, and when we came back home too tired to cook, Sunny's dad would order in pizza with extra chilies on the side. But ever since we'd moved out last year, their guests had been few, and my mother-in-law had retreated into her own paranoia and telephone gossip while my father-in-law spent most of his time in his study.

I knocked on the door even though it was open. He was sitting behind a mahogany desk that was far too big for the cramped room, and staring at a computer screen. "Surinder," he said. "Come here, help me with this." He pointed to the screen. "I can't get this working." I walked around the desk and clicked a few buttons showing him how to end the non-responsive program. "You make it look so easy," he said, looking at me over his reading glasses. "Sit down." He pointed to the leather wing chair that he had picked up at an antique store the last time we went shopping together. "We'd had it reupholstered and edged in brass tacks, refinished to its original splendour until the chair looked like it belonged in a grand library from some other time when art and literature were as important as commerce, when the art of conversation was as important as the content. But here in this space the chair looked captive, a prisoner of this ten-by-ten room. My mother-in-law hated his penchant for old things and relegated them all to his study, which was now brimming with bookcases and first-edition finds, the dust layering and insulating shelves and nooks. "How are you, my dear?"

"I'm good."

He nodded. "You look good, yes, but are you?" he asked again, this time pulling a bottle of Scotch from the bottom of drawer.

"How many have you had?"

"Not enough," he said. "Your mother is driving me crazy. All this cleaning and cooking, and for what? To entertain people we don't even like?"

I smiled. "Maybe the two of you need a holiday, get away for a while."

He shook his head and sighed. "This is what we've worked for. This is what your mother wants."

I tried to imagine him as he was when they lived on Vancouver Island—big glasses, pot-belly, a striped tie and a white short-sleeved, collared shirt. That was how Sunny had described him and it was very unlike the wiry old man who sat before me now. Even though I'd seen photos of him, I couldn't get my head around the contradiction that this man who loved books, recited Rumi and adored Picasso had spent his youth in a mill, smelling of cedar and sawdust. I stood up and ran my fingers across the row of books, turning my head to read their spines, wondering what was new in his collection.

"Looks with its sidecurved head curious what will come next. Both in and out of the game, and watching and wondering at it." He paused, waiting for me to pick up his recitation.

"Backward I see in my own days where I sweated through fog with linguists and contenders, I have no mockings or arguments.... I witness and wait." I pulled the book off the shelf and cracked the spine, inhaled the musty pages and old words. "I see you're reading Whitman again."

He smiled. "It suits my mood. My age." He blew the dust off the chess set that was sitting in the bay window, all the pieces still locked in play from where we'd last left them a month ago. "I believe it is your move," he said.

"We don't have time. Mom wants you to move the cars."

"Come on now. Just one move."

"All right," I said, shaking my head.

He waited and watched—a breath, a sigh, dangling from his mouth as my hands hovered over pieces, plotting a course. "Too bad Sunny doesn't play anymore." He took off his glasses and wiped the lens on the untucked end of his dress shirt. "You know I taught him and Kal when they were boys. They were good. They even entered tournaments."

"He never told me that," I said, sliding my pawn into play. "Why did they stop?"

"Because Kal wouldn't let him win."

"Check," I said, sitting back into the chair, my arms crossed.

He drummed his fingers against his lips and leaned over the board. "Clever girl. Very clever girl." He scratched his balding head, looking utterly stupefied and pleased as I left the room.

That evening's dinner party was like all the others. All the guests huddled in groups, soda-fuelled children played hide-and-seek in the hallways, and the men—Sunny included—stood in the living room, their never-empty glasses in hand, while I sat a prisoner of my kitchen mates, who crowed and delighted as they listed the births, deaths and marital status of relations as if they were accomplishments.

Occasionally I looked around, peeking into the living room that smelled of warm alcohol and aftershave, that hummed with hockey talk, and fortune hunting. Talk of new cars, luxury cars, sports cars. German or Japanese? Selling land, buying land, old country and new country, buying low and selling high, tearing down and building up. Kal was stuck in the middle of one such conversation between two uncles who were debating the longterm value of real estate over mutual funds, their voices blurring the ends of unfinished sentences. Kal just nodded, agreeing with them both, stepping back from their encroachment of his personal space. "Yes, Uncleji, you have a point." He leaned against the wall, and opened the nearby window, closing his eyes momentarily. I saw him exhale, and it almost took my breath away.

I heard my mother-in-law call from the other room. "Surinder!... Where did she go now? Always disappearing when I need her help."

Kal looked up when he heard my name. I smiled, and lifted my hand in a hesitant wave. He mouthed "How are you," and as I left to join my mother-in-law in the kitchen I thought how much it looked like "I love you." I mouthed it to myself, letting the words roll over my tongue, tap my palette and hollow out my throat like a long kiss. I remembered his kisses. His mouth, the soft part of his lips, a hesitation, an inclination, an instigation of what came next. I wondered if he remembered when we were lovers or if he had forgotten those few weeks in university, when the summer heat was unbearable, when our bodies pulling off each other's felt like peeling flesh. I wondered if he'd forgotten the time when I was not his cousin's wife. When I was his friend, when I was his lover. When I was his.

Sunny thought it was inappropriate for me to have a male friend, even if it was his cousin, and shortly after we were married he insisted that I not be seen with anyone but him. Though he'd always been possessive, it was his mother who had encouraged this development, chiming in his ears all the things that people might say. One evening when I chose to go to a movie with Kal rather than sit and watch television with her, she complained to Sunny, conspiring against me, telling him how bad it looked for a married

woman to be out with another man. When I came home, Sunny was waiting for me, demanding to know why I had gone out without his permission. I could tell by his rambling accusations that he was drunk and that
any defence I offered would fall on deaf ears. He would not be appeased,
and abruptly stopped my half-hearted attempts with a closed fist to the
face. I fell back in shock and pain, not being able to distinguish which had
caused more hurt.

The next morning he'd sent me flowers at the office. I watched those
flowers wither and fall away from themselves, and let the remains sit in a
crystal vase until the water converted the stems to sludge, the bitter odour
reminding me to throw them out. Before tossing them away, I'd pulled at
the cloying petals, landing on "he loves me not." I avoided telling Kal what
had happened, and after a time our friendship buckled in the silence and
I was relegated to the position of another man's wife, our talk limited to
family matters.

Occasionally Sunny invited Kal and his girlfriend Irmila to dinner, even
though we both disliked her politics, the controversies she spun for the
sake of conversation, if not for the controversy itself. She seemed to enjoy
the way Sunny loosened his tie when she engaged him in capitalist debate,
locking her eyes on him as she seduced him with opinions, connections
and names. She dropped names as if they were articles of clothing, and
word by word, confused men like Kal into believing that her anger was
passion. Her lack of beauty was diminished or made invisible by her avail-
ability and willingness, both of which were subtle and vulgar.

"Meena. Let's get going." Sunny was standing at my side, keys in hand.

"But your mom… she expects us to stay and she needs my help."

"I said let's get going." I nodded and went to offer up excuses to his
mother, who was on the verge of tears at our leaving early.

"But you haven't even had dinner yet."

"I know, but Sunny's tired."

"Well, at least take some food home." She reached into the kitchen
cupboard and pulled out assorted Tupperware which, unlike my mother's

collection of recycled yogurt containers, had matching snap-on lids. "How many rotis?" she asked, handing me the tinfoil. "Wrap them tight so they don't dry out." She stacked the containers of daal into a bag, which she handed to me with a heavy sigh. "He just got here and already they're leaving," she said to my father-in-law, who came to my side and kissed me on the cheek.

"We'll see you soon, hmm?" He pulled me to his side and walked me to the door. "Everything okay? You look upset."

"No, not upset. It's just. I should go… He's waiting. You know how he gets when he has to wait."

My father-in-law nodded as if he were having trouble remembering or not wanting to remember. "Visit soon, hmm? We have a chess game to finish."

I told him that I would and rushed out to meet Sunny, who was already waiting in the car, engine started. He pulled out before I even had my seat belt on, rolling down the window to wave at some acquaintances who had honked, his smile fading as soon as the tinted window shut.

The windshield wipers squawked, pushing the rain into fanning ripples of blurred visibility. Sunny leaned forward, squinting into the narrow band of light on the road, the car veering back and forth over the yellow line. I stared out the window, my reflection overlaid on the passing night. I thought to tell him to slow down, but instead pressed my right foot into the mat as if I could brake for him, as if I could make him stop. Once before when he was drunk and I was insisting he let me drive, he'd pulled the car over and with no hint of emotion told me to get out, leaving me on the side of the road in the pouring rain. By the time I'd made my way home, I was cold and wet through, my sari laced in mud, my mascara running down my face like black tears, my hair dripping in tangles. Humiliated and angry, I packed my bags and returned to my mother's house, staying only until she insisted on returning me to the Gills, as though I were something that didn't belong to her anymore. Sunny's mother had stood at the door, greeting us in obligatory hugs before ushering us into the family room, where Sunny and his dad were seated on the leather sectional. As we dipped countless digestive biscuits into our tea, watching the crumbs resurface and cling to the sides of the teacups, our parents made small talk around our marital problems, lightening the burden of blame. I sat glancing at the walls, which were covered with black tapestries depicting Ram and Sita, their outlines cheapened with sequins, while Sunny sat in the corner, watching the hockey game that was muted on the TV, occasionally looking up when he heard his name mentioned. We listened, letting their talk wrap around us, joining us in something that was not love.

The minute we got home, Sunny took off his coat and picked up the phone.

"It's late," I said.

He didn't answer.

"Who are you calling?"

"Checking my messages."

I could tell by his expression that whatever message he was waiting for and had been waiting for was still not there. Jasmine hadn't called. She'd moved on. He dropped the phone into the cradle and retreated to the den, telling me he had some work to finish.

"Now? At this hour?"

"I didn't hear you complain when I paid off your mom's mortgage," he said, shutting me out.

I stared at the closed door, watching the light beneath shade with his passing step, wondering whether to go in and try to lure him from his bad mood, but instead reached for the stack of mail and sifted through the magazine subscription renewal notices from *Better Homes and Gardens* and *Canadian House & Home*. After we'd first moved into the loft—which Sunny had agreed to buy as an investment—I'd set out to make it into a home and spent every weekend amassing paintings, art pieces and furniture. I was hoping to fill the open space, but no matter what I filled the emptiness with it wasn't enough and eventually I hired a contractor to frame walls and rooms where none had been. "Rooms have purpose; they contain things," I told Sunny when he baulked at the idea and expense of adding freestanding brick walls to support a second-storey master suite.

Sunny hated the bright colours and dark wood I chose and wanted a palette of black and white. I told him the world wasn't black and white, even though I knew his life was. He believed in a choice of opposites: yes and no, right and wrong, love and hate. There was no in-between for him. He once told me that this ability to act quickly, deduce situations and calculate risks to come up with the best possible outcome was what made him successful in business. It was what would make him the youngest partner in the law firm. It was what made him somebody.

I knocked on the study door, waiting for a word before opening it.

I leaned in the doorway. He was looking out the window, Scotch on the rocks in hand, his back to me. "I'm going to bed."

"So go." He didn't turn around.

I sat down in the club chair across from his desk, wringing my hands, unsure of what to say or where to look. He still didn't turn. I heard him clamp down on a piece of ice, fracturing it into small pieces.

"Are you thinking about her?"

Now he turned. His jaw flickered before his eyes did. "Not now, Meena."

"Why? Why don't we ever talk about it?"

He stared at me impatiently. "Because I don't see the point."

"You don't. Of course *you* don't. Tell me Sunny, what do you think it says about you that you married me because your parents made you?"

He fisted the glass down and walked around the desk, grabbing my wrist, twisting it slightly before pulling it to his mouth in a kiss. "Hmm, probably as much as it says about you, Surinder." I yanked my hand from his mouth and stood up to leave, his temper defeating mine. "Come on, babe. Don't look so upset. You and I are more alike then you think." He reached for my hand. "We do what we need to do to get what we want," he said, pulling me back hard and fast, taking what he wanted—always taking.

That night I wanted him to stop, but like all the other times I just lay there and let him; the only time he told me that he loved me was when he came. He only loved me in the leaving.

3.2

The day before Sunny and his parents left for India, the sky finally fell. It had threatened snow since Christmas, and now it delivered, covering the streets and cars in mounds and piles. Everything was lost and white. Cars were abandoned and shops closed early; children stayed home from school and took to the local hills, sleds and crazy carpets in tow. Sunny stared out the window watching thick flakes swirl to the ground in varying degrees, his eyes measuring accumulations. As day turned into grey light, the city tunnelled into a deep quiet, a dreaded calm like the sound of power lines and televisions turning off late at night when sleep was still hours away.

Sunny reached for the phone. "Delayed. Cancelled." That was all he said when his mother called to commiserate about the weather conditions. When she had suggested the trip, I'd answered with an appropriate hesitation, telling her that I couldn't get the time off from work. Her disappointment was short-lived; she remembered my body's response to India—the nausea that had plagued our first trip was reason enough for me to avoid a second one. I'd spent that entire month white-fisted and body-clenched, dripping with heat and exhaustion while touring the holy temples that dotted the vast country. The stench of feces, pollution, dirt and decay sank into me like weighted stones, altering the way I breathed to short inhales and long exhales that left me in a perpetual state of light-headedness. I was drawn into the sinkhole eyes of beggars; Sunny reminded me not to look at them, not to encourage the child beggars, the blinds beggars, the lame beggars, yet I stared into their eyes looking for something beyond the want. Whenever I would stop to stare, Sunny would cuff his arm in mine and pull me along.

His mother's sympathy for my illness thinned to irritation, and the following year, when I hadn't produced a grandchild, she told me it was during that trip that she'd realized I was too weak to conceive. Then she began consulting with gurus and various other holy men on what was to be done about my fertility. I was told to drink rosewater tea and forego the consumption of any meat. I wore a roped necklace of charmed talismans stuffed with fennel and garlic that left a noosed imprint on the back of my neck long after I'd taken it off. She and Sunny's aunties concocted large vats of herbal remedies and would stand over the steel pots stirring like old hags at cauldrons. After a time I stopped humouring her homeopathy and threw out whatever she gave me, occasionally placating her hopes with missed periods that signified nothing. I grew to enjoy her disappointment when she saw my tampon wrappers in the wastebasket. I thought it was the least she deserved after I realized that she had taken an indiscreet inventory of all that was hidden in my room. Once I'd caught her in the act of looking through my dresser drawer, her hands slicing through layers of lingerie as if she were looking for evidence of something. I waited until she'd left before trying to assess what she had taken this time, but found nothing gone, perhaps because there was no longer anything to take that I had not already given up. A few months after the wedding my father-in-law had found one of my half-filled journals among her things and without telling her, handed it back to me like an offering. "Put it somewhere safe. Somewhere secret," he'd said. I hadn't written a word since.

Sunny turned on the television, flipping through the weather channels—looking for a prediction beyond the police warnings to stay off the roads—and the images of cars lying nose down in ditches or crunched in the highway pileups of whiteout conditions. The power flickered, dimming the room in a lower wattage, a softer light. I sat down next to him and lifted his arm over my head, around my shoulder, searching for some warmth, staring at the screen light on his face. He pulled me closer, so my head rested in the crook of his neck. His breath was slow and tense. "It'll be fine," I said. "I'm sure it'll all be gone by tomorrow." He nodded, but I could tell he wasn't at all assured. He flipped through the stations, pausing on CNN and the BBC, any station that had devoted itself to 9/11 by providing endless commentaries on the events of just a few months ago.

"Is it the flight? The flying?" I asked, recalling the footage of the plane crashing into the tower, how the initial shock of it had silenced us into staring at the screen all day and all night.

"No, it's not that."

"It's okay if it is. I know a lot of people who are scared of flying now."

"I said it's not that. I'm not scared. Okay." He sat up, and pressed his hands against his forehead. "I'm just tired. I'm going to bed." I waited for him to ask me to come with him, to put his arms around me like he had in those nights and weeks after 9/11 when neither of us could stand to be alone, but he didn't.

On the morning of the terrorist attack, Sunny had called me from the office, telling me to turn on the news. I'd sat up in bed and flicked on the television, and was confused by the dust and chaos. Sunny and I were quiet, staring at separate TV screens, holding receivers to our ears for an hour before I asked him to come home, and when he did we sat on the sofa watching the news coverage in disbelief, stopping only to translate the events to my mother who had called asking what had happened. Sunny told her about it in clinical terms, in ways he thought she could understand, and as he spoke, I imagined her on the other end standing in her living room, wide-eyed, TV on, the images flickering in her dilated pupils as she experienced it just like every other person being fed the intravenous live news feed. We fell asleep in front of the television and when I woke up the only light in the room was the glare of the screen, the snow and hiss of it. I switched it off and lay in Sunny's arms, our bodies curled into each other until morning came. We spent the next three days in bed tangled in each other, confusing love and desperation until the shock of it, the universal shock and compassion of it all, turned Sunny's fear into anger. He stayed up late watching television, indoctrinating himself with misplaced patriotism and like so many others took refuge in telling anti-Muslim jokes and watching the late-night Bin Laden comedy sketches. When I'd scold him for it, his rebuttal was: "They'll get what they deserve. Everyone does."

The sound of cars slicing through slush and ice woke us before our alarm clock did. I got out of bed and grabbed my robe, yanking it on as I looked out the window.

Sunny sat up. "Well?"

The street below was cut into an imperfect grid of black and white, and edged in piles of dirty, plowed snow.

"It looks fine. I'll call and check."

He kicked the blankets off and got out of bed. "Call my parents and let them know as well."

After I'd confirmed the flight departure, Sunny showered and raced around the loft, packing his carry-on, looking for his camera equipment, asking me to get him things from this room and that room, refolding all the shirts that I had already folded until finally all the bags were packed with anything he might possibly need for his six-week stay.

"I think that's everything," I said.

Sunny patted his coat pockets, checking and triple-checking his wallet, his keys, his passport in his almost OCD way. Threes. He did things in threes when he was scared, and everyone that knew it pretended not to notice.

"Ready?"

He nodded three times.

Kal and I drove Sunny, his parents and their luggage to the airport. My mother-in-law had four suitcases and two trunks stuffed with my old Indian suits, which she would donate to the poor. "We will buy new things. So many things." She said it like a promise, showing me pictures of the newest fashions that she would bring back. I tried to be thankful.

She baulked when the luggage attendants told her that her suitcases were over the weight restriction and huffed when they insisted she open the bags and remove some items. I told Kal and Sunny to go and buy an extra bag from the airport store while I pried the luggage keys from her and opened the biggest suitcase, which promptly popped open when I undid the latch. Bright-coloured saris and chunnies spilled out of the case like streamers out of a clown can. She yelped, embarrassed as other passengers looked on. "I am donating these," she said to anyone who was listening. "They are for the poor."

My father-in-law knelt down and helped me sort through the clothes and repacked them into the new bag. "No good deed goes unpunished," he said, laughing as we locked the case and loaded it onto the conveyer belt.

Sunny hurried us along, reminding us all that they had a plane to catch.

At the security gate my mother-in-law hugged me. "Don't forget to check on the house every day." She handed Kal and me a list that included alarm codes and bank account numbers, then reviewed them with us in huddled secrecy. "I'll call every Sunday. Like clockwork," she said, hugging me in a real embrace that left me feeling a little guilty that I couldn't wait for her to leave. As she continued talking, repeating her houseplant-watering schedule, Sunny checked his newest cellphone compulsively, and when it was time to leave he put his arm around my shoulder and kissed me the way a brother would kiss a sister. He saw Kal watching and kissed me again, this time hard on the mouth so that I felt it like a branding or a bruise. Kal looked the other way.

3.3

After Sunny left, the snow melted in drifts, icing over at night and then melting into downhill streams that collected in murky puddles at the foot of storm grates already plugged with plastic bags and dead leaves. The city returned to its grim prospects of grey skies and slivered light. The homeless came out from their shelters and slept on the street; the commuters went back to work, and walked by as if the street people weren't even there. Adam—the homeless man who sometimes slept beneath our building's awning—had a white tumbleweed beard and blue eyes as clear as a seer's, and any time he saw me he smiled and tipped his hat and I dropped in whatever change I had. Sunny only gave him grim looks, but Adam said he preferred that to being ignored—it was better, he said, than the concerted effort most people made to not notice, "to look away, look away."

Every time I saw Adam, I thought of Liam, and the homeless people he used to befriend. I remembered his big toe sticking out of his dingy sport sock when he took his shoes off and gave them to the man who lived by the dumpster. Every time I drove by that dumpster or saw a shoe dangling by a lace from an electrical wire, I smiled and wondered whose shoes they were.

A few days after Sunny's departure, I cleaned out our closets and donated all of our old shoes to charity, saving Sunny's new Ferragamos for Adam.

"Happy late Christmas," I said, handing him the box.

He smiled, opening it cautiously, lifting out each shoe as if it were a piece of art, something delicate and breakable.

"Well, put them on," I said.

He tossed his broken runners aside, pulled the shoes over his callused soles, and strutted down the street singing "Stayin' Alive" as if he were John Travolta in *Saturday Night Fever*. I watched him until he turned the corner. Then I went back inside smiling, and took the stairs instead of the elevator. The phone was ringing when I got in. It was Sunny's mother again. Sometimes she needed me to wire her money, but mostly she talked about how hot it was, how dirty it was and how jet-lagged she was. At some point in the call, I would pretend that the connection was bad and repeat "hello, hello... are you there?" until one of us hung up, usually me. But this time I didn't bother and let the call go to the answering machine. I listened to her message, which began and ended with "Hello... Surinder... " As I heard her repeat my name I felt bad, and I lifted the phone just as she hung up. I dialled her back at the number she'd just left, and waited for the call to connect. Sunny answered. I hung up and sat with the phone in my lap, half-expecting him to call back and ask me why I'd hung up on him. But of course he didn't have call display; he didn't know it was me and he didn't call back.

In those first nights without Sunny, I went to sleep on my own side of the bed, but eventually slid into the warm space between the pillows—legs and arms sprawling, taking up space. His absence made room for me and as the week progressed, I spread myself out more and more, leaving my clothes on the floor wherever I'd undressed, filling the fridge with all the foods he hated—Gouda, sushi, anything with garlic, anything that smelled. I did my laundry in one load, not separating the whites from the coloured, and ate crackers in bed without worrying about crumbs. I went to see the foreign films that he would never go to, and one night for the first time in years I went out with my colleagues for drinks after work.

It was game night and the pub was packed with the soon-to-be middle-aged and pot-bellied men staring at the large TV screens, pints swishing in their hands as they lamented missed goals and bad calls. They patted one another's backs and bought pitchers, talking to one another out of the sides of their mouths, their eyes never off the puck for more than a second.

"What'll you have?"

I leaned into the bar, barely able to hear myself over the rowdy crowd. "A beer."

The bartender looked bored. "What kind?"

I looked around to see what other women were drinking. "Stella."

I clinked glasses with my co-workers and guzzled one pint and then another, enjoying the sudden buzz of alcohol and male attention. I wondered if that was what my life would have been like without Sunny, if this is what my life would have been like if I'd never met him. A tall blond man sat on the empty stool next to me and shook my hand. His palms were sweaty, and his breath was loose. He leaned closer and said something directly into my ear. I nodded, though over the constant hub I couldn't make out a word he said and wasn't sure what I'd agreed to. He bought me a beer and talked some more. I sipped and nodded.

"Meena, is that you?"

I turned around to see who was calling me and elbowed my beer off the table and onto myself. I reached for a stack of napkins and blotted the stain. "Kal, what are you doing here?"

He looked slightly horrified. "What am *I*? What are *you* doing here?" He looked at the blond man sitting next to me and grabbed me by the elbow. "Does Sunny know you're here?"

"No, of course not. It's just a work thing." I waved to my co-workers that I was fine. "He's a friend," I shouted.

They nodded and went back to watching the game. The blond man moved down the bar and chatted another girl up.

Kal handed me some more napkins. "Look at you. You're a mess."

"It's no big deal." I dabbed at the beer stain that had spread and soaked through my white blouse. "Stop looking at me like that."

He shook his head. "Like what?"

"Like that. Like you're disappointed in me."

He didn't disagree. "Cover up, will you? I can see everything and so can everyone else." He held his jacket in front of me.

"Well, what are you even doing here?" I asked.

Kal pointed to a group of Indian hockey-jersey boys sporting baseball caps and goatees. Some of them were Sunny's friends. "Watching the game."

I put on my coat and grabbed my purse. "You're probably right, I should just go. I'm a mess."

He followed me out of the pub. "I'll drive you."

"I'm fine. I'll walk."

"Come on. Sunny will kill me if he found out that I let you walk."

I turned around. "Sunny... Is that all you care about? What Sunny will think?"

"It's not like that and you know it."

"Fine. Then let's go," I said, walking across the street towards his truck.

Kal opened the door and I slid in next to him. As he started the engine, I unbuttoned my coat and then my blouse.

He glanced my way. "Meena, what are you doing?"

"Stop looking and just drive." I slipped the blouse past my shoulders and pulled my coat back on, fiddling with the clasp of my bra, trying to undress and dress with the discretion of a Grade 8 girls' locker-room version of myself.

"Meena, what the hell?"

I shoved Kal in the arm. "I said don't look. I'm soaked and stink like beer, okay?" I pulled off my blouse and bra, yanking them through the sleeve of my coat like a magic trick. "Voila." I buttoned my coat up to the very top and fastened my seat belt. "That feels better."

Kal looked at the bundle of clothes on my lap. "How did you do that?"

"It's a girl thing. We can all do it." I smiled and shoved the bra and blouse into my purse. "I just haven't had to do it for a long time."

He smiled, his mouth curled on one side like he was thinking or perhaps remembering the times when we used to undress in such haste. "Meena, when was the last time you went out?"

"You mean for fun? Before tonight?"

He nodded and waited for an answer.

I sighed, not bothering to calculate. "It's been a long time... Sunny goes out but, well, he'd rather go alone."

"Why don't we go out?"

"I don't know, you tell me." I was giggling for no apparent reason other than the beer buzz.

"Well, do you want to?" He glanced at me, then the road and then back again.

"What, like now?"

"Yeah, sure. I'll take you home. You can change and we can go out, like we used to."

I stared at him as if he should know better. "Things aren't like how they *used* to be."

"I know. But that doesn't mean we can't go out. We used to have a great time together. Remember that one night we went and heard the Matthew Good Band play."

"I remember. That was before anyone had even heard of them."

He nodded. "It was amazing." He reached into the glove compartment and handed me a CD. "Have you heard their newer stuff? "Strange Days" is amazing."

"Yeah, I love that track." I put the CD—*Beautiful Midnight*—into the deck and we both listened and sang along to every other word.

We started listening to it all over again. When it reached "... and you're gone," Kal turned the music down, nodded emphatically and pulled over. We had reached my building. "We should go out," he said. "Tonight. We absolutely should... There's this new place in Gastown, great live music and..." His cellphone rang before he could finish. I could tell by the way that he talked, his voice flattering, that it was his girlfriend Irmila. She'd lived in Hong Kong most of her life but moved to Vancouver when Hong Kong returned to Chinese rule. This was the footnote that seemed to be added to her name whenever anyone spoke of her. As if being from Hong Kong made her more special or less Indian. Her accent was intriguing, a cadence that was foreign but not at all like the Bombay British accent of other Indians. It was staccato, and overly formal, devoid of contractions and slang. It hinted at aristocracy and, like the rest of her, was difficult to place. "She's not like other Indian women," Kal had told me. She was older than him and had never been married—and in fact when they'd started dating, she'd told him that she was not the marrying kind. As if to prove how different she was, she liked to boast that she was the only Indian person who lived on Commercial Drive, the old Italian strip that was now being revitalized by granola crunchers and New Agers. She could read auras and when I first met her she said mine was blue, but didn't explain any further.

Kal nodded on the phone, smiling at me. Apologetic already.

He shut the phone and before he could say that something else had come up, I told him: "Another time, then."

It wasn't until a week later that I saw him again. I was in a coffee shop, contemplating writing in a journal that I had bought from a nearby store, when he and Irmila walked in. She was asking the dumbfounded barista if their coffee beans were fair trade. He called over another employee, who then went to the back to ask the manager. As they waited, Kal seemed bored by the whole thing. He glanced around, saw me in the corner and perked up, as if I were the shot of caffeine that he needed. He tapped Irmila on the shoulder and motioned my way. She nodded and he walked over, dragging a chair from another table.

"Small world."

"The beans are fair trade." I pointed to the sign.

He nodded and looked back at Irmila, who was in deep conversation with the manager. "She'll figure it out." And in just a few minutes she had, and was sauntering over with two cups of coffee to go.

"You remember Sunny's wife," Kal said.

She put the coffee on the table. "Of course, Surinder with the blue aura."

"Meena," Kal corrected.

"You're a writer?" she asked, looking at the journal.

I tucked it into my bag. "Hardly."

"Oh, that's too bad. I long for someone to talk books with. I adore writing. I wanted to be a writer once, after I read Tolstoy, but that was before I met Marc, who taught me to paint. So many colours." She sighed, in a way that made me understand that Marc was a former lover. She was the kind of woman who struck me as having many lovers, men and women alike. She was all about experience. Poor Kal.

"Meena, Irmila's having a thing tonight. You should come."

Irmila's laugh was throaty and elegant. "Kal, it's not a thing." She leaned over him and handed him his coffee, touching his shoulder, fingering the collar of his shirt, every movement a request. "It's a showing at the gallery where I work, and you should absolutely come. Everyone will be there," she said, in a way that made me wonder who "everyone" was.

When I told her I couldn't she insisted, writing down the address on a napkin for me, reminding me several times before they left that they both hoped to see me there.

The address on the napkin had almost worn off by the time I thought I was in the right neighbourhood. I remembered that she'd said it was off Main Street, in another up-and-coming neighbourhood that hoped to be the next Yaletown, but by the looks of it was years away from evicting the vagrant element that lurked in the shadows of rundown buildings whose former purpose and history peeled away with placards. I walked up and down the same city block, trying not to look lost, before I found the gallery. It was on the second floor of a brick building that, according to the sign, had once been a bank. The narrow stairwell was filled with people who were smoking with one hand and drinking with the other, moving and swaying as I shimmied by them.

It was Kal who saw me lingering in the doorway and invited me over. His longish hair was slicked back and he was wearing an untucked plaid cowboy shirt. It was trendy in a second-hand, I-don't-care-about-fashion way, and when I looked at Irmila in her vintage lace blouse, flowing skirt and hiking boots, I knew she must have bought it for him. He rarely wore anything but a white T-shirt and jeans. He was naturally simple and easy, often unshaved, and here he was complicated by her. He smiled and took my coat. "Did you find it okay?" he shouted.

I nodded encouragingly. Speaking against the music and background noise was pointless. The studio had brick walls and reclaimed wooden floors. Cocktail waitresses circulated and guests looked thoughtfully at the photographs that were hanging on the walls. Humanscapes—that's what Kal had told me the photographer said they were. Close-up portraits that were meant to evoke an interpretation of each life by following the shadows and lines of the face, the imprint of smiles, the furrows of worry, the sorrow in eyes. Occasionally Irmila saw me and raised her glass, but she never actually came and said hello. She was in her element, talking with a group of highly intellectual-looking people in corduroy blazers who I presumed had a string of useless degrees and could talk about philosophy and economics with an equal amount of ease. She leaned into conversations, and she touched men's knees and held women's hands when she spoke. Everything about her was a flirtation and proposition. Her friends were all one note, loud and passionate, their opinions clear-cutting paths of righteousness. "The U.S. funded the Taliban during the Soviet–Afghan War... they wanted to get the Soviets out because it's *all* about the oil. It's all about who controls the oil man." Everyone nodded, adding in obscure footnotes and intellectual asides; some touted conspiracy theories, suggesting 9/11 had been engineered. "War is good for economies: the rich get richer and the poor keep dying." The woman who'd said that looked my way and stared me up and down as my high heels punctuated the floor. Kal introduced me. She nodded, still staring at me as though I didn't belong. I looked away and spent the evening on the outskirts of various conversations. I nodded and smiled, sometimes in no general direction, almost embarrassed by my ridiculously expensive shoes and postal code, ashamed that I knew more about designers and celebrities than I did about politicians and foreign policy. Eventually I walked around the room and in and out of conversations without contributing a word, content to linger in the lines of the photographs, to absorb myself in someone else's view of the world... until I saw him.

He was standing in the corner of the room talking to a woman with an asymmetrical haircut. He still talked as if he were conducting an orchestra rather than a conversation: his hands opened and sliced the air with both passion and indifference. His blue eyes, framed in wrinkles, bracketed an easy smile that had softened with age and yet to me he seemed wholly unchanged. I stared at him so intently that I felt everything else disappear. Sound felt like heavy furniture and walls melted away. Kal saw me staring and leaned over my shoulder, whispering, "That's Liam." I nodded and took a sip of my drink, whispering his name in the rim just so I could feel it reverberate on my lips. "He's the photographer."

I looked away, trying not to look interested, trying instead to radiate the detachment that everyone else at the gallery seemed to show. "How does Irmila know him?"

"She met him in London. I think he was freelancing for some magazine that she worked for at the time."

"Do you want me to introduce you?"

I grabbed his hand as he got up. "No. No. That's not necessary."

"Later then," he said, wandering off to join Irmila, who was beckoning him like a child. I stood against the wall, staring at Liam through the shifting crowds of clinking glasses and cliquey conversation until he turned towards me with such purpose that I thought perhaps his name had escaped my lips. He stared through me in the type of look that can elongate moments and rooms. I looked away, and when I looked back he was gone. I scanned the room. He was talking to Irmila. She whispered something in his ear. He laughed and looked at me as though I were in on the joke. I was horrified and humiliated in ways that I had forgotten, and blindly turned around and ran down the stairs, pushing past the cigarette smokers, who were now hard-packed against one another. I rushed down the street and in a few minutes I heard his footsteps behind me, his voice call out. I didn't look back, and eventually his footsteps stopped.

3.4

The next day when I arrived home, Liam was standing on the sidewalk in front of my building. I recognized him from a distance—his casual stance, hands in his pockets like a sheepish adolescent—waiting for me the same way he always used to.

"Irmila told me where you lived." I stood motionless but for the jingle of keys in my hand. "Don't worry. I didn't tell her anything."

"What's there to tell?"

"Why did you run away last night?"

"Liam, why are you here?" I asked.

"To talk."

"About?"

He rubbed his hand across the nape of his neck, dishevelling his already unkempt hair. "You're not making this easy."

"Am I supposed to?" I asked, brushing by him towards the door.

"Do you want me to go?"

I pressed my code into the security panel, opened the door and stood holding it. "No... don't go."

He followed me into the building, both of us quieted by the small space, the awkward formality of an elevator, which forced us to look up and watch the small-screen news bites—scenes of 9/11 and political debates on the promised war on terror. I tried not to watch it. When I did all I could think of were the jumpers, who'd looked like black birds falling from the sky.

"Where were you, when it happened?" I asked.

"London... The whole city just stopped, you know? Everyone watching the news, no one talking, people crying. For a few days it felt like life had changed, but then things don't ever really change, do they?"

I didn't answer.

"How about you? Where were you?"

"Here, of course. Always here."

The doors slid open. With Liam walking behind me, the short distance to the loft seemed longer, yet neither of us tried to fill the silence. I unlocked the door and he followed me into the entryway, staring up at the vaulted ceilings, the wooden beams and steel rafters. He threw his jacket over the edge of the sofa and wandered around looking at everything from a distance as if he were in a museum. Arms folded behind his back, he stared out at the million-dollar view. He said nothing, occasionally pointing or gesturing at some place where we had once been, careful not to touch the glass.

"So, this is your husband?" he asked, picking up a picture of Sunny on a nearby table. "Irmila told me you were married."

"And you? Are you married?" I asked.

"No."

"Why not?"

"Why not?" He laughed, and shook his head as if he were trying to come up with a good idea. "I guess I'm just not the marrying kind."

His answer collided with the recollection of Irmila not being the marrying kind. I wondered at the coincidence. I wondered if they'd been lovers. She was just the type of woman he would have loved. Her accent and eccentricities were reason enough. I imagined them drinking bottles of wine, talking of nothingness like it was nothing, making love on a velvet divan or a Moroccan rug after doing exotic drugs and drinking elixirs. I suddenly hated her.

"Do you want a drink or something?" I asked, trying to be casual, to be grown-up about seeing him.

"Yeah, sure. Your husband won't mind my being here, will he?"

"He would. But he's out of town." I went into the dining area and opened the liquor cabinet while Liam circled the apartment. I leaned over the sideboard and exhaled, realizing that I had been holding my breath, rationing it since I'd seen him outside the building. "Is red wine okay?" The words came out fast, almost flustered.

"Sure, whatever... This place is amazing. Looks like you've done really well for yourself."

"We do all right. Sunny's a lawyer and real estate developer."

"And you? Are you a famous or soon-to-be famous writer?"

I looked up. "Neither. I gave it up."

"Why?

I uncorked the wine and reached for two glasses. "Just didn't think I could make a go of it."

"Did you try?"

"Sometimes you don't need to try to figure out that you'll fail."

Liam was rifling through the pile of CDs on the table next to him. "Hip hop? R&B? Since when?"

"They're Sunny's," I said, handing him a glass.

"So is everything in your life sunny?"

"Ha. Very funny," I said, trying not to look at him even though I knew he was looking at me, pulling me back in. I was flushed with just the thought of him.

"Do you love him?" he asked, looking at his picture again.

I tightened my face. "He's my husband."

"That's not an answer."

"It's my answer."

"Did you ever love him?" He watched my expression for the answer that was buried in my long pause, and I hated that he could still do that, that he could see me without even having to try.

"Why does it matter?"

"Because it does."

"Does it? Still?" I sat down, staring out the window as I explained the details of my marriage, surprising myself with the honesty and clarity with which I replied to his question, with which I told him everything. He was quiet, and I wasn't sure if he was sad or disappointed in me. "And what about your love life?" I asked.

He sat down, his body turned to mine as if he were settling into a long conversation. "It's not as interesting as yours."

"Try me."

"I had a girlfriend for a few years and well, it just didn't work out."

"Why?"

"We just grew apart, wanted different things."

"Like?"

"Like... I don't know... Do I have to know?"

"Well, yes. Don't you want closure?"

"No such thing." He took a sip of his wine. "You and I are proof of that."

I paused, surprised and frightened by his honesty. "So, if you're not here for closure, what are you here for?"

"I don't know." He stared at me until I looked away. "When it comes to you, I never knew."

"Did you want to?"

"Want to what?"

"I don't know." I sat up, as if my posture could straighten our talk and keep us in line. "Your photographs," I said, changing the subject. "They're great. I always knew you'd make it."

"Well, I've hardly made it. Half the time I have to tend bar to pay my bills."

"Is that what you did after high school, bartend?"

"Yeah, among other things." He was playing with the remote control and accidentally turned on the CD player.

He turned the music up. "I still can't believe that the new wave, post-punk, alternative girl I remember married a guy who listens to Puff Daddy."

I reached for the remote. "I guess that's because I wasn't the same girl you remembered."

He held the remote away from me. "And are you now?" He asked it like a dare, turning the music off when I didn't answer, when I wouldn't be affected.

I shrugged and got up. "I don't know; I'll let you decide... That's why you're here, isn't it?"

"I guess I just always wondered what happened to you."

"Well, you left and my life moved on."

"I only left because I couldn't stay."

"And I only stayed because I couldn't leave."

"Couldn't or wouldn't?"

"Both... I did try. I went looking for you the next week, but you were gone already."

"Would you have really gone with me?" When I told him that I would have, we both fell silent until I let what might have been fall away from us. "Is that why you ran away last night?"

I nodded. "You said you'd wait."

Liam stood up and knotted his fingers into the belt loops of my jeans, pulling me closer with just a look and a slight tug. I felt his breath on my neck and watched his thoughts grow in the slow up-and-down movement of his larynx. Only small words could escape him.

"Can I stay?"

I saw him every night for the following two weeks, and each night resembled the night before. We made feverish love. Quiet and violent. Sometimes on the floor, other times up against a wall, or on a table, pants around our ankles, shirt buttons undone, arrested arms and legs, knocking paintings sideways and oriental vases from their decorative stead. We never talked after. We straightened the couch cushions, put on our clothes, not quite able to look at each other as though we were surprised by what we had done, surprised by what we could do to each other. At other times—usually early in the morning, when we were only partly ourselves, surrendering to the consciousness of waking dreams—we made love slowly, deliberately, fingertips tracing the shadowed portions of our bodies. His collarbone, the curve of my hips, the slope of his back, every bit to be memorized and remembered—until the phone rang, alarming us and reminding of us of our reality. Neither of us moved; we both knew it was Sunny. Liam rolled

onto his back, turning away from me, his silhouette outlined in darkness.
"When will he be back?"

"Soon," I answered.

3.5

Liam was staying in a converted-factory studio above a string of barred-windowed shops that never seemed to open. In the day the cobble-stone alleys were full of sleeping homeless men, and at night the space filled with the sounds of cheap, high-heeled prostitutes and drunken men speeding away in cars. "You get used to the noise," he said one night, after police sirens and flashing lights had startled me awake. I lay back down, listening to his breath overlap mine, following the flashing lights that flickered over his face and crawled across the dingy walls dotted with dirt-squared outlines where pictures had once hung. I wondered if they had been his pictures or someone else's. Aside from the row of boxes stacked by the wall, very little in the apartment was actually his. Even his couch was a hand-me-down from the landlord. When I'd first come over, I was unnerved by his barren living style and his half-packed life, and I opened and closed cupboard doors looking for some permanence—only to find his locked suitcase in an empty closet. I hadn't asked him about it but I hadn't stopped wondering why he lived as if he were on his way somewhere.

I slipped out of bed and opened up one of the boxes, sifting through his books and photographs. There were postcards of blue-water beaches, some postmarked and others not, some written on and others not. There were photos of him with long hair in Montreal, pictures of him with a shaved head in who-knows-where, pictures of people I didn't know, women I didn't know, pictures of him acne-faced in junior high school and even pictures of me then and now, all of them piled together in loose stacks of memories and moments that had no sequence, chronology or currency. The previous day, after Liam had developed some of his pictures, he'd handed me one that he'd taken on one of our morning-afters. I was wearing a black slip, sitting with my knees pulled up to my chest, my head against the window as if I were looking for someone, longing for someone. "This is how I'll remember you," he said. I smiled, even though for him I was already becoming a memory.

Now as I leafed through his belongings, letting each picture fall carelessly into the box, I wondered how long it would be before that picture of me was placed on top of the pile, something to be remembered and forgotten, something to be boxed and collected and carted around from city to city. "Meena, come back to bed." Liam threw his leg across the blanket where he expected my body to be.

"In a minute." I stared out the window, thinking backwards and looking down at the street, which was lit only by a flashing vacancy sign. I wondered if Harj still lived in the area. I hadn't received a card from her in years and though I had no reason to think harm had come to her, every time a woman was reported missing in the Downtown Eastside, or an unidentified body washed up on the shores of the Fraser River, I worried helplessly that it was her. Even now I wondered if I'd recognize her if I passed her on the street. Perhaps I'd walked by her dozens of times with nothing but a vague sense of familiarity. I rested my head against the cold window, my fingers running along the crack in the glass, listening to the wind that whistled through it until I couldn't distinguish the sound from Liam's breath. An hour later, Liam lumbered out of bed and turned on the coffee maker, going through his usual production of yawning and stretching as he went. "Did you even sleep?" he asked, sitting down across from me and looking, like me, at the sliver of opaque moon that was woven behind the lightening sky.

"No, not much."

"What's wrong? What's on your mind?"

"Nothing."

"It doesn't look like nothing."

I sat up, sighing and stretching, weary-boned, as if I my skin had been wearing me and no longer fitted. "I was just thinking about Harj, wondering where she is."

He was quiet for a minute. "Have you ever tried to find her?"

I shook my head and curved my back like a cat before slumping back into myself.

"Why not?"

"I don't know. I guess I'm scared... I mean, what if I found her and realized she's not who I remember? What if nothing I thought or felt about her was true and all these years I'd built her up in my mind to something she never was?"

Liam got up and put on the T-shirt that was lying on the couch where he'd thrown it the night before. "Are we still talking about your sister, or are we talking about us now?"

I didn't answer and went back to staring out the window.

"Is that why you were looking through my stuff?" he asked.

I shook my head. "I'm sorry. I shouldn't have done that."

"Did you find what you were looking for?"

"I don't know. I don't know what I expected to find." I got up and poured myself a cup of coffee. "I don't know much anymore," I said, taking a sip.

We spent the rest of the day meandering through Stanley Park taking pictures, sitting on benches and drinking coffee out of to-go cups. While Liam took pictures of people who passed by, zooming in on their faces with discreet lenses, I sat nearby writing about him in my journal, occasionally watching the way he examined the angles and shifted his perspective. "Depth of field. It's all about depth of field," he yelled when he saw me looking on. "Come here. I want to show you." I tossed my coffee cup into the trash bin and wandered over. He held the camera in front of my face, adjusting the lens for me. "How far away things are even when they're close up and vice versa." He held his hand over mine and pressed the shutter release. He pulled the camera away and showed me the picture we'd taken of a young woman pushing a baby carriage. Her eyes were tired, almost vacant.

"She looks sad."

Liam zoomed in on the image. "Really? I don't think so. I think she looks thoughtful." He put the camera down and smiled at her as she walked by with her sleeping baby. "Thoughtful. For sure."

"Do you want kids?" I asked.

"Yeah. Definitely." He lifted his camera up again and took a picture of me. I pulled strands of hair away from my face and smiled. He put the camera down. "No smiling for the camera, remember. It looks forced."

"Sorry." I frowned. "Is that better?"

"How about you—do you want kids?"

"Sunny can't have kids." I looked away, distracted by a group of tourists taking pictures at the nearby lighthouse, all of them smiling.

"That's not what I asked," he said. "If you could have kids, would you?" He was holding the camera, poised to take a picture.

"I don't know. I want to and I don't."

"Hmm, that's a theme for you."

"What is?"

He smiled behind the lens. "Indecision."

"Oh, shut up." I took the camera from him, turned it on him and clicked off several shots before I saw Kishor Auntie waving in the distance, walking towards me in her salwar kameez and windbreaker.

"Shit." I handed Liam the camera and took a step away from him.

"Surinder?" she asked.

"Hi, Auntie."

"I thought that was you. I told your uncle: 'That looks like Surinder standing there with that camera.' And look, I was right." She smiled and pointed backwards. "My nephew is here from India. We are showing him the sights." I waved hello. "So, have you heard from your mother, from Sunny? You must miss them, hmmm?"

"Of course. But they're fine. Everyone's having a good time."

"It's been so hot. Record temperatures, so I'm told."

"Yes. I heard the same."

She looked at Liam and spoke in Punjabi. "And who is this?"

I shifted my stance, obscuring her view of him. "Someone I work with."

When she smiled and nodded, eyeing him up and down, I could tell that she was suspicious and that nothing I said—none of my polite inquiries about her nephew—even registered with her.

"Okay, then. I will leave you to your work. Tell your mother hello for me."

I didn't exhale until she fell from sight. "Fuck."

"Who was that? And why did she keep calling you Surinder?" Liam asked.

"It's a long story. We should go," I said, handing him his camera bag before walking off towards the car.

Liam threw the bag over his shoulder and rushed to catch up. "Meena, what's the matter? Who was that?"

"She's a friend of my mother-in-law and the world's biggest gossip. She's probably on her cellphone telling the whole world that she saw us together."

Liam grabbed my arm, slowing my pace. "Relax, she didn't see anything. It'll be fine."

"No, it won't. You don't know how she is. I can only imagine what people are going to say."

"Who cares what they say?"

"Me." I was yelling now and not sure why. "I care. I'm married, remember? I have a husband."

He took a deep breath and let it out slowly. "And where does that leave me..."

"I didn't mean it like that. It's just Sunny. He's..."

He shook his head, pausing on a word before dropping his eyes. "He's your husband. I get it... He's your husband and you're going to stay with him and I'm just what, some guy?"

"I didn't say that."

"No. You didn't need to. You don't need to say a fucking thing." He started walking in the other direction, yelling backwards. "I thought you'd changed."

"I have changed."

"No, you haven't. You still can't make a decision to save your own life. Everything is about everyone else."

"You've got no right to say that," I yelled, arresting him with my voice. "You've no idea what it's like being me. Being Indian and all the shit that comes with it."

Liam turned around. "You know what, your right. I'm not Indian, but you've managed to give me quite a fucking education in it, so I may as well be." He grabbed my arm. "Meena, life is full of choices. That's not about being Indian. That's just life."

I pulled back. "And what do you choose besides yourself? You never unpack. You never stay anywhere. Don't you ever get sick of running away?"

"Don't you?"

Liam and I didn't talk much that night. We spoke in routine details: Which foreign movie to rent. What wine to drink with the takeout tandoori that was too spicy. What time we had to work the next day. What... Which... How... All our questions, long or short, were dismissed with short replies. It wasn't anger that quieted us—it was my doubt. He had no answer for it; it wasn't a question.

3.6

I waited at Serena's front door, sniffing the ends of my hair, wondering how long it would take before I smelled of the curry and onions that seemed to punctuate the entire neighbourhood. Down the street, Sikh fundamentalists had turned another teardown rancher into a makeshift gurdwara. Most religions fractured into sects because of scripture interpretation, but this division of belief was based on tables and chairs: the moderates had wanted to sit on chairs in the dining hall, and the fundis had wanted to sit on the floor. Both sides rioted and drew their kirpans to settle the matter in an embarrassing display that caught worldwide media attention. I was amazed how many people became fundis after the riots. Even Serena's mother-in-law became an Orthodox Sikh. When she returned from a pilgrimage to India, she was gursikh: she was reborn. She wore her kara and kirpan, but she had trouble with the kes and still went to get laser hair removal done on her face.

I rang the doorbell again before remembering that Dev hadn't fixed it yet. Serena's husband rarely fixed anything other than Scotch and soda for himself and his trucker friends. I knocked, looking up at the green mildew stains on her peach stucco house, and wondered how long before the entire building would be covered in mould. How long before the lazy bastard saw the state of his home. Every time I saw the lingering stains, I thought of the time I had come over to find Serena on a ladder, pressure-washing her house. When I asked why Dev wasn't doing it, he popped his head out the door and said that women were always saying they could do whatever a man could do. He laughed as he scratched his belly. "Fifty:fifty, my marriage is fifty:fifty." I didn't laugh, and as I helped Serena down from the ladder I asked him if that meant that he would be making dinner. A week later she'd had her third miscarriage.

I knocked repeatedly until my five-year-old niece opened the door.

"Masi Meena, guess what?" she said, breaking free from my stifling hug.

"What?"

"I lothst my tooth." She displayed a gummy smile, sticking her tongue out of the newly vacant space. "And the tooth fairy left me a dollar."

"Meena, is that you?" Serena yelled from the top of the spiral staircase in a tone that reminded me of the way my mother had called out to me when I was a teenager returning late from school. "Simran, bring your Masi upstairs and then go finish your spelling," she ordered.

I smiled and mussed her hair, remembering the frustrations of being so full of energy when no one else was.

Serena was sitting on the floor folding laundry, and barely looked up when I came into the room. "Look who's here. I was beginning to worry about you; I haven't heard from you in weeks."

"I've just been busy... Can I help?" I offered, looking at the neatly stacked piles of laundry.

"Oh no, it's fine... Arjun!" she yelled to my nephew. "Come and pick up your laundry!"

Arjun sauntered in a minute later, his pants slung low on his hips. "Hi, Masi."

"Hey, A.J." I resisted the urge to hug him.

"Did you finish your homework?" Serena asked, shooing him off with his pile of laundry. "Do you want some chai?"

"Sure." I followed her into the kitchen. "Where's Dev?" I asked.

"He's sleeping."

I bit my lip when I saw new bruises on her arm. We never talked about it—there was no point. She had tried to leave him once, when A.J. was a baby, but my mother, who was grieving the loss of Harj, had convinced her to stay. I wondered if she bore her family's betrayal anew every time Dev hit her. I suspected the failed attempt to leave had hurt her far more than he ever had.

She saw me looking at the bruise and pulled her sleeve over it as she reached for the phone.

I could tell by the well-placed "hah" and "achcha" in Serena's speech and by the muffled Pindu Punjabi emanating from the receiver that it was her mother-in-law on the phone. Dev's mother was as tacky as the dandruff-flaked hair that she pulled back into a netted bun. She had something to say about everyone and as the eldest in-law in our family she was entitled to her opinions and a giant dose of ass-kissing. She was upset when my mother had told her that I was marrying Sunny; she'd wanted me to marry her nephew from India. Marriage was the easiest form of immigration and she'd brought her extended family over marriage by marriage, member by member, building a dynasty of ancestral strangers who shared only title and land. Some had said that she'd only married her son into our family to secure five Canadian brides for her nephews, yet it was only my refusal to marry into her family that infuriated her. She'd arrived late for my wedding and never offered to help my mother in the kitchen as the other women did. When my mother had served tea to Sunny's family before hers, she'd stormed out of the house, screaming that she had been insulted enough for one day. My mother had scurried after her, offering apologies so that Serena wouldn't feel the brunt of this bezti. Now, whenever I saw her, she would make sure to tell me how her nephew was, how many sons he had and how beautiful his wife was. She'd then ask me how I was and when I was planning to have children. When I didn't answer, she'd offer me a smile to match her cunning; my apparent infertility was her retribution.

"Who was she gossiping about this time?" I asked as Serena set the phone down.

"Dev's cousin Balbir... apparently he just told his parents that he plans to marry his gori girlfriend."

"And what did they say?" I asked.

She dropped the tea bag into the boiling water. "What could they say but yes. He's their only son."

"Such a double standard; it's okay for him to marry a white girl, but yet no one talks to their cousin Rajinder because she married a white guy."

"Our double standard is their gold standard."

"Dumb Punjabs."

"Why do you always have to do that?"

"What?" I asked.

"Make fun of everyone who doesn't believe what you believe."

"You don't believe that shit either."

"Of course not. But saying it doesn't change how they are."

"So you'd prefer me to be silent, like you?"

She sighed. "Meena, why haven't you returned my calls? Mom and I have left you messages at work, at home and on your cellphone."

"I told you, I've been busy."

"Yeah, I know you've been busy. Kishor Auntie called my mother-in-law today... Why give people like them something more to talk about?"

"I don't know what you're talking about."

"She saw you with some guy."

"He's just a friend. I can't help what people say."

"Meena, stop it. I'm not stupid." I folded my hands across my chest and looked away, guilt settling in my stomach. "Sunny isn't going to be gone forever. He'll be back in less than a week." She paused as if she were waiting for me to say something. "What are you thinking?"

"I'm not thinking. For once I'm not thinking, and I'm happy."

"I can't believe you," she whispered. "You're so naive. What do you think will happen when Sunny finds out? What do you think people will say?"

"I don't care what people say."

"How can you not care? For God's sake, Meena, think of Mom. Do you really want to put her through this?"

"I have thought of Mom. I've always thought of Mom. I've always put her needs ahead of mine, but I can't keep doing that forever."

Serena opened and closed cupboard doors as if she were looking for something but wasn't quite sure what. "I can't believe you. You're so selfish. You just can't go off and do whatever you want in life with no regard for anyone else."

"Why not, why can't I?" I pressed.

"Because that's not..." She slammed the cupboard door shut. "It's not fair."

I stood in the silencing truth, watching the chai churn and rise until she pulled it from the stove to strain it. I sat down and stared out the kitchen window. My niece was kicking rocks and playing hopscotch alone in the cul-de-sac. Other children rode their bikes around her, zipping about in figure eights.

"So, what are you going to do?" Serena sat down, handing me a cup of tea.

I cupped the mug with both hands and blew the steam away before taking a sip that burned my tongue and stripped me of the need to talk.

3.7

I met Liam at the Chinese restaurant across the street from his studio apartment. It always smelled like warm noodles and the windows were covered in steam regardless of the weather. Coming in out of the rain, I clamped my umbrella shut and shuffled and excused myself through the dinner rush, leaving a trail of raindrops behind me. Liam was sitting at our usual corner table staring out the window, though there was nothing to see. I sat down across from him and drew a love heart in the condensation; he smiled and said nothing, and we both watched it crack and bleed into itself. His smile faded slowly, but the lines remained, settling into his skin. His eyes were tired—the blue thinner, diluted and watery, as if the colour might spill over the rims. Everything about him was worn and tired—disappointment personified.

"Are you packed?" I asked as I undid my coat and hung it on the back of the seat.

He nodded.

I kept talking, trying to make him speak, to draw him out. I told him about my day at work, about the rain, the traffic, but he seemed to want none of it and slumped further into his seat. "Are you excited about the shoot?"

"Yeah, it'll be a nice change. I need to get out of the city, get away from here."

I stared around the restaurant, listening to the clatter of dishes, pretending to read the Chinese lettering on the wall hangings. Luck. That was the only one I knew for sure.

"When do you leave?" I finally asked.

"Tomorrow morning. I'll take the early ferry."

"You'll be gone a week?"

He nodded. "Maybe more. It depends how long the shoot takes... You know you could still change your mind and come with me."

I fiddled with the napkins and packages of soy sauce, trying to ignore the tension and silence between us. We hadn't argued since the day we'd been seen at the park, but we hadn't really talked either. Everything about us was suffering like rain.

"You know I can't."

He leaned forward and picked up his tea, sipping slowly. "So, what... he'll be back when?"

"Tomorrow afternoon."

"Perfect timing." He put his cup down. "And then what? When are you going to tell him?"

"I don't know." I looked at the window again, wanting to wipe the heart away, wanting to draw it again, to make it good.

"You are going to tell him, aren't you?"

I reached for his hand, locking his fingers in mine. The waiter interrupted before I could attempt an answer and gave us the laminated menus, pointing to the specials, the photographs of dinner combinations A, B and C. I glanced at it, telling Liam to order for me like he usually did. When the waiter had left, Liam didn't reach for my outstretched hands, and I dropped them onto my lap, lacing them together like a child waiting to please, waiting to be told what to do.

After dinner we stood outside the restaurant beneath the ripped awning watching the rain fall in all directions, the wind pushing it this way and that. Liam flipped up the collar of his coat and inhaled to my exhale, our breath taking from each other.

"Look, I'm sorry about tonight. Dinner and everything. I'm just tired. I should probably go." He stuffed his hands in his pockets and waited for me to say something. I stared at his building across the street as though I had only just noticed the stains on the brick work, the yellowed glass, the graffiti wall that said "I wuz here" in big, fat, swollen lettering.

"You sure you don't want me to stay tonight?" I asked.

He looked away. "Probably best if you go... I've still got to pack my equipment and stuff."

I nodded, grimacing that it was fine before hugging him in one arm, aware that our bodies didn't touch, that there was distance between us.

I took a cab home, watching the city pass in a rain haze. The rain that made me invisible, that made us divisible. Even when I got home, I stared out the window, tracing raindrops on the glass with my fingertips, unable to see the city. Thin clouds that pulled apart like spun sugar covered the tops of buildings, obscuring the streets below and hiding the sky in grey fibres that made me want to unravel.

I sat on the sofa and listened to the building moan as if it were doing so in service of all its inhabitants. It was only after Sunny left that I'd noticed the reverberation of water in the pipes, how the sound of waves and rivers rushing through the walls made me feel like I was drowning, made me want to hold my breath.

I reached for the phone, called my mother and lied. I told her I'd been sick. I lapped up her sympathy.

"You should rest. You don't eat enough. Have you eaten? You should make some tea. Add in extra fennel. It soothes the stomach. That's what your Masi does."

She didn't stop for an answer and I offered only the occasional "achcha." That was enough for her to know that she was heard, that someone was there, and she kept talking. I lay down on my bed, believing her. Believing that all I needed was rest.

After hanging up the phone I sat in the bath, my body slumped over the edge, the side of my face pressed against the cast iron tub. I wanted to cry but couldn't. I conjured up sadness, pulling moments back from the past. My father dead on the ground, Liam walking away, my handwriting crossed out with indelible ink. I zoomed in on moments, finding new moments, new worlds inside each one that had never really existed. Narration and omniscience, dialogue and monologue in my own mind like a Technicolor imagination, a melodrama that could not make me cry, the same way that *Casablanca* couldn't make me cry anymore. "I've seen it too many times. I know how it ends," I'd once told Liam.

I pulled myself out of the tub and lay down on the bed, naked and wet, staring at the ceiling fan as it spun round, the chill cutting like a knife slicing layers of skin.

The phone rang. I sat up and flipped on the lamp before picking up the receiver.

It was Liam. He seemed upset.

I adjusted my eyes to the light. "Where are you?"

"Outside. Can I come up?"

I looked out the window. Liam was standing in the rain, looking up. The rest of the street was quiet; even the homeless had left for shelter.

I buzzed him into the building and waited at the front door.

He held me close.

"It's okay. I've got you, you're fine... We're fine." That was all he said before we went to sleep, our bodies folded and encased, with his head between my breasts, my leg over his thigh, his arm around my waist, my fingers drifting down his back, charting the notches of his spine, tracing the spread of his ribs, filling in the hollows.

In the morning he was gone, and I wondered if he was ever there or if I'd dreamed him. I turned my face into the pillow, inhaling. Then I plucked fine hairs from the sheets, blowing one from my fingertip like an eyelash. Make a wish.

After I got out of bed, I got dressed and cleaned the loft. I scrubbed the toilets, the floors and then the bathroom sink, rinsing away Liam's razor stubble. I vacuumed and dusted, picking up the knick-knacks and cleaning beneath them. I opened windows until the bedroom no longer smelled of sex and longing and then when everything else was done, I pulled off the bedsheets and crumpled them into a ball, pressing my face into them one last time before tossing them into the washing machine. I wandered around the loft, my eyes sweeping for signs of Liam.

He was gone. It was like he'd never been there, like he'd never happened, like he'd been an event, not a person.

3.8

Kal and I stood at the arrival gates, watching Sunny and his parents walk through the sliding glass doors towards us, all of them weary-eyed, switching their loads from one hand to another and craning their necks to see through the mass of smiling people holding flowers for loved ones. I waved and stepped out of the crowd.

Sunny hugged me with both arms. "God, it's so good to be home."

His mother nodded vigorously. She was hobbling with her carry-on bag, which Kal quickly relieved her of. She straightened her leg, flexing and pointing her toes, stumbling to one side as if she were about to topple over. I caught her by the arm. "My sciatica. Such a long flight." My father-in-law made a mocking face when she wasn't looking. I hugged him briefly before returning to my mother-in-law's aid. "My legs, my legs." I hooked my arm in hers and helped her sit down.

"We'll be home soon." I motioned to Kal and asked him to get her some water. She made a production of not wanting us to go to any trouble. "No ice," she said, yelling it repeatedly as he went to get her some anyway.

"You and Dad stay here and Sunny and I will get the luggage."

Sunny and I waited hand in hand at the carousel, watching the luggage drop down the slide. I stared up at the flight information—the ever-changing arrivals and departures, delays and cancellations panning across the bottom of the screen like tickertape—and I read each detail as if it meant something.

"Did you miss me?" Sunny asked, pulling me closer, his arm about my shoulder, loose but still possessive.

"What kind of question is that? Of course I did." When he didn't say anything I looked up at him. He had a dingy tan, as if layers and weeks of filth had solidified on his flesh and even yellowed the whites of his eyes, making him look suspicious, making me feel suspect.

I smiled as I pulled away, pointing to the luggage. "I think those are ours."

Sunny's mother hobbled over, directing us on how to stack the suitcases on the trolley so they didn't topple over. "Wait until you see all the saris. Such fine embroidery; there is nothing like it here. Oy, be careful with that one," she said to Sunny. "That bag has the parshaad in it... a blessing all the way from the Golden Temple for you, Surinder. For your children."

Kal grabbed the rest of the bags and loaded his truck with the luggage, while Sunny's parents piled into the back of my car. "Oh, my joints," Sunny's mother said. "My arthritis was so bad there that I didn't get out of bed for days. Ask Sunny. Sunny, isn't that right?"

Sunny nodded and shut the door. He reached for my keys. "I'll drive."

"It's okay. You're probably tired."

"I said I'll drive."

I nodded and sat in the front seat listening to my mother-in-law's chatter subside into sleep. Phlegm rattled in her throat. My father-in-law stared out the window, adjusting his glasses and eyes to the light. "You okay, Dad?"

He smiled. "Oh, fine. Very fine."

Sunny's mother unpacked her suitcases, covering the carpet with swatches of silk and satin—the clothes she had bought—while I put on the water for tea. "And this one is for your mother, and this one is for your oldest sister and this one is for you," she yelled from the family room.

EVERYTHING WAS GOOD-BYE

Kal came into the kitchen holding the box of sweets that my mother-in-law had brought in her carry-on bag. "And this little piggy went to market and this little piggy stayed home and this little piggy went wee wee all the way home," he mocked. I snapped him with a tea towel and told him to be quiet before we both got into trouble.

"Oh, all the fun is in here! What are you two laughing about?" my father-in-law asked.

"Nothing," I said.

My father-in-law slapped Kal on the back. "Tell me, how is my nephew? Has he found a wife yet?"

"Are you asking me or him?" I asked.

"You, of course. You are his cousin-brother's wife, his bhabiji. It is your duty to find him a wife."

Kal waved his hands in refusal. "No thanks, Chachaji. I don't need a wife. I have a girlfriend."

My father-in-law dismissed the remark with a sour face. "A girlfriend is not a wife... Look at Sunny and Meena. Don't you want what they have, what he has?"

Kal didn't seem to know how to answer and I looked away, not wanting to watch his struggle or interpret the meaning of his silence.

"Girlfriend. Nonsense," Sunny's father continued. "You know I was eighteen when I got married. I never even saw your Chachiji's face. The day after the wedding, I left for Canada. I didn't see her for two years."

"Things were simple back then," Kal said.

My father-in-law paused with faraway eyes. "Some things were simple, yes, and some things were complicated... but we made it work. It was our duty." He looked around. "Isn't that right?" he shouted to my mother-in-law, who was talking with Sunny.

"What, heh?" she yelled. "Kal, I need you. Come here."

"Duty calls," he said, excusing himself.

My father-in-law reached for a glass from the shelf.

"What can I get you, Dad?"

He moved me out of his way. "I can get it." He poured himself a glass of tap water and gulped it down. "Much better than India's."

181

"Did you have a good time? See all your old friends?"

He nodded. "Yes, old is right. We are all very old now."

"I didn't mean it like that."

"I know." He sat down on a nearby chair. He looked thinner, his chest slightly concave as if parts of him had disappeared into himself and the only mass left was what little air there was in his lungs. Every time he went to India he seemed to come back a little less himself.

"Are you sure you're okay?"

He nodded and patted his heart with his whole hand. "It's the coming and going of it." He looked at me, but his eyes were elsewhere. "We were not meant to leave the people we love so many times."

"No, I don't suppose we were." I kissed my father-in-law on the cheek, pressing my hand on his shoulder as I walked by. He held my hand and patted it with his own, in that paper-thin way old people have when they offer empathy for the luxurious problems of youth.

I went downstairs and shut myself in the washroom, flushing the toilet every few moments so I wouldn't be bothered. I reached into my purse looking for my phone, becoming frantic when I couldn't find it, knowing that Liam was somewhere waiting for me to call. I dumped the contents on the floor and sifted through the side pockets, hoping that it was there, that it had slipped inside the lining. After a few minutes I gave up, went back into the living room and asked if anyone had seen my phone.

Sunny produced it from his pocket. "Who's Liam?"

"What?" I was sure my face went red.

"Liam. He's on your display." Sunny flipped the phone open before handing it back to me. "He's called, like ten times."

Kal glanced at me. "Liam... isn't that the new guy at work. I remember you mentioned him to me?"

I stumbled. "Yeah. I've been helping him out until he gets up to speed."

Kal and I were quiet for a moment.

"Well, aren't you going to call him?" Sunny asked.

I shook my head and dropped the phone in my bag. "Maybe later... Are you ready to go? You must be tired?"

Sunny looked at his watch and agreed. "It's 3 A.M. in India," he said to his mother, who was yawning herself.

"Better you go. Get some rest," she said.

The apartment seemed different with Sunny in it and as he moved about the bedroom changing out of his clothes, his presence surprised me as though he were a shadow appearing and disappearing from the corner of my eye—slightly out of sight, out of reach. I picked up his clothes as he dropped them, taking the change out of the pockets and folding everything into a neat pile on the leather bench in front of the bed. I sat down and ran my hands over the leather, thinking of how only a few days ago I'd made love to Liam there. I looked up, catching Sunny's backside in the full-length mirror across from the bed. His body was chiselled, his upper body overdeveloped by brutish workouts and protein shakes that did nothing to enhance his thin legs. "Chicken Legs," I'd teased, before realizing how sensitive he was about them.

He pulled the sheets back and got into bed. "Are you coming?"

I lay down next to him. He put his arm around me and fell asleep. I waited until his breath was loud and his eyes had rolled beneath their lids before moving his arm and creeping out of bed to call Liam. I shut the door behind me and turned the television on. The screen light flickered through the dark living room. I dialled and waited, my palms sweating on the receiver, my breath amplified and reverberating in the mouthpiece. The call went to voice mail. I hung up and dialled again. I paced the length of the room, then sat down on the edge of the couch. Voice mail. I hung up and dialled again. I got up, paced some more and sat down again, pulling at strands of hair, twirling them between my fingers, cupping the receiver, pressing it into my ear. "Pick up, pick up," I whispered over and over, rocking back and forth ever so slightly, every time listening to his casual voice on the other end, so cavalier, so fucking cavalier in his "It's Liam... leave a message or don't" bullshit. I slammed the phone down.

3.9

Wrecked with jet lag, Sunny napped most days and retreated to his den late at night to catch up on missed work, consider new investments and watch online porn. One night, after I'd refused him, he got out of bed and went into his study. I heard him make himself a drink, turn on the computer, lean back in his chair and then nothing, nothing but the silence and the ache of a man before he comes, the moments when moments seem to open and close, collapsing on themselves. I closed my eyes and thought of Liam's body fused on mine, how when it was over neither of us moved and we would lie there, entwined and helpless.

I reached for the phone and called him, skipping the formalities of greetings when he picked up. "I miss you."

He was silent. "I miss you too."

"I'm sorry about the other day. It was hard to talk and Sunny–"

"It's okay," he said, cutting me off on Sunny's name as if he didn't want to hear it, to imagine it.

I stared at the ceiling, the dark of the room. "I miss you."

"I know... I do too."

We were quiet, full of short sentences that amounted to nothing but the punctuation of absence: "I miss you," "I love you," "I want you," "I'm sorry." The three-word strings tugged and pulled at us, superseding the need for talk and explanations, justifications and ramifications.

"I should go. I just wanted to hear you." I imagined him nodding, staring out the window, or looking at the pictures he'd taken that day, retouching them, making them better. "When will you be back?"

"Soon."

That was all he said.

Over the course of the next few days, I had long conversations with the idea of him, rehearsing all the things that I would tell him when we were together. When I was at work, I wrote out my thoughts in longhand, making him into a story, and when I read it back it frightened me so much that I shredded the papers into bits and tossed them into the trash, only to mourn them five minutes later. I retrieved the fragments and stuffed them into my purse as if I were stuffing my heart back into my chest.

When the wait was unbearable, I called him from my closed office door and from the washroom stalls of restaurants where Sunny and I dined with his parents, just to hear his voice on the answering machine, relieved that the sound of him matched my memory. I held the line, listening to the dial tone until the recorded voice told me to hang up, to try my call again, to ask for assistance.

3.10

I walked by a lingerie shop on Robson Street, transfixed by the lace-and-satin window dressing, the poster of a woman wearing a black bustier and fishnet stockings, lying across a bed, her hair tousled and mouth parted. She had a look about her, wanting and vulnerable, a certain surrender. I wanted to be her, and turned back and opened the door to the shop. I fingered the fine lace intimates, bypassing the Valentine's Day markdown items that looked tawdry, used almost, the way burned-down candles and dirty wine glasses look on the morning after. Everything in the store smelled like roses and talc powder, so delicate that I was afraid to touch them. The salesperson noticed my hesitation and came over.

"Can I help you?"

"What's on the poster?" I pointed to the window. "Do you have that?"

She nodded. "Yes, just. It's brand new." She pulled one off the rack. "This one looks about your size," she said, measuring the cups against my breasts. I was embarrassed, even though I was the only customer in the store.

"Here we are." She handed me the panties. "Do you want to try the stockings as well?"

I nodded and followed her around the store as she picked up an assortment of other things that she thought I might like.

"Is it a special occasion?" she asked, helping me into the change room, which was both cabaret and brothel in its decor of draped red velvet. All it lacked was a stripper pole.

"An anniversary," I said, without thinking.

"Well, let me know if you need any sizes."

I undressed and pulled the flimsy garment off the hanger, avoiding my naked self in the mirror. I fastened the countless hooks and eyes, and snapped the garter on the stockings, plumping my breasts into the wired bustier cups. I slipped my high heels on again and stepped back, looking at myself in the three-way mirror. I cupped my breasts and pouted, smiled just enough, closed my eyes halfway until I looked like what I was, an adulteress on her way to another man's bed.

Liam was never as I'd imagined him. He was tired and unshaven; his clothes were wrinkled and still smelled like the sea's salty decay; his smile when seeing me at his door was half-hearted, his embrace part relief and part torture.

"I missed you." He said it like a confession, something to be ashamed of, something he didn't want or had no choice in. We stood there in each other's arms, silent, eyes closed, almost swaying, anticipating the rhythms of each other. "Come here," he said, pulling away. "I want to show you what I've been working on."

"These are the new ones?" He was standing behind me, but I could tell he was nodding, waiting for approval. The images were stark and haunting, black-and-grey landscapes, rain and clouds, a medieval sort of dirt. "What do you call them?"

"Human residue." He pointed to a crushed pop can tangled in seaweed on a beach. "It's representative of what we leave behind. Environmentally. And then this one," he said, pointing to a reflection of a naked woman in still water, "is about emotional residue. How place and person aren't singular, how we assign memories to place and how that place becomes a symbol or a metaphor for something and... well, you get what I mean."

I turned around. "I do... they're beautiful."

"You're beautiful." He put his palm on the side of my neck until I strained to it, surrendered to it. When he kissed me, my mouth parted, my eyes closed, everything about me stripped away. I thought of the woman in the poster, the lingerie still sitting in the bag by the door. I didn't want to be her. I just wanted to be his.

Afterwards we lay on our backs, cigarettes in hand, the threads of smoke rising above us, twisting and weaving its haunting canopy over our naked bodies.

"What are we doing?" I asked.

Liam exhaled a ring of smoke into the air and watched it ripple before he reached across me and butted out the cigarette, extinguishing the orange glow, the dying sparks. I got up, sheets wrapped around me as I picked up my clothes, which lay in a puddle on the floor.

"Do you have to leave? You just got here."

I dropped the sheets and pulled on my clothes, quickly fastening my bra. "Sunny will be waiting."

"So, tell him that you're running late."

"I can't. He already suspects and I can't risk it."

Liam rolled over and turned towards me. "Risk what?"

I sat on the edge of the bed next to him, my hand in his. "You."

"Tell him... Leave him already."

I sighed. "He's not the kind of man you can just leave."

He pulled me towards him. "Then just stay. Spend the night."

I kissed him and got up, slipping on my blouse. "You know I can't. If I don't get back he'll be... well, you know how he is."

He sat up in bed. "No, I don't know. Tell me, how is he, Meena?"

I sighed and reached for my purse. "He's not you."

"Have you been with him yet?"

I shook my head and turned around. "No. I told you already that I haven't, that I won't. That I– "

"That you'll what?" He got up and pulled on his pants, stretching his T-shirt over his head. "What will you do? He's your husband. Are you really going to be able to tell him no?"

I didn't answer.

"If you did wouldn't he suspect? Can you really risk that, Meena?" He was staring at me, his eyes burrowing, accusing. "I mean, can you really risk anything?"

I reached for him and he shoved me away.

"Is this how it's going to be? You come by and we fuck, what, a couple times a week?"

"No. Is that what you think this is?"

He ran his fingers through his hair, his hands arrested behind his head for a moment before he dropped them. "I don't know what this is."

3.11

Neither of us spoke of his leaving, though there were traces of it everywhere. Open boxes had been sealed and put into storage; his passport, which was always tucked between T-shirts in his bedside drawer, now lay face down on the dresser; his suitcase, usually housed in the closet, now lay open-jawed on the bed. Half empty, half full? I still couldn't decide, and as I'd watched him pack over the course of the week, I'd wondered if even he could.

"Where will you go?"

"I don't know. East. I'll figure it out as I go."

I imagined him hitching across Canada the way he'd told me he'd done after high school, riding in beat-up vans and trucks, walking for miles, buying prepackaged gas station food, eating at rest stops, sleeping in cheap motels.

"Do you need money?"

He pushed by me, stuffing more clothes into his suitcase. "No, I don't need your money. I'm fine without it." He pulled out dresser drawers, tipping the contents onto the bed, sorting them into loose piles. He emptied his medicine cabinet, tossing the half-empty bottles into the trash. I stood in the middle of the studio watching him move from task to task with the urgent precision of a planned departure.

The studio was as bare as it usually was; his bed was unmade, the fridge almost empty, his unwashed coffee mug in the sink, the shades half drawn, yet as he packed, pulling at his belongings, closing them into cases, I felt his leaving. It settled in my chest, echoing like a heart murmur.

I picked up a pile of his photographs. Pictures he'd taken of me. Pictures I'd taken of him. Black and white. "Don't forget these."

He didn't look up. He didn't take them from me.

I held them out farther, shaking them like an offering. "Here's your fucking human residue." My voice bounced off the walls and back at me.

He snatched them from me, shoving them into his already crammed duffle bag so that the photographs folded and collapsed on themselves. There was quiet except for the sound of a persistent car horn. He ducked his head out the window, yelling at the cabbie that he would be a minute.

"So this is it? Just like that."

He zipped up his duffle bag. "No, not just like that, Meena. You and I were never *just* like that." He picked up his suitcase and slung his bag over his other shoulder.

I watched him leave the building, and as the cab pulled away from the curb, I ran outside, my arm half extended like a desperate a plea for him to come back or a frantic reminder that he had forgotten something. Someone.

After he'd left, I drove around the city, feeling as if I were sitting with a ghost, as if he were there next to me not speaking, not answering my thoughts. "What do I do?" I asked it over and over again. "What am I supposed to do?" No answer. Of course no answer. "What are you going to do now, Meena?" I slammed my foot on the gas pedal and drove faster. I thought of the way Liam and I used to drive to the beach when we were teenagers, my feet on the dashboard, windows rolled down, hair flying, singing along with the songs on the radio. We were almost free.

The sun was going down as I finished circling the Stanley Park Causeway for the second time. The sky was silver and gold, clean-lined and layered, reflecting itself onto the glass towers and office buildings that crowded the downtown core, that boxed everyone in. Inside those towers people were looking out of their floor-to-ceiling glass windows and watching the light change. They were also glancing now and then at wall clocks and soon, like me, they would see that it was time to go home, time to watch reality television and the local news while only partly aware that they would simply be wasting time, waiting for the next day, the possibility and inevitability of it all. The thought would scare them to death. It did me.

When I got home Kal and Irmila were over and Sunny was talking loud, trying to open a bottle of champagne that uncorked just as I walked in.

"Hey, good timing." Sunny motioned for me to come quickly, handed me a glass and filled it with the champagne that was frothing out of the bottle neck.

"What's all this?" I asked, not quite looking at anyone straight on.

Sunny poured glasses for Irmila and Kal. "Well, do you want to tell her the good news or should I?" Sunny asked, his glass poised for a toast.

Irmila held out her hand, displaying her ring finger. "We're engaged."

"Engaged? Wow. I had no idea the two of you were so serious."

Kal put his arm around Irmila, who seemed taken aback by my comment. "Well, we are," he said.

"Of course. Of course you are. I didn't mean it... I'm sorry, I've just had quite a day." I felt dizzy and hollow, nauseous from crying. Sadness had become a physical thing. "Can you excuse me for a moment?" I handed Sunny my glass and rushed into the bathroom, where I gagged dry heaves. My face was red, my eyes were puffy from crying. "Allergies," I would tell Sunny if he asked me why. I splashed cold water on my face, trying to snap myself back into the pretense of marriage.

Sunny knocked on the door. "Babe, you okay?"

I ran the water. "Yeah, out in a minute."

When I emerged, Irmila and Kal were sitting comfortably as if they intended to stay a while. I sat across from them, only half listening to the details of how he had proposed, how she'd said yes, when they would be married, how happy his parents were, how they loved her like a daughter. As she spoke, gushing like an ugly schoolgirl who'd finally got a date, Kal stared at her, falling deeper into every word, looking at her with a love that surprised me.

"Meena, I thought we should take these two out to celebrate. I made reservations for seven." He looked at his watch. "We should probably get going." Sunny put his arm around Kal, and slapped his back in just the way that the leading man would do in the old Hollywood movies that Liam and I used to watch.

Irmila smiled all during dinner, talking over everyone, laughing with her head back and eyes closed, the conversation pivoting around her. She was entirely herself and when she asked the server how each meal was prepared, if the greens were organic, if the salmon was fresh or farmed, I could tell it bothered Kal because he joked about it, and then afterwards they bickered in a playful way, pawing at each other like kittens. I said very little for fear that I would say too much, that my smile would crack into a thousand sorrows, and occasionally I went to the ladies' room to cry in the privacy of a stall.

When I came out the last time, Kal was on his way to the men's room. "Your eyes. They're red."

"Allergies. It's the pollen."

"Meena, you're not allergic to anything."

I looked over into the dining room. "I should go back in."

"Irmila and I had dinner with Liam the other night."

"Who?" I asked, pretending to look through my purse for something.

"Meena, don't. Not with me."

I looked up. "What, Kal? What would you like me to say?"

"I know he's gone."

"And–"

"I know you must be upset, but… it's better this way."

"Better for whom?" I asked, walking away before he could answer.

3.12

I felt the SkyTrain's motion in the sway of my head. I could tell by the curves and the long stretches of straight track when it was time to get off and knew that it was soon but not yet. I opened my eyes as the door slid open and shut, watched everyone readjust to make room for more passengers. The train was crammed with college students laden with books and with middle-aged women wearing comfortable shoes and carrying their emptied bag lunches and high heels in gym bags. They were the type of women who sat behind reception desks and had not changed their makeup and hairstyles in years. They had their heads buried in grocery-store paperback novels, Harlequin romances or bad mysteries—anything that took them away from their life, this commuter life where on each train ride they came up against their misspent youth, which had got them to no place but here. Every time a group of teenagers got on the train, laughing and exaggerated, trendy and rebellious in the way they touched and flirted as if they were entitled, these women looked on with the bespectacled stares of librarians. But the men on the train—in their poorly tailored suits and scuffed shoes, their newspapers stuffed into the side pockets of worn briefcases—didn't notice much and stared straight ahead with weary astonishment. I wondered where they were all going and if they would be relieved when they got there.

The train doors opened and closed and the mix of men and women, young and old, filed in and out, the exchange as easy as breathing. Those who remained sat tightly, moulding their round bodies to the small squares seats, pulling and tugging at the hems of their spring raincoats, not wanting to infringe on their neighbours' space yet looking up occasionally to find some eyes to look away from. I, too, pulled in my imaginary borders, closing them around me as I looked out the window, staring into my opaque reflection, faceless until I suddenly heard my name like a question. It was Irmila.

Since I'd last seen her she'd cut her hair, and she was now sporting long, blunt bangs that made her look more severe and sophisticated than I remembered. I'd avoided her and Kal since that night at dinner a few weeks ago, and seeing her now only seemed to remind me of Liam's absence, the pit and ache in my stomach since he'd left, the lingering guilt and want of him. I shrank into myself, willing myself to disappear, hoping she wouldn't come over, but within an instant she was sure of her recognition and trotted down the aisle, carrying a brown bag of groceries overflowing with vegetables, excusing herself as she brushed by glazed commuters.

She sat down with a huff in the handicapped seat next to me. "Hey, Surinder. What a surprise. You on your way home?"

I nodded. "Yeah. I was out visiting my mom."

"She lives in Surrey, right?"

"No. Delta."

"Oh. It's almost the same... so many Indians. I don't know how you can stand it."

I didn't bother answering. She was all about rhetorical questions. "How have you been?" I asked.

"Busy." She made a dramatic eyebrows-up face. "We've been planning the engagement party and it's just out of control. I wanted to keep it small, but Kal's parents want this big, Indian-type... You know how it is. Everyone on the guest list is an uncle or an auntie. Plus work is just madness." She knelt down and picked up one of the apples that had fallen out of the bag and was rolling away. "Organic... do you eat organic?"

I shook my head that I didn't. "Sunny isn't into it."

"I never ate it before either, but Liam got me into it. You remember him. I think you met him, that photographer at the gallery that night... anyways, I was talking to him the other day and he—"

"You talked to him?"

"Yes, we talk all the time. We're old friends."

"Did he ask about me?" I asked, without thinking.

"No, why would he?" She stood up, bracing herself against the metal rail as the train slowed and the next stop was announced.

"No reason."

She threw her purse over her shoulder. "This is my stop," she said. "We'll have to get together some time soon." I could tell by the way she crinkled her eyes that she was only being polite and probably made the false promise of "let's do lunch or coffee" every time she bumped into anyone who might be remotely useful to her in the future. "Say hi to Sunny for me," she said, and plowed into the rush of commuters getting off the train. I nodded that I would and watched her being carried off in the crowd, wishing she'd be trampled. Ever since her engagement, I'd hated her more than she deserved, and now that I knew that she talked to Liam I hated her for that too.

When I got home I plopped onto the couch, ordered in my Chinese cravings and flipped on the news, watching it in several times zones. The barrage of media images from 9/11 that still plagued the screen numbed me, and I flipped through them, passing the commentaries so fast that they blurred into sound bites. I reached for the remote and pointed it at the TV like a gun, pressing the button as though I were pulling a trigger.

I sat back, staring at the packets of sweet-and-sour sauce, the chopsticks, and fried rice that littered the table like a drug addict's paraphernalia. I threw it all back into the grease-stained bag it had come in, tossed it in the trash and sprayed air freshener across the room, masking the odour so Sunny wouldn't complain about my eating it again. "Careful," he'd said, patting my stomach. "You've put on a few. You're going to get fat if you keep eating that shit."

After cleaning the kitchen, I went to bed and pretended to sleep, listening for him at the front door, stabbing his key into the lock. He stumbled up the stairs, his keys rattling as they hit the table beside me. I could tell he was standing over me, a shadow, undressing, layer by layer. He slid in beside me, his whisky lips on my neck telling me that he missed me, his legs spreading mine, his face an inch from mine, fucking in measured thrusts until I pushed him back, telling him that I didn't feel well. He pulled out and rolled over, jumping out of bed when he saw the sheets were stained in blood. He rushed to the washroom. "Jesus, Meena, why didn't you tell me you had your period?"

"I don't." I followed him into the washroom, blood trickling down the inside of my thighs. I tried to speak, but my words loosened to nothing and the room disappeared into a thousand pinholes.

When I opened my eyes Sunny was crouched on the floor next to me, phone in his hand. "Meena! Thank God you're okay."

"What happened?" I tried to get up, but couldn't.

Sunny put the phone down and helped me up. "You passed out and hit your head. Does it hurt?" he asked. I winced that it did. "I'm going to take you to the hospital to get checked. Here, lean on me," he said and helped me get dressed.

"How are you feeling now? Are you okay?" He kept asking this all the way to hospital, glancing at me every few minutes, reaching for my hand as if he were checking to make sure I was still there.

It was two hours of waiting in the emergency room before my name was called. "About time," Sunny said, glaring at the admitting nurse who had told him to "sit down sir," every time he approached the desk asking why it was taking so long, his voice growing louder as he complained that others were being seen before me. But even after I'd been admitted and had donned a paper-thin hospital gown, we waited, listening to the sounds of the other sick and injured that were only partly contained by the draped partitions—the sounds of low moans and dry coughs, the sounds of respirators and the steady beats of cardiac monitors. Sunny read back issues of *People* cover to cover while I closed my eyes, pulling up the blankets and untucking the hospital corners, pretending to rest so he would stop asking me if I needed anything. He hadn't been this attentive since our honeymoon.

On the way to the hospital he'd been clenched with emotion, driving fast and zipping around corners, and he was red-eyed when he told me later that he thought he'd lost me. "I don't know what I'd do without you."

I opened my eyes when I heard Sunny pacing the bed's perimeter, complaining about the wait. "Why don't you go get some coffee? You look exhausted."

"I'm not leaving you here alone."

"I'll still be here when you get back. Besides, I could use some tea. Can you bring me some?"

He nodded and kissed me on the forehead. It was only a few minutes after he left that the doctor pulled back the partition, pronouncing my name in syllables as he read it off the clipboard. He flipped through the chart, reading my blood-work results, clicking and unclicking his pen before underlining something. He shone a light in my eyes, telling me to look left to right, up and down and made a note on his chart. He felt the small bump on the back of my head. "How are you feeling now?"

"Okay. Better."

"It'll hurt for a bit, but you don't seem to be suffering from a concussion or anything serious like that."

I smiled relief, but he didn't notice because he was looking at the chart again.

"It says here that your last menstrual cycle was some time ago. Is that correct?"

I nodded, telling him that my periods were always irregular and stress made it worse.

"What kind of stress?" He perked up.

"Just the usual. Is something the matter?" I asked.

"Well no, not really. Your test results are all good, but… they also indicate that you're pregnant."

"Pregnant?"

"Yes, about eight weeks."

"What? I can't be… what about the bleeding…"

"Spotting and fainting are not that unusual for a first trimester, but we'll schedule an ultrasound just to be sure everything's fine."

I nodded, barely listening as he went on about prenatal care, vitamins and birthing classes. I placed my hand on my stomach as if something would be revealed to me besides my fear. Sunny came back in holding two coffees, worried when he saw the expression on my face.

"What is it? What's wrong?"

Before the doctor could speak, I told him it was nothing.

But when we got home I couldn't look at him. His sympathy only made me retreat further into my own guilt, into the quiet of secrets that could not be kept.

3.13

I stood at the departure gate waiting with the red-eyed to board a flight to Montreal. I'd packed while Sunny was sleeping, moving around him on tiptoes, frightened that he would wake up before I left, that I might have to answer to him. I packed only what I needed immediately, thinking that if I needed anything else I could replace it when I got there, or learn to live without it. I called my mother from the airport. She scolded me for calling so early—the ringing phone had alarmed her. I imagined her sitting up in her bed, wild and frightened, her loose hair spilling over her shoulders, unruly strands curled at her temples like fine silver threads. "I'll see you this weekend... Dinner on Sunday, don't forget, and remind Sunny." I nodded, even though by then I would have put thousands of miles between us.

I checked my wallet for my ID, boarding pass and Liam's address several times, touching each like a talisman. In the days after I'd learned of my pregnancy, I'd tried to call him, but only ever got his voice mail. I'd listen to his voice, "This is Liam. You know what to do," and each time I'd wondered if I did know what to do and hung up wondering for hours after. Hours, during which I would have dinner with Sunny, talking about the random details of our days, listing them, embellishing them, adding them up, as if after some time they would appreciate and eventually perhaps be worth something and we could say, like so many aging married couples did, that it had been worth it. That having been there with each other despite ourselves was a worthy accomplishment on its own.

Whenever Sunny talked about the future, near and far, I'd hide my eyes, ducking into myself the way a bird would tuck its head under its wing to protect itself from the rain and cold. A few days before deciding to leave I called Liam again, prepared to tell him everything, but this time my attempt was greeted by an out-of-service recording. I told myself that it was better this way; I needed to say it to him, see the reaction in his eyes when he learned that he was to be a father. Hearing his silence in the distance wasn't enough. I had to go to him. I'd imagined that he'd be relieved to see me, elated by the news of my pregnancy. He'd swing me around in his arms, my feet dangling in the air. We would live together in a Victorian townhouse, which we would lovingly restore. We would put the baby in the stroller and walk around the neighbourhood at dusk or window-shop on the weekends. We would grow old and never even know it.

Worried and anxious, I hadn't slept the night before, but now was too restless to sleep on the plane, so I sat flipping through the in-flight magazine and monitored our flight path on the seatback screen. I wondered what the weather was like in Montreal, if there would be snow on the ground. I hadn't packed for it, not even gloves; the practicalities of this trip had got lost in my hurry, and if they hadn't been perhaps I would have lost my courage in the planning. "Just go," I'd told myself. "Just go."

A little boy in the seat ahead of me popped his head up and down, peeking through the headrests, smiling a silly cracker-encrusted grin. His mother was rocking a baby in her arms and whispered to the boy not to bother the nice lady, in the kind of voice that mothers often use when their children are embarrassing them. The boy kicked his legs and thrashed backwards, knocking his seat into the reclined position. The woman stood up, baby still in her arms, and apologized.

"It's all right, really," I told her, offering the little boy a smile. "It's a long flight."

She looked relieved. "Do you have children?"

"Actually no, not yet. But I am expecting." It was the first time I'd said it and I was amazed at the ease with which I'd said it. I wanted to say it again, to wrap my mouth around each word and digest it slowly.

"How far along?"

"Ten weeks."

"Congratulations. You must be very excited."

"I am. We are." I told her that I was on my way to Montreal to see my husband, who was a photographer, and I was somewhat surprised at how easily the lies formed and how comfortable they felt, how later they lulled me into a dream that left me only once we landed. Liam was not my husband. My husband was in Vancouver. By now, Sunny would be at the office, sitting at his desk, talking on the phone, toying with his pen, rearranging papers in piles, unaware that I had left him. I felt sorry and sad for both of us.

While others rushed to the baggage carousels, I sat in the waiting area listening to the French and English flight announcements of arrivals and departures, summoning the courage to keep leaving. It was a process, not an act. I had to do it bit by bit. I set my watch to Montreal time. I took off my wedding ring.

The taxi driver pulled over, pointing to the address that I'd given him. It was a rundown Victorian carved into apartments, the gabled roof lined with birds. The kind of place inhabited by university students with radical views and big dreams, old women with sad immigrant pasts and gypsy-king men like Liam. There was a dusting of snow on the steps and on the plastic patio chair that sat by the front door. It looked like the place that Liam had told me about, only he had left out the crumbling state, the missing bricks in the facade. He always made everything seem better than it was. Even me.

I rang the bell. No one came. I sat on the stoop, my suitcase propped by the dirty screen door. I watched people pass like time. An old woman with an ill-fitting silver wig and a map of a face, deep lines, red lips, a mask of years. She did not smile. A young couple in love, their hands in each other's pockets, lips mashing. I had to look away. A little girl in a red wool coat walking with her mother, staring back at me as if she knew why I was there. Her breath made smoke.

After an hour, a bearded man wearing layered T-shirts and a toque stopped at the steps of the old Victorian, his bike slung over his shoulder. "Can I help you?"

"You live here?" He nodded and I stood up, moving out of his way. "I'm looking for Liam."

He picked up his bike and walked up the steps, dropping it wheel-first onto the front porch. "He hasn't been around for months." He pulled out his keys and unlocked the door, turning away as though he'd either forgotten or didn't care that I was even there.

"Do you know where I can find him?" I asked.

"Not sure. Last time I heard from him he was in Vancouver."

I nodded. "Right, Vancouver." I turned around, hobbling down the steps, my luggage tumbling behind me, my feet frozen into the point of my shoes as I walked away, yanking my suitcase wheels free through the cobblestone streets, heading west.

Sunny was sitting in the shadows of the living room, staring out the window into the lit apartments across the street, watching the comings and goings of other people's lives, no more interesting than our own. People watching television in the dark, the room lit by flashing images, couples fighting in muted gestures, all of them existing side by side in small rooms, quiet and contained. I had been gone less than a day, yet the back and forth of time zones and memories left me feeling like my whole life had played out in one day. Perhaps this was what people meant when they said their life flashed before their eyes.

"You're back."

I dropped my bag by the door. "Things didn't go as I planned."

He turned towards me, the grinding of his jaw visible in the half-light. "I bet."

"Pardon?" I stepped back as he stepped forward.

"What do you think I am, stupid? Did you think you could keep it from me?"

"Let me explain."

"No. You don't need to. You see, our doctor called today." He paused, waiting for me to speak. I fell mute. "He wanted to book your ultrasound."

I could see his eyes now and turned away from them. "I was going to tell you."

"What? What were you going to tell me? That you're a fucking whore?" He grabbed me by the shoulders and shook me back and forth, my head snapping first from the motion and then from his fist. I fell back, stumbling over my suitcase. He grabbed me before I hit the ground and pinned me against the wall, my throat in his hands. "Who is he? Is that where you went? To be with him?" He let go, kicking me as I slid down the wall gasping for air in the dark, my breath overlapping his.

3.14

The next morning I left, carrying the same suitcase that I'd come home with. I checked into the Fairmont Hotel wearing movie-star sunglasses to hide my eyes, now mottled in green and yellow, edged in what looked like a thick line of black marker. The attendant at the front desk tried to be polite about it, pretending not to notice my broken-down appearance, speaking to me with well-scripted manners.

"How long will you be staying with us?"

I dismissed him with a shake of the head. "I'm not sure."

He smiled, clicked a few keys on his computer and handed me a key, pointing to the elevators, reminding me of the amenities—the fine dining, the swimming pool, the spa. I nodded, rushing him along.

I drew the curtains shut and lay on the bed as if it were an island and I was stranded and content that I'd washed up on its shore, that the tide had released me from its ebb and flow. I stayed there for hours, observing the subtleties of light, the gradual blue darkness, ignoring the occasional thought to call home. Home. It was a mocking word, as small as a kind gesture and as large as an ocean. I whispered it, trying it on, wrapping it around me as I cocooned. I thought of my baby nestled deep inside my body, lying in the dark of me—defenceless, only the size of a bean; pink gelatinous matter, tissue and blood, I thought of the laminated pictures of fetal development posted in the doctor's office. By now my baby had eyes, ears, the beginnings of limbs; paper-thin, see-through skin; and a brain that was developing, making connections. "When will she dream?" I'd asked the doctor.

"She? You think it's a girl do you?" The doctor was listening for a heartbeat but gave up, saying it was too early to hear.

"Dreaming. Not for a few more months."

Ever since then I'd been wondering what she would dream of. If she would see me there; if when I slept, she and I would meet in the dark subconscious, in that lonely space of Sufis and saints where wisdom is something a child sees through a crack in the door before it's closed and the meaning of what was there is lost.

I closed my eyes and pulled the covers up. My body ached in the aftermath of the previous night. Bruises made visible and ugly by each passing hour, phantom pains taking their shape, marking territory, branding. I hated him for it, and yet every time I felt the pain or caught sight of a bruise, I was grateful for the reminder. I wouldn't go back.

I woke with the panicked sensation of not knowing where I was. My eyes startled open, blinking hard, adjusting to the flat morning light before my thoughts organized it all into some non-sequential order—last night, the night before, years before, falling back into me as if they had existed outside of me, orbiting when I slept until the gravity of my wakefulness pulled them all back in.

I stayed in the hotel room for days, ordering in minimal room service—Premium Plus crackers and orange juice with no pulp. I couldn't keep much down. I watched the daytime drama of soap operas, sometimes without the sound, just so my eyes had something to follow, something to keep them from welling up and spilling over the brim. When my phone rang, I didn't answer it. Sunny would have called my mother or Serena to say I'd left, to tell them to go and find me as if I were some dog to be rounded up. Each time it rang, I stared at it, listening to the rings, waiting for it to click over to voice mail. Sometimes I listened to the messages—my mother's faraway voice, searching, bent with worry and fear. "Come home. Just come home." I closed my eyes, trying to find my way back, my way forward. I didn't call her. It was better to just disappear, to fall away, to leave her with her questions rather than give her the truth of what I'd done.

It was Kal who found me. He'd tried every hotel, called in favours, asked around at my office until someone told him where I was. When I opened the door to let him in, he stared at my face with a pained expression that was both guilty and sad, the exact way he looked as a child when we'd broken my mother's favourite vase and were confronted with her loss.

"It's okay," I told him.

He walked around the room, and fingered the drapes aside. A triangular shard of sun cut across the bed. He turned, dropped his hand, and the light disappeared. I hadn't noticed before he'd arrived that the room smelled stale, like warm sheets and sleeplessness, like the sick and unattended. I asked him to open the window and collected the crumpled tissues on the nightstand and threw them into the trash. He watched me stack the room-service plates in neat and clattering piles. "How long are you planning on doing this?" he asked.

"I'm not doing anything."

"Well, how long are you planning on *not* doing this then?"

I climbed back into bed. "Why are you here?"

"You're not going back to him, are you?"

I shook my head and bit my lip, cracking the scab that had formed over the split. I bit down harder to stop the bleeding. "No."

"When are you going to tell your mom about the baby?"

"He told you?"

"Yeah. He asked me to find you."

"So that's why you're here?"

"No. I came to take you home. Your mom, your sisters, everyone's worried. I told them that I'd come and get you. That I'd make sure you were all right."

I shook my head. "I can't."

"You have to." He sat on the bed and reached for my hand. "I'll go with you."

My mother couldn't look at me. My face was still swollen, eyes shining blue and purple like the inside of a faded seashell. She didn't ask me what had happened. Serena made tea, placing it on a silver tray on the table in front of me, handing it to me when I didn't reach for it on my own. It went cold in the silence. The phone rang, piercing into the quiet, and Serena went to answer it, whispering into the receiver to one of my sisters or maybe to Masi that Kal and I were there. I listened as if she weren't talking about me, as though I didn't know what she was going to say next.

My mother sat on the edge of the couch, shadowing my face with her hands, fingertips tracing air.

"What has he done?"

"It's not what he's done. It's what I've done."

She dropped her hands as suddenly as a marionette whose strings had been cut. "What? What could you have done to deserve this?"

I didn't answer.

"That's what I thought. You don't need to protect him. I will call your Mamaji. He will settle this." She stood up, determined, talking in run-on sentences about what should be done.

"Mom. No. There's nothing to settle." I paused, trying to slow my breath, trying to put my thoughts in order, to find an easy way. "I'm not going to work things out... I can't."

I looked at Kal. His silence opened a door.

"Mom, I'm pregnant... It's not his baby."

Her face fell. The words aged her.

"I'm sorry," was all I could say.

"What people said... it was true." She looked at Kal like he was an accomplice. "And the father—who is he?"

"His name is Liam."

She refused to look at me, and stared out the window. "Leee-aaaam." Her voice was quiet and mean. "That same boy. What people said… they were right." She stared at me in controlled anger, waiting for me to answer. "All this time. You lied… What were you thinking?"

"Mom, I love him."

She was unmoved, so I told her again, so that this one time there could be no misinterpretation. "Pyaar."

She stared behind me, looking over my shoulder, somewhere into the past.

"Love? You always believed what you saw on TV, what you read in books… those silly stories… It's not real, Meena. This," she said, fisting her heart, "this is what's real. This is love. A mother's love for her child, that is real… and now look what you've done," she said, her face crumpled in sobs. "You've thrown it away, and for what?"

I placed my hand over my stomach. "For this… Mom, I'm going to have the baby."

"Alone?" Her voice was pinched in contained sadness.

"You raised us alone."

"I didn't do it alone. It wasn't the same… Your Mamaji, your Masi, I had family."

"So do I."

My mother turned to the side, refusing to meet my eyes. "You ask too much. You have always asked too much."

I stepped back slowly, distancing myself as I'd always done. Kal reached for my hand and whispered "Let's go." He said it a few times before I moved, before I made my way outside.

"Go where?" I asked as we drove away from the house and turned off the street.

"You can stay with me for a while."

"What about Irmila?"

He reached for my hand. "What about her? It'll be fine."

I waited in the foyer of their East Vancouver rental while Kal went upstairs to explain my situation to Irmila. They spoke in harsh whispers that tapered at the end. I tried not to listen, instead staring at the walls, which were adorned with Egyptian prints on papyrus and questionable local art that was as colourful as the neighbourhood residents whose loud voices and reaching eyes penetrated my skin as we'd walked by. "Hey, pretty lady, where you going?" they'd asked. I'd turned around and answered "I don't know," and though Kal was right there, his hand in mine, I'd never felt more alone.

3.15

The day I packed to move into my own place, Sunny locked himself in the den. He didn't come out even when I knocked on the door to tell him I was leaving. I leaned my head against the door, listening to the sound of him on the other side. I imagined that he was sitting in his leather chair, staring out the window, the way he often did when he'd been working too many hours.

"Sunny. Please. Open up."

No answer. Compared to his rage, his silence was unsettling, a harbinger. A few days earlier he'd turned up at Kal's house, argued with him about my staying there, and called me a bitch and a whore. "And you," he said pointing his finger in Kal's face like a madman, "you were supposed to be like my brother." His face was red, the veins in his neck protruding, so hot and wiry that I thought if I put my hand on them I'd feel his pulse, be able to slow it down. He'd left in an angry rush, speeding away in his car, leaving us with the silent fatigue of him, the perpetual exhaustion of not knowing what to do.

Now I knocked again. An offering. An explanation of why. I talked into the door. When he didn't answer, I left with my belongings packed into the back seat of my car and drove across the bridge into Kitsilano. I'd put a down payment on a Craftsman house with "potential," which I would come to realize was only a euphemism and real estate term for a fixer-upper. At first I would call Kal when something needed doing, but one night when the hot-water tank burst and my basement was filled with two inches of water, Irmila suggested I call someone else—"a professional," she'd said. I hadn't called him since and eventually he'd stopped calling me. I told myself it was for the best.

Night was the hardest part. The house settled into its bones like an old woman; its moans and whispers kept me up. I sat up in bed and called Serena, who updated me on family happenings. Whenever she said things like "Oh, you should have been there," she would go quiet afterwards, the silence full of apologies and condolences. "Don't worry, Mom will come round," she assured me after one such sequence. I nodded, forgetting she couldn't see me. "Meena, are you still there?" I told her yes, but that I had to go, and hung up.

I reached for the baby booties I'd started knitting to go with the blanket my mother had sent. I threw the ball of yarn across the bed and consulted the knitting-for-beginners, instructions that I'd torn out of a magazine at the doctor's office. When we were children, my mother had knitted while we watched television. The click of her knitting needles sounded like the crack of my grandmother's false teeth, and I flinched each time she crossed the needles in a loop, as if part of me were being caught up in her weave. She always started her knitting session by tossing the loose ball of yarn onto the floor, and within an hour would have collected it in needled rows of tight stitches that amounted to nothing but the satisfaction of repetition. Each night she would look at her stitches and stretch the warp flat, and when she saw me watching would hand me the last unbound stitch and let me unravel the whole thing. To my recollection, she had never finished anything until now. When I received the blanket, I called and thanked her. She asked me how I was feeling and I told her that I was fine, because she deserved that much, even if it was a lie.

Now as I crossed the needles, looping the yarn, I wished she'd taught me how to knit, I wished she'd had the time. After an hour my hands grew tired and I got out of bed and put the knitting away. I looked out the window. The last few blossoms on the trees rustled, falling in graceful turns, twisting their way down on the edge of a breeze. I traced their path with my eyes. Down the street a car started and crept forward slowly. The window rolled down and the driver leaned out as if he were reading house numbers. I ducked back behind the draperies when I realized it was Sunny. I rarely saw him without the presence of our lawyers, and even then he didn't look at me. He spoke about me as though I weren't there, his words a riddling of bullets. "She can have the car; she can have the Chippendale chairs—but not the dining room table." When I'd remind him that I didn't want anything but the divorce, he would pause, restrain himself and then continue on with his list, cataloguing our life, dividing us up, drawing things out, re-inserting his presence in my life one piece at a time.

After a few minutes, I peeked through the side of the window. He'd parked, switched his engine off and was watching the house, looking up into the lit windows. I picked up the phone as if it were a weapon and put it down only when he drove away. I felt my heart give way, collapse in fear, and I rushed downstairs to check the locks. I slept with the lights on.

When I came home from work the next day a moving truck was parked in my driveway. A crew carried boxes and filed in and out of my house. I shimmied by the men, my growing abdomen scraping by a stack of boxes.

"Excuse me," I said.

A man in a plaid shirt and ball cap looked up. "You the owner?" I nodded and he thrust a clipboard in my face. "Sign here."

I signed. "What is all of this? And how did you get in?"

He pointed to Sunny's name at the top of the requisition form. "He left it unlocked for us."

"He did? He doesn't even live here," I explained.

"Look lady, we just deliver the stuff. Okay. You got questions, you can call the office."

I nodded and moved out of their way, watching them stack boxes and bubble-wrapped breakables next to a growing mountain of furniture. I picked up the phone and called Sunny. He was calm when I asked him what he thought he was doing.

"It's your stuff. From the settlement."

"Yes, I know that, but how did you get into the house?"

"I don't know what you're talking about."

"They said that you let them in."

"Did they?" He was quiet for a moment. "Well, they're wrong. Maybe you left the door unlocked or something. Apparently pregnancy makes women absent-minded."

"Sunny stop it… I saw you last night. I saw you."

"Stop. You want me to stop—no, Meena, I haven't started yet. You think you can just walk away. No. Things aren't over until I say they are."

"What's that supposed to mean?"

"You figure it out," he said, and hung up.

I sat on the sofa, phone in hand, watching the men stack the rest of the boxes against the wall before leaving. The next day I had the locks changed.

3.16

Tej ran a razor blade through the packing tape, slicing the box open. She dug her hands into the Styrofoam chips, pulling out pieces of fine china. "Are you sure you want to do this?" she asked, carrying them outside to where Serena was pricing items.

"Yeah. Time to start over," I said, bending over and lifting up a box of glassware. "To let go." I hadn't opened the boxes since Sunny had had them delivered, and finally after a month of staring at the piles and stacked furniture knew I had to get rid of them, to remove him from my life a piece at a time.

Serena yelled from across the lawn like a referee calling a foul: "No lifting for you. Go sit down. We got it."

"I'm fine," I assured her and unpacked the box, adding it to the rest of my belongings that were strewn on the lawn. It felt strange to bargain the value of things, to watch the piles of designer decor fall into hands of junk collectors and treasure hunters. They held crystal up to the light, inspecting the diamond cut of the glass, and tested out the dining room chairs as if they were Goldilocks.

"How much for this?"

I recognized the voice. It was Irmila. She was wearing a paisley strapless summer dress, and flip-flops. Her hair had grown and grazed her tanned shoulders, making me wonder if she and Kal had been on vacation or had spent their summer lying on the beach. "This one? How much?" she repeated, holding up a hand-painted ceramic vase from Chile.

"Thirty-five," I said.

She perched her sunglasses on her head and squinted. "Surinder? I mean, Meena, is that you?"

"How are you, Irmila?"

"Good. Wow, look at you." She stared at my abdomen with the same amount of shock that everyone did. "I didn't realize you were so far along. When are you due?"

"Not until October."

"Wow, you still have a ways to go," she said, counting off the three months on her fingers. "A Libra or maybe a Scorpio, just like Kal."

"How is he? Kal?"

"Good, really good," she said, admiring the house. "*We're* doing well. We're thinking of buying a house soon… I forgot that you lived in this neighbourhood. Kal will be so surprised when I tell him that I bumped into you… Thirty-five, then?" she asked, reaching into her wallet.

"Tell you what, just take it."

"No, I couldn't really."

"Please."

She thanked me and tucked the vase under her arm.

Kal knocked on my front door later than evening, the same vase in his hands. He handed it to me when I opened the door. "I gave it to her," I said.

"And I am giving it back." I invited him in and he took off his coat while looking around the room. "I haven't done much decorating yet."

He turned towards me. "You've been busy. I mean, look at you." He paused and smiled. "You look great."

"You seem surprised."

"Not surprised, happy. Pregnancy suits you."

"Thanks."

We were both quiet for a moment.

"So Irmila tells me it was quite a yard sale."

I smiled at his small talk, almost surprised that we'd been reduced to it. "Yeah it went well. Whatever we didn't sell we donated to charity."

He nodded, and looked out the window, pressing his palm against it. "These are single-pane windows. You'll want to change them before the winter. I can look into it if you like."

"Thanks, but I've already hired someone to do it before the baby comes."

"The *baby*." He whispered it slowly, the word popping from his mouth in syllables. "I still can't get used to the idea."

"The idea of what?"

"You as a mother."

"Tell me about it." I laughed and motioned to him. "Come, let me show you the baby's room." The sound of our footsteps filled the space that conversation should have. I opened the door to the nursery. "Serena helped me decorate."

"It's a girl?" he asked, glancing at the stack of baby clothes on the dresser.

"Yeah. This is her at twenty weeks." I showed him the ultrasound picture, outlining her features. "Pretty amazing, isn't she?"

Kal looked right at me. "Yeah, she is amazing indeed."

I put the photo down and smiled. "It's good to see you again."

"I don't know why I haven't come around sooner. I just—I'm sorry."

I fiddled with the stack of baby clothes, unfolding and refolding the tiny pink sleeper sets. "It's okay. You have your own life and Sunny is your cousin. It's all complicated. I get it. I really do." The baby kicked. I winced and reached for the door jamb to steady myself. I rested my hand on my stomach, pressing in on her foot. Kal watched, mesmerized. "You want to feel?" He nodded and placed his hand on my stomach. "That's her head," I said, moving his hand. "And that is a foot." His hand jumped with her kick. "I swear she does somersaults in there."

He placed his palm back on my abdomen, both of us quiet as we imagined her universe in mine. His face brightened as she squirmed beneath his palm. "Wow. That's so amazing. You're lucky." He moved his hand away. "Irmila doesn't want kids."

I sat down in the rocking chair. "Maybe she'll change her mind."

"Maybe… But sometimes I wonder if we should even get married. How do I know that she's the one?"

"If you're looking for advice on love, you're probably asking the wrong person. I've managed to make quite a mess of things." I tried to laugh.

"Did you love Liam?

I shook my head and smiled. "I did… and I do."

"How do you know?"

"I don't know… With him, I mean with us… love was a lot like faith."

"So, what, you just believed?"

"Yeah, sort of."

"And that was enough?"

"It had to be."

Kal paused and looked out the window. "Meena, Liam called the other day. He asked about you."

"What did you tell him?"

"Nothing… It's not for me to tell."

I didn't say anything.

"He's living on the Sunshine Coast now." Kal reached into his pocket and handed me a piece of paper.

"What's this?" I asked, taking it from him.

"It's his phone number. I thought you might want to call him."

3.17

My contractions started in the middle of the night and by the time I called Serena my water had broken and I was delirious with fatigue, crying for my mother, desperate for something or someone to numb the rolling pain of steady contractions, the tension and pull of being split from the inside out.

Once I was admitted to the hospital, the nurses examined me, telling me not to push even if I wanted to. After a few minutes they called the doctor. The baby was breach and kicking to come into the world feet first. Serena propped me up, telling me to breathe. The nurse administered an iv drip to slow my contractions. "Is there anyone you want us to call?" she asked, a preface to the explanation of complications and "sign here" forms being thrust in my face. I motioned to Serena to get me my purse and handed the nurse Liam's phone number.

By the time I was allowed to push, I was only half alert, pain taking my mind to other places, pulling me back, tossing me away. Moments were like rooms, long and narrow, something to get lost in, something to run out of. I dreamed with my eyes open.

It was two states of physicality, opposing forces so strong that even inside the pain there was a fervour and an ecstasy where my thoughts deferred to the design of my body and being. Serena held my hand, said things—reassuring things that, once said, evaporated into my screams of being broken and torn.

Three hours later, Leena was turned and tugged from me. My body relaxed and spasmed in the shock of afterbirth. The intense cold trauma of being two and then one settled on my skin like a thousand needles. I held her for a moment, felt her against my breast, fists batting at the air. I couldn't hear her screams. The moment was outside of sound. I fought joyful fatigue. My eyelids were weighted. My body, now sewn, felt full of stones. I slept in a flood of night.

When I woke it was to the soft shapes of dawn, to the sound of Liam's voice. He was holding Leena in his arms, staring out the window. "It's okay. I've got you. You're fine. You're fine."

3.18

L iam spent most days and some nights at the house until some nights became every night and his staying was no longer a question. When he moved in, he dropped his suitcases at the door, his definitive arrival our homecoming, Leena's birth an impetus for everything. He unpacked quickly, hanging his clothes in the closet, piling his books on the nightstand, storing his camera equipment in the hall closet, and when he was done he sat down next to me and looked around the living room, his eyes acclimatizing.

"Are you sure this is what you want?" I asked.

He looked at Leena asleep in my arms and put his arm around my shoulder and pulled us both into his quiet embrace, then kissed the top of my head. "Yeah, this is all I want."

That same night Liam stood over the crib watching the rise and fall of Leena's chest, his finger tracing the outline of her rosebud lips, listening to her soft breath and deep sighs, all the while waiting for her to stir, waiting for an excuse to pick her up and hold her.

When she stirred, he brought her into bed, snuggling her between our warm bodies, and we stayed like that for weeks, existing around her in a pattern of feeding, sleeping and diaper-changing.

When we woke up, the past seemed to recede and for the first time we made plans that were only partly about ourselves.

"We could tear down this wall. Open up the space." Liam took out a measuring tape. "What do you think?" I didn't answer. "And out here," he continued, opening the patio doors, "we can build Leena a playhouse, plant roses, maybe some honeysuckle. I already talked to Kal about it."

I folded my arms across my chest. "Did you now?"

"And up here… " he was running up to the third-floor attic, "would be your writing studio. You could put the desk here, by the window," he said, measuring the space. "It'll be perfect."

"Liam, I don't know."

"Just picture it… just try and see it."

"I am trying. I just don't see the need for it. I don't even write much anymore."

"Meena, I remember your stack of journals. You write."

"Keeping a journal is not the same as writing."

"Is that what you think or is that what your mom told you?"

"Don't bring my mother into this." Liam followed me down the stairs. "You've never even met her. What do you know about me or my mother?"

Liam stood behind me at the patio doors where only a few minutes ago we'd been making plans, talking about the future as if the past were another place far from this tree-lined street, far from this house, far from our family. "Look, I didn't mean it like that." He put both his arms around me. "I just want you to have all the things that you always wanted. That's all."

"I know. I guess I just miss her… I miss talking to her. Sometimes I call her just so I can hear her pick up, just so I can hear her say hello… and then I look at Leena, how beautiful and perfect she is, and wonder why my mom doesn't want to know her own grandchild. I hate her for that… but I still miss her."

"She's your mom. Of course you miss her. I still miss my mother and she left when I was six." He went on to tell me that after high school he'd found her address in his father's things and hitched a ride to Saskatoon. When he'd arrived at her house, she was in the backyard, pinning a load of laundry to dry. He'd watched her for a while, not saying anything, mesmerized by the everydayness of the moment—the sheets billowing, the dust gathering, the sunlight in her eyes. "When she saw me she didn't say anything but my name. And even then it was like a question, her voice raised on the end... We went inside, she made coffee and I sat at the kitchen table staring at the fridge covered in some other kids' artwork... You know, I'd had all these questions for her, about why she left, but for whatever reason I couldn't ask them."

"You didn't ask her anything?"

"No. It didn't seem to matter anymore... When I left she gave me a hug and told me that she thought about me every day."

"Have you talked to her since?"

"No. I don't see the point."

"The point is she's your mother."

"But she didn't want to be my mother. That's why she left. She didn't have to tell me for me to understand it... I could tell by the way she looked at me, the relief in her eyes when I said I was just passing through."

"Well, maybe she's changed."

"People don't change—not really. Sometimes you just have to make it easy for them and let them go."

I nodded, though it didn't seem easy at all. I couldn't let go the way he could, because it wasn't what I'd been taught, because no matter what my mother told me, no matter how harshly she spoke to me or did not speak to me, I knew that she hadn't let me go, not really. When Harj left home, she could have done what other parents might have done, and removed every bit of her daughter, cutting Harj out of family pictures, burning her clothes and books until nothing was left but the haunting of a smouldering pyre. But she hadn't done this to Harj, and from what Serena had told me, I knew that she hadn't done this to me either. My winter coat was still in the closet, my worn paperbacks still lay on the bedside table, and my pictures still rested on the mantel.

All of us—Harj, my father and I—remained with my mother like ghosts, our photo images slowly bleached by the sun, fading away until we became stories. And though they too were fading from my day-to-day life, their voices were still tucked into the corners of my mind, where regrets play on the present and sharpen tongues into bitter daggers that bite everything and taste nothing. My family's voices, my doubt, their hopes, my insecurity, our dreams all returned half-dead, mummified into new dread, until some days I didn't want to get out of bed and I nudged Liam to answer Leena's cries.

Liam left me to sleep, telling me that he understood what I was going through. He'd read countless baby books, and had become an expert on both infant brain development and post-pregnancy hormonal imbalances. When I'd get weepy and sad, he'd bring me tea in bed. "Probably just a touch of the baby blues. You'll be fine."

Now as I lay in bed, listening to him in the other room playing with Leena—blowing raspberries on her belly, anticipating the sound of her short squeal—I wondered how he understood so much when I didn't.

I got out of bed and joined them in the living room, which was strewn with rattles, burp cloths and Liam's photography paraphernalia. I picked up one of his cameras, lay down on the floor next to him and Leena, and held the camera an arm's length above us, taking a series of self-portraits that Liam would later frame and hang throughout the house.

3.19

The first snowfall held the city in its breath, casting a tinsel chill across the sky, a silvery glaze on windows and a rosy glow on children's cheeks. The streets were lined with wreaths, the street corners dressed in charitable causes and the shop windows adorned with nostalgic scenes of foil-wrapped Christmas gifts beneath perfectly trimmed trees. As I walked down Robson Street, past all the windows filled with packaged hopes, I knew that mine would go unopened and wondered what my mother would say when Serena gave her the gifts I sent, what she would make of the picture of Leena.

I meandered in and out of shops, buying a few more things even though I'd already finished my Christmas shopping. Both Liam and I had been extravagant, especially with Leena. The hall closet was already crammed with gifts for her and every time Liam brought home another, trying to sneak it in, the others would tumble out onto the floor.

"She's too young to even remember this," I'd told him when we decorated the elaborate tree.

He'd smiled, that smile that always made me feel two steps behind, and said, "But *we* will."

This was what I thought as I lined up to pay for another rattle to stuff into her stocking. Around me, shoppers pulled out their wallets and the cashiers conversed with one another about their own Christmas plans as they counted back change. "You're so lucky you're off early, Harj," one cashier said to another. I dropped the rattle when I saw her, and as I bent over to pick it up she walked by me, the scent of her Lily of the Valley perfume lingering. I stared at the front door that she'd just walked out of and left my purchase behind to hurry after her—in and out of stores, across streets, observing her from a safe distance until she was about to enter the train station and I thought I'd lose her. I called out.

She turned, squinting at me as if I were out of focus. "Meena?"

We didn't hug. We stumbled in our own surprise, grasping at the familiar in each other although we were so obviously unfamiliar—listing the details of our lives over the din of commuters, every other word muted by passing traffic and the street performer who played classical violin for pennies. Every time I looked at her, really looked at her, she lowered her eyes and the rush of the oncoming cars swept her hair across her face like strands of cobwebs. She wasn't as I had remembered her—still tall, but now somehow stretched, as if all of her features had been pulled up; her once-chiselled face now seemed edgy, her cheeks like cliffs and her eyes like caverns.

"Do you have time for coffee?" I asked.

She looked down the street, a little unsure, before saying, "Sure... I know a place close by."

We sat down by the window, our table pushed close against the next one, where a couple sat talking on their cellphones, shopping bags crowded around their feet.

"Don't you hate that," Harj said, without waiting for a response. Her questions were always statements, leading you into ways of being and thoughts that weren't necessarily your own. "I hate it when people talk on their phones instead of talking to each other." She said it just loud enough that the couple heard and inched their chairs away from ours. "So, how's Mom?" She asked it in a matter-of-fact way that was almost cutting.

I unbuttoned my jacket. "She's fine. I don't see her much since... " I paused and Harj waited, gesturing for me to continue, hurrying me along, nodding in an I've-heard-it-all big sister manner as I explained what had happened.

"So she wrote you off too."

"No. It's not like that. She didn't write me off, and she didn't write you off either. She just needs time."

"Well, kiddo, I hate to break it to you but I haven't talked to her for over fifteen years. That's a lot of time." She took a sip of her coffee, and her cup banged against the saucer when she put it down.

"You could call."

"She didn't want to hear from me just like she doesn't want to hear from you."

"That's not true." I thought of Leena and how nothing could ever keep me from my daughter. My mother always said that one day I'd understand and I wondered if I was finally beginning to. "We're her daughters. We're all she has."

"Well, good thing she still has four more she can talk to." Harj leaned her face against her cupped palm and stared out the window. "Remember when we were little we used to fog up the bathroom mirror and draw all over it? You only drew love hearts and happy faces."

"And you wrote swear words."

She laughed at the recollection. "It wasn't all bad."

"No, it wasn't... You know, we all missed you. After you left. I'm sure that if you called now..."

She shook her head no, tossing the idea away, and we fell into silence, allowing other people's conversations to filter into ours, picking up awkward threads about movies, Christmas plans and books, small talk filling up space, taking up time.

"So..." She paused, straining for something. "You mentioned you were writing. What is it? A tell-all book?"

"Hardly... there's not much to tell."

"Who are you kidding?"

I smiled. "Apparently no one... I guess I just feel kind of funny writing about family... That's probably why my work is all over the place... It's all pretty raw and kind of scary."

"Why scary?"

"Mostly the idea of anyone reading it."

She sipped her coffee. "Truth is a scary thing."

"You sound just like Liam."

"He must be a pretty smart guy then."

"Yeah... he's been really encouraging. We've even talked about my going back to school after maternity leave."

"That's great. You were always a good writer. I remember your diaries were very detailed."

I sat stunned for a moment. "You read them?"

She laughed again. "Only the good parts... but seriously, I'm really glad you have someone to support you. Lord knows we didn't grow up with that."

"Mom did her best."

"We all do," she conceded.

Later, when we headed back to the train station, I wondered if I would be like her, looking in on the past as if it belonged to someone else. When she answered all my questions with vague answers, I knew she was content to end our conversation, leave everything unsaid and undone. Somehow I understood this self-imposed exile that kept us all in a loose orbit of one another, the controlled distance a delusion of freedom. We stood on the platform together, watching people rush back and forth in steady determination. When our trains pulled in on the opposing tracks, we hugged briefly, both of us heading in different directions.

3.20

I was getting dressed, tying my sari for the third time, trying to get the folds even, when Liam came in. He stood in the doorway, tapping his watch. "The babysitter's here."

"I just can't get it straight," I said, tucking the pin through the folds. "Maybe we should just forget it. I don't want to go anyways." I flopped down on the bed.

"We already missed the wedding. We can't miss the reception as well." Liam picked up the pile of fabric on the floor, sat down on the edge of the bed, and handed the material to me. "They're our friends."

I sat up. "Irmila is *not* my friend."

"Well, *Kal is*. He's always been there for you and besides if it wasn't for him we might not even be together right now. So hurry up and get dressed."

I didn't move.

"Come on, Meena. We've been through this already."

I still didn't move. "I just think our going is a bad idea."

"Why? Is this still about Sunny?"

I nodded. I hadn't seen him since Leena's birth, though at times when the phone rang late at night and no one was on the other end I was sure it was him. Once when Liam and I had come back from taking Leena for an evening walk, I thought I saw his car turning off our street, but Liam was sure I was imagining things.

"It'll be fine. You said it yourself. It's a big wedding. We'll be seated at different ends of the banquet hall and we probably won't even see him."

I raised my eyebrows, still not convinced. "Tell you what, let's just go and see how it is. If you feel uncomfortable, we'll leave."

"Ohhhh-kay." I got up reluctantly.

"It's just weird," I said. "All those people... I haven't seen most of them since I left. I can only imagine what they'll think when they see us."

"They'll think what they want to think. People do."

I nodded, and fiddled with the sari pleats obsessively. "I suppose."

"It'll be fine. Now hurry—we'll be late."

I grabbed his wrist and checked the time. "No we won't. It's Indian standard time: everyone will be late."

He turned me around and pulled me closer. "Well then, in *that* case," he said, wedging his fingers at my waist, pulling at the pleats. I smacked his hand away. "We don't have time. I still have to do my makeup and put on my jewellery." I reached for an armload of red-and-white bracelets. "Not to mention I haven't told you about the party rules."

"What rules?"

"Well, they're unwritten rules about propriety. Indian people, married or not, do not show any public affection."

Puzzled, Liam ran his hands along his perfectly stubbled jawline. "But love is the plot line of every Bollywood movie."

"Yes, but no one actually kisses in a Bollywood movie. They may sing and dance about love, but there is always a cleverly placed tree or a fuzzy camera shot to obscure any moment where a kiss should be... Anyways, back to the list:

"No touching
No hand holding
No hugs
No kissing
No eye contact
No visible affection

No flirting

No talking to women, and

No allusion to the fact that we are more than friends."

"So I should pretend that I'm your brother?"

"Yeah, kind of. Oh, and you have to get my drinks for me because women aren't supposed to drink."

"Okay. So I'm to act like your brother and your bartender?"

"Yeah, pretty much."

"Will your mother be there?" he asked.

I nodded.

"And does she know that I'm coming with you?"

I nodded again.

"Is she okay with it?"

I paused. "She'll have to be."

On the way there he asked me to teach him a few words of Punjabi so he could speak to my mother, and by the time we got there he'd mastered some phrases.

"Sat Sri Akal." Liam folded his hands and knelt down to touch my mother's feet just as he'd seen people do in Hindi movies. She grabbed his shoulder to stop him from the embarrassment and dismissed him with a hasty "Hello."

We sat at a table at the back of the reception hall, close to the balcony doors above the entrance—the congregation place for all the fringe Indians, including the divorced and interracially married couples.

"So this is what you meant?" Liam said as an auntie walked by, her whiplash stare so obvious that it seemed to crane every neck our way. Though we hadn't tried to draw attention to ourselves, it seemed that everyone knew we were there and yet pretended that we weren't, all of them walking around us, making a point of not talking to us.

After dinner Liam and I congratulated Irmila and Kal, who were receiving their guests in a long line. Irmila hugged and kissed everyone without managing to touch anyone. When it came time to embrace me, she leaned in, her lips poised but only hovering over my cheek. Kal hugged me tight, whispering in my ear that he was so glad we'd come. It was enough to have made the evening worthwhile.

As we made our way back to the table, I saw Sunny sitting with his parents. His father saw me looking and smiled in that ironic way he always did. The upturn of his mouth and the slight shrug of his narrow shoulders suggesting he was somehow responsible for life's small agonies simply because he understood them, accepted them.

"I need a drink. You want one?" Liam asked after we were seated. "That him?" he said, gesturing towards Sunny, who was now staring back at us.

"Maybe we should go now."

Liam glanced at Sunny. "Don't let him intimidate you Meena. We don't need to leave because of him."

I nodded, and he squeezed my hand before getting up to go the bar. I watched him walk through the crowd and wait in the drunken lineup of middle-aged men and thought how out of place he looked. When he got to the front of the line, Sunny walked over and stood in front of him. I saw the exchange, the way a person witnesses an accident waiting to happen. There were words. Words that I could only read in the faces of those around them. Liam took his drinks from the bartender and turned back towards Sunny and said something. Sunny puffed up and made wide-armed gestures that seemed to say, *You want a piece of me?* Liam walked back to the table.

"What an asshole," he said, taking his seat. "I can't believe you were married to him."

"What did he say?"

"Nothing. It doesn't matter. Forget it," he said, downing his drink and then mine.

By the time the bhangra music started, Liam had consumed enough rum and Cokes to think that he was Hrithik Roshan.

"Come on, Meena," he said, getting up and reaching for my hand.

I crossed both of my hands over my chest and flatly refused. "I don't bhangra."

"Come on, stop being such a gora… All you have to do is walk in a circle, screw in a light bulb and open a door." He mimicked the motion with his hands and attempted to pull me onto the dance floor.

"Stop it, everyone is staring at us." I whispered it so harshly that he let go of my wrist and stepped back as if I had struck him. I reached for his hand. "I'm sorry. I just think we should go home now." I saw Sunny still watching us from a marked distance and the way he looked at us made me feel like he'd been tracking us since we'd arrived. "Please, let's go," I suggested. I was pulling Liam towards the nearest balcony exit when I saw Sunny closing in on us with a long and steady stride.

"Meena! Meena, aren't you going to introduce us properly?" Sunny asked. He grabbed my arm as we went through the doorway. I smelled the alcohol on his breath and saw it in his eyes in the way he struggled to focus.

Liam shoved him away. "Don't touch her."

"She's still my wife." Sunny shoved back.

"Not for long." Liam leaned in to Sunny's face.

Sunny stepped back, stiffened his lip and lifted his chin. "Oh, a fucking tough guy, huh?"

"Come on Liam, let's go." A crowd was beginning to form around us and I knew it would just be a minute before everyone inside the hall heard.

"For fuck's sakes, Meena, did you really need to bring him here? Are you trying to make a fool of me?"

"Meena doesn't need to *make* you look like a fool—you manage to do that on your own." Liam curled his hand into a fist.

"Come on, let's just go. This isn't the place. Think of Irmila and Kal," I urged, trying to pull him back from the scene that had formed around us. We turned and started to head towards the narrow staircase that led down from the other end of the balcony, but Sunny blocked our way.

"Well, I hope you enjoy her more than I did." Sunny laughed, looking to his friends for approval. "I guess some guys like leftovers."

Liam stopped, turned abruptly, and punched Sunny in the face. "The only leftovers are what I leave of you, you piece of shit."

Sunny teetered, stumbling back a few feet, hitting the balcony railing before straightening up. He smiled as he cracked his neck to each side, then lunged at Liam with a fisted grip. The crowd inhaled and stepped back as if they were one person, gasping as the two struggled. Liam had Sunny in a chokehold and Sunny was sputtering, his face red, veins protruding.

"Sunny, Liam, stop this. Stop this right now!" I yelled.

Young men from inside the hall rushed outside to see what was happening, their shouts alerting others to come and see. I pleaded for Sunny and Liam to stop.

"Meena, get back." Liam waved me aside with his free hand. Sunny elbowed Liam in the stomach and turned around, swinging blows, punching him repeatedly until Kal came rushing out, pulled him off and dragged him back through crowd, telling him to calm down.

"Okay, show's over. Everyone go back inside. Everything's over," Kal said, dispersing the crowd. "Jesus, Sunny, get it together. This is my wedding."

"Fuck that." Sunny spat blood in Liam's general direction. "Fuck them."

Liam was doubled over in pain, his hands on his ribs. He stood up slowly, wiping his bloody mouth on his sleeve. I put his arm over my shoulder and helped him up, balancing his weight on one side until he could stand on his own.

"You better watch your back," Sunny hollered. "If I ever see you again I'll fucking kill you."

"Save it, you motherfucking piece of shit."

Sunny pushed Kal out of the way. "What did you say?"

"You heard what I said."

Sunny barrelled into Liam's chest, pile-driving him against the balcony, pushing him over the edge. I leaned over the railing, screaming his name as he hit the ground like a bird falling out of the sky.

3.21

I paced the floors of the peach hospital corridors before retreating to the waiting room, where the pasty walls whispered all the bad news that had been delivered there. I held my head in my hands, trying for a prayer. Kal and Irmila were huddled by the reception desk. Irmila's eyes were red and tear stains cut down her face, drawing fault lines through her makeup, cracking her veneer. "I just can't believe it," she kept saying. "How could this happen?" When Kal put his arms around her I wanted to close my eyes in the envy of such an embrace—the little words and small assurances that made her stop crying momentarily. "It'll be fine," he whispered in her ear, the same way Liam had always told me, the same way I'd told him when he'd stuttered on my name, his throat clotted by blood. "Stay with me," I'd said. "You'll be fine." I'd said it over and over, convincing myself that the distance in his eyes was not an end.

I curled into the pay-phone booth and called the babysitter, crumpling my sobs between twisted tissues and false reassurances. I crossed my arms over my chest, pressing my forearms against my engorged breasts to stop the letdown of milk that tingled at the mention of Leena's name. The nurses at the nearby station offered me downturned smiles when they heard me ask about the baby, when they saw the bloodstains on my sari. If this was the beginning of sympathy, I thought it too soon and looked away.

The sun still hadn't set. It lingered on the edge of the horizon, burning the last of that spring day into a thin line of red until finally it slipped into shadow and the hospital grew quiet and reflected itself back in the large windows. I pressed my palm against the glass, watching everything behind me as if it were in front of me. Even the clock on the wall reflected time backwards. How many hours had it been? How long had we been here? I tried to add it up, but could only manage subtraction. I could only calculate the loss. Irmila and Kal were sitting in the 1980s' waiting-room chairs, resting their heads against each other's, staring at the paintings on the wall—paintings of fruit and flowers. Mostly still life. Like my face in front of me.

I turned around when I saw Serena had come in with my mother.

"What are you doing here?"

"Meena," was all she could say. Her face was small and sad, her silence trembling.

"What? What do you want?"

Kal stood up. "I asked them to come... You can't go through this alone."

"Go through what alone? Just what do you think I'm going through?"

My mother reached out her hand and I knocked it away. She grabbed my hand and held it, locked in hers. Part of me wanted to tell her to go, but my rage turned in on itself and I collapsed, leaning into her arms, sobbing insults and injustices until she held me so tight that words could not escape and my mouth hung open in woe.

We sat in a row, all of us staring at the clock, observing time. Every second and minute measured, counted and added into a prayer or wishful thought of what would come after this moment and then the next. "Time passes slowly when it is all that you have and all that you wish for," my mother said, patting my hand in hers.

Someone was calling my name. Everyone stood up. It was the attending physician. He spoke in muted tones. His eyes were small and clinical. Tired. The kind of tired that makes you think only of home, of your bed, of the people you love, the tired that unchecked makes you weep like a lovesick fool, the tired of crying eyes and worn-out hearts, the tired of the destitute, the tired of standing outside in the rain without an umbrella waiting for a bus, the tired of mothers with too many children and too many mouths to feed, the tired of hopelessness, the tired of bad news, so much bad news.

I closed my eyes. The doctor continued to speak, more technically now. I didn't need the details. I couldn't hear his words beyond the loss. I couldn't hear anything but Liam's voice, his whispers breaking inside me like waves of grief, receding to the quietest parts of my mind. Everything fell away from me.

The doctor motioned to a young nurse.

I followed her down a long, sterile hallway towards a double set of steel doors. She kept looking back at me, making sure I was still there, the painful proof that I could exist without him.

The doors opened and closed me in.

Everything was quiet now.

Liam was lying on a metal gurney in the middle of the room with the remnants of medical heroics around him. As I walked towards him, I lifted my hand to my mouth, choking back mournful cries, muffling the sound that only the dead can hear—the sound of wind before it wakes you.

Kal came into the room after me.

"Meena."

I turned around, unable to speak. My mouth was full of screams, yet clamped by terror. Kal reached for me and I pushed him away, draping myself over Liam's chest. I shuddered, calling his name, sobbing until there was nothing but the vibration beneath grief—a deadened sound like fists against ice.

3.22

Clouds drifted across the morning sky like shapeless spectres. I pulled the sheers across the window like a shroud, as if I could dampen the haunting, but it lingered in the stillness of the house and in the inanimate sounds of the ticking clock, the creaking floorboards, the leaky faucet that Liam had meant to fix.

The phone rang, splitting the silence into two realities—one for the living and one for the dead. Kal answered, speaking in a low tone: "Not so good... she cried all night. I think she may be asleep now... I'm not sure... I think I'll stay. No, I know that... Can you even hear yourself... You're worried about the honeymoon when Liam was just killed..."

As I lay on Liam's side of the bed, listening to Kal argue with Irmila in frustrated whispers, the phrase "Liam was just killed" wounded me. I whispered it like a non-believer, wanting to hide in denial, but everything spoke to his absence—even Leena. She had cried out in the middle of the night and when I rushed to the nursery and peered into her crib, I was surprised to find her in a deep slumber. I remembered my mother telling Serena not to worry that A.J. often cried in his sleep. She believed that when babies slept they returned to God, where they assimilated all their past lives and purposes to this one. That they cried when God returned them to our care. I ran my fingers through Leena's black ringlets and wondered what she dreamed of and if she saw her father there. I thought of all the things she would miss. She was only six months old. She wouldn't even have the pleasure of remembering him.

I got out of bed and walked into our ensuite. Liam's razor was by the sink, his towel and clothes still on the floor. I'd always nagged him to clean up after himself, but now was glad that he hadn't. I didn't want to forget that morning. I'd showered and was standing in front of the mirror looking at how my body had changed. As I turned, I saw Liam leaning up against the door. I didn't like him seeing me in my slackened skin, and pulled my robe in front of me. He walked up behind and put his arms around me and stared at our mirrored image, said that he too was amazed how one life could change him so much.

A shadow fell across the mirror and like a hopeful fool, I spun around, uttering Liam's name. I turned back, trying to hide my disappointment from Kal. "Meena, the police called. They need a statement." I wondered what more I could tell them that I hadn't the night before. I didn't want to talk to them again and see them scribble my loss in a few notations on a spiral pad that they would flip shut and hardly remember but that I would never forget.

"Not now," I said. Short words were all I could manage; small meanings contained things, hid the quake in my voice. I wondered what to say in the wake of death. It was like trying to speak a language that had no words. "I need to check on Leena," I said, and walked across the hall to the nursery. She was awake, staring at the sunspots on the ceiling, batting her fists and legs as if she were trying to reach them. She smiled when she saw me. I picked her up, and sat down in the rocking chair, holding her against my chest, my hand cradling her head just as I'd done when I came back from the hospital. I sat there for hours, rocking back and forth, lingering in the false sense of momentum, allowing the motion to console us both.

My mother came in and offered to take her from me so I could rest but I shook my head, unwilling to put her down even when Serena came in and sat down next to me. "The arrangements..." she began. I raised my eyebrows, disinterested in this process that was taking Liam from me in fractured steps. "The hospital..." She stopped when she realized that I didn't want to talk.

When the woman at the hospital had handed me his personal effects in a brown paper bag, I'd stared at her in disbelief, wondering how there could be so little left. His clothes, his wallet, his watch. I wanted to yell at her, to throw the bag at her, but instead I clutched it to my chest like it was everything.

"I've made some calls," Serena said. I nodded, biting down on my lip, grateful that I would be spared such things. But my own thoughts were of little comfort—they flattened and stretched out like time, like eternal questions that began and ended with *Why?*

3.23

The house was full of whispers. Fragile movements and gentle footsteps gathered like dust in corners. Grief filled the rooms like grey morning light. It was palpable.

I had no real sense of how much time had passed. Time had a different set of rules for the dead and grieving: every second was an emptiness burrowing in my marrow, and every hour left me more fragile than the previous one.

Days and nights passed in this hazy state of denial and understanding, broken only by the small consolations of bouqueted apologies, their constancy conveying multiplying regrets, their acrid smell only contributing to my grief. I'd pull at the petals, plucking them off one by one, letting them fall to the ground for Leena's amusement.

"Such beautiful flowers... and you've ruined them," my mother said as she swept up the remains. "Why? For what purpose?"

I shook my head, unable to answer.

"You should get dressed. People will be coming over soon."

"What people?"

"Serena, her mother-in-law, a few others," she said as she tossed the petals into the garbage can.

My sisters, even Harj, had come over every other day, all of them bound to me by the hierarchy of events that bring Indian people together—the birth of sons; the marriage of sons; and death, any death. Death, in its infinite and final design, healed and humbled the living. Sometimes I talked to them and at other times I let my mother tell them how I was. She took some pride in recounting my details. As if knowing that I woke at three in the morning, and wept until five, that I could not eat solids without throwing up made her the mother who had not abandoned me. As if knowing these things absolved her. She'd all but moved in, insisting on staying in the guest room. "It's not good to be alone," she'd said. When I reminded her that she was alone, she said it wasn't the same though she couldn't articulate how it was different.

When people came over to pay their respects, my mother made tea and accepted the apologies I stumbled over. "Sorry." Sometimes, to their discomfort, I repeated their apology over and over until it distanced me from them and all I could hear was my own apology. It was my fault that Liam was dead. If I had never married Sunny, Liam would never have been dead. If I had never agreed to go the party, Liam would never have been dead. If I hadn't had an affair with him, he wouldn't be dead. I spent hours in those regrets, hoarding them and nesting them into some half-life, everyone looking at me with the gravity reserved for wounded animals and the terminally ill.

That afternoon Kishor Auntie and Serena's mother-in-law came over to pay their respects. They came out of obligation to my mother, acting like bereaved Bollywood heroines, searching private sorrows in order to seem sufficiently upset by my loss. They sat down, drank their tea and ate their biscuits, talking of my life as though I weren't in the room. When I got up to leave, my mother reached for my hand, gently urged me to sit down and fixed the white chunni that had slipped from my head. Kishor Auntie continued her commiserations: "And Sunny? Who would have thought that he... that this kind of thing would happen?"

I stood up and walked away, not wanting to hear any more about what she'd read in the papers, what she'd heard at the temple about the charges against Sunny. "Manslaughter." Just the sound of the word made me want to vomit.

"Meena!" my mother commanded

"No, Mom. I'm not you." I looked around at my sisters, who were moving in and out of the room like ghosts, tiptoeing around the memories of the dead—in the same way we'd tiptoed around the memories of my father, in the same way we'd built our lives around my mother's grief.

"I can't do this. I don't want to be good at this… and why are you even here? You didn't even know him," I said to Kishor Auntie. "Neither of you did. You should both be ashamed."

As I walked out, I heard my mother apologize for me, saying that I wasn't myself. I wondered if I'd ever been myself.

"Stop apologizing for me," I yelled back at her. "All you ever do is apologize for us. When are you going to see that we never did anything wrong? None of us." I said it to hurt her, to push my pain away, and she took it, carrying my burdens, holding me up through his passing.

"His passing." Someone had said it on the phone the other day, and though I couldn't remember who, I couldn't help remembering the phrase every morning when I reached for Liam's watch on the nightstand, almost forgetting that it no longer kept time. He'd been wearing it when he fell, and though the face was cracked and the metal links were mangled, the second hand still moved—stuttering back and forth, commanding time in a new sequence. Each second was only an insignificant pass amounting to nothing.

I held it to my ear, trying to establish that rhythm, attempting to adapt to the falsetto.

3.24

The following day I went to the crematorium alone. Liam hadn't believed in funerals and in a way I was glad—I didn't want anyone else to see our ending. But as I stood by Liam's side in the surreal periphery of parting, I wondered if the reason my mother had kept pictures of my father in his casket was because they gave her some proof of an ending, so that beginning again was not a betrayal. There I stood, unable to let Liam go, wondering why people said good-bye like this when only silence answered back. He didn't seem real. None of it seemed real, and I kept closing my eyes and opening them, hoping that it wasn't, wishing it wasn't so.

When the funeral director told me that it was time, I panicked and wondered if I should go with him. I'd been to many a service where the loved ones accompanied the body to the furnace, where they wrapped their grief around the heat that converted flesh and bone to cinders, yet I knew I couldn't do it and I waited in the silence of the room, watching the silver-tipped dust float in and out of the light and nestle into the cracks of picture frames and burnished wood.

After an hour the funeral director returned to tell me that the "process"—that's what he kept calling it—would take several hours, and suggested I return another day to collect the remains.

"The remains," I repeated.

When I didn't move, he gently reminded me of the consultation we'd had in which he'd given me brochures detailing the *process*.

"Of course," I said, even though I hadn't read his brochures. I didn't want the cruel details, not then and not now.

"Have you given any thought to the columbarium?" He asked as I got up.

"No."

"Well, perhaps it might still be an option you may like to consider. Many families take comfort in having a place where they can visit their loved ones."

"Perhaps," I said, though the idea of interning his ashes behind a marble plaque in a wall with hundreds of other souls horrified me. I couldn't leave him there. It wasn't what he would have wanted.

I left the chapel and walked slowly towards my car, and would have been oblivious to the rain if not for the scent of coaxed earth. I paused to watch a funeral procession make its way out of an adjacent chapel in huddled groups. Black umbrellas opened all at once, blooming in the rain. I watched them move along the cobblestone path, across the green lawn, to the nearby cemetery, and I followed them, to stand on the outskirts. A little girl fidgeted, turning her head in towards her mother's body—an almost in utero embrace.

"Earth to earth, ashes to ashes, dust to dust." The pastor's voice was calm and open. The silence that hung between his words was like the loss itself, present but inaudible. He didn't eulogize, he didn't proselytize: he simply bore witness like we all did. These people, whoever they were, were dignified and austere in their grief and I took their strength as my own, mourned their loss as my own.

After the service, when all the guests had left, I remained behind, standing in the rain, looking at the gaping hole in the ground as if it were an open sore, and repeated the only prayer I'd ever learned:

Ik Onkar
Satnam
Karta purukh
Nirbhau
Nirvair
Akal moorat
Ajuni saibhang
Gurparshad
Jap.

FOUR FOR TOMORROW

4.1

The seasons are changing in me, around me—life has become a perpetual solstice. The cold of it drives me to my bed for an afternoon nap. I always get sick when the seasons change. Harj used to say that it was my body revolting against time, making a desperate attempt to slow it or stall it somehow. She said I was never ready to let go. As a child I mourned the slack of a tulip stalk, sobbed for bleeding roses, lamented the crackle of autumn, and for winter I had no words. I took to my bed with a spring chill, a summer cold, an autumn flu or a winter's worry, hibernating under the billowy warmth of the blanket that my mother had stuffed with cotton batting. I remember how she drew the needle in and out of the quilt; she had a rhythm. Everything does, and when I find mine I can venture out again. I wonder when that will be, if that will be. I feel I've been under for as long as Liam has been gone.

Leena climbs up on my bed. "Mama, can you tie my cape?"

I sit up to take the white pillowcase she is holding. "Playing Hansel and Gretel again?" I ask, knotting the ends. She nods as I tie the makeshift cloak around her shoulders. She read "Hansel and Gretel" last week, and the day after she announced that she was much smarter than Gretel and would have scattered rosebuds or blossoms on the path—something that was brightly coloured yet bitter to eat. "All you need now is a basket," I say, getting out of bed. "Let's get one from the kitchen."

I hand her the basket, lead her into the garden and watch her scatter the petals along the ground. Such a sweet way back to a mother who hides her tears in smiles. I try to keep my grief hidden from her, but I know she sees it, just as I saw it in my mother's eyes—a thin veil of ice over water, a tipping of elements that held her in balance.

I pick up the clipping shears from where I dropped them yesterday and attempt to resume clipping the rose bushes. Under Kal's short tutelage Liam became a novice gardener and was learning to trim the roses so they would twine into the lattice fence. I hated gardening, and every time Liam asked me if I wanted to join him, I asked him why he bothered with something so anticlimactic. So much effort for such a short bloom. "The seasons are a metaphor for life. Each stage falling into the next with no thought of an end," he answered.

"With no thought of an end," I mutter as the blooms fall to my feet. I kneel down and sift through the soil and clutch the heart-shaped petals in my hand and wonder about this seasonality, the succession of days building into life. I wonder if we survive the cycles of life or whether we just surrender into each with our regrets tucked into something new. I clench my fist like a choking memory, the petals stain my hands and the sugary smell of spring lingers even after I try to wash it away.

"Mama, come find me!" Leena yells from the far corner of the garden.

"Coming!" I follow the trail that she's left; her way back is my way forward. I jump up onto the tree-house ladder's lowest rung and grab Leena's spindly ankle. "Nibble nibble... who is nibbling at my house?" I say, laughing as she pulls her legs up in a giggle fit.

"No fair, I wasn't ready yet!" She tosses her unruly locks from her face, jumps down from the ladder and scatters the last of her blossoms on the ground. My mother tells me that Leena looks like me, except for her eyes. His eyes. Liam's eyes. She says his name now.

Leena drops her empty basket, picks up one of the dead canes and swats the air with it. "Mama, when is Uncle Kal coming to pick me up? I want to play pirates!"

"Did someone say pirates?" Kal asks from the deck, before running down the stairs. Leena laughs as he chases her around the garden with his hand hooked in his shirt like a claw. He lifts her up and shakes her upside down until a few pennies rattle out of her pockets. "Ah, treasure," he says, turning her upright again. Dizzy now, she staggers like a drunken sailor, picking up her loot.

Kal walks over and kisses me on the cheek, takes the shears and shows me how it should be done. "Did you finish that writing assignment?"

"No, I wasn't in the mood."

"Well, maybe while we're gone. I thought I'd take Leena to see that new Disney movie she's been on about."

As we talk, Leena tugs at Kal's shirt and waits as patiently as any four-year-old can before yelling that it's time to go. I wave from the door, blowing kisses, reminding them to have fun and to be back before bedtime.

The house is too quiet without her. I turn on the lights in the kitchen, the television set in the living room and the stereo in my bedroom, hoping that some task will be illuminated in these acts. I open the closet door; Liam's clothes are all lined up in a row. They don't smell like him anymore and I wonder if it's time to give them away. My therapist suggested I do this years ago as part of the healing process, but every time I threw something away or packed up a box for charity I felt I'd lost him all over again and ended up rummaging through thrift-store bins until I had bought everything back. I run my hands along the collar of one of his favourite shirts and try to imagine someone else wearing it. The idea fills me with dread and I shut the closet door.

It is six o'clock.

I sit at my desk and try to write. No words come.

I sort through a stack of books and stare at the draft of the memoir that I wrote before he died. "You're almost there," he'd said as he read the pages, dropping them in a pile as he went. I wanted to correct him and say "We're almost there," but never did.

It is seven o'clock

I call my mother. She is reading the flyers. She tells me where apple juice is on sale. We share silence.

It is seven-thirty.
I call Serena. I leave her a message. The rambling kind that, when it ends, does so abruptly.

It is eight o' clock.
I wait at the front door for Leena to come home. She arrives, candy-faced and sugar-smiling. Overtired, she struggles for sleep.

It is nine o'clock.
I make myself a cup of chai. I watch television even though there is nothing worth watching.

It is ten o'clock.
I wonder if Kal will be coming back. I want him to but don't know how to ask. There are so many questions in the asking that neither of us has answers for. We just take what the other one can give. And even then, we take it quietly. We say nothing after. We lie separately, staring at the ceiling, far from each other's arms, the space where Liam and I lay a chasm between us. Just as he falls asleep, I nudge him awake; I never let him stay. I tell him that Leena still comes into my room when she has nightmares and I don't want her to find him in my bed.

Although this is true, he knows it isn't the real reason that I won't let him stay but accepts it anyway. Accepts me any way.

It is ten-thirty.
I pick up my cup of cold chai and go downstairs to reheat it for the third time. I know I won't drink it. I'll just watch it turn in the microwave, listen

to the oscillating hum over rain, count the rain drops that hit the window, watch them spread into veins that stretch across my reflection and wonder why all I know how to do is wait. But for what I still don't know.

It is eleven o'clock.

A knock at the door.

"Is it too late?" Kal asks.

"No, it's fine." I open the door barely the width of half his shoulder. His arm scrapes the door jamb and rain beads off his jacket onto the hardwood floor.

"One hell of a storm tonight," he says as he hangs his coat up. "Leena asleep?"

I nod and follow him into the living room, where he turns off three of the four lamps before sitting down. "She had a great time at the movies. Thanks for taking her."

"I had a good time too. She's a great kid… Liam would've been proud of the way you've raised her. She's pretty incredible."

A silence follows. I never know what to say when he speaks of Liam so I say nothing.

"You know I love her like my own." Kal puts his arm over my shoulder and pulls me closer. "I love you both like–"

I raise my shoulders, pushing his words from my ears.

"What is it?" he asks.

"Nothing." I rush out of the room as though I've suddenly remembered that I've left milk boiling on the stove.

"When, Meena? When is it going to be something?" He follows me into the kitchen.

"What about Irmila?"

"What about her? She's the one that filed for the divorce."

I take my cup of chai out of the microwave and tip it into the sink, watch it circle the drain. "You could work things out."

"What's there to work out? We don't want the same things."

"And by things, you mean kids."

He nodded. "You know I want a family. I want what you have."

"You mean what I had."

"No, I mean what you have right now. You're so lucky to have Leena... Sometimes I think you spend so much time missing Liam that you can't feel anything for anyone else."

"This isn't about me. It's about you... You could still work it out with Irmila if you wanted to."

"No. It's too late. You know her. She's always thought that I loved you and well, now I realize that she's probably right." He presses his body against mine and I close my eyes to the weight of him, wondering who is giving and who is taking in this portrayal of love, in my betrayal of love.

Afterwards, I shower. I know the pulse muffles the sound of my tears and the soapy water excuses my red eyes. When I emerge, Kal is half-dressed. I wonder if he heard me crying this time.

"Do you hate me for this?" he asks, stretching his sweater over his head.

I find it difficult to answer the question and look away as he buttons his pants. In a way, I do hate him. I hate both of us for being a reminder of everything we've lost. Even my mother warned me, asking me what I would tell Leena when she was older. Would I tell her that I was once married to the man who was imprisoned for killing her father? A man who was Kal's cousin. "The wounds are too deep, too close," my mother told me. "You cannot heal one another." I tried to take her advice, but couldn't.

Kal is waiting for an answer. Unlike Liam, he is frightened of my silence. "I don't hate you, I just don't know what this is. Are we friends? Are we lovers? I just feel like I can't give you what you need."

"What I need is you."

"And is this enough?" I ask.

"It has to be," he says, walking out the door.

I rush down the stairs after him. "Kal, wait."

He stops at the front door. "I'll wait, Meena... I've always waited."

I let him go, but stand at the closed door with my hand pressed against it until I hear Leena's voice behind me.

"Is he coming back?" she asks, her eyes half obscured by the tumbling curls she refuses to let me cut.

I smile, scoop her up in my arms and brush the hair from her eyes. "Yes, but not today."

"Is he going to be my daddy?" I smile, though inside I feel old wounds opening.

"You have a daddy," I say, placing her into her bed, smoothing out her rumpled sheets. "He loved you very much."

She looks at Liam's picture by her bed. "Does it hurt to be dead?"

"No," I answer, punctuating my answer with a kiss on her nose before getting up to leave.

"What does it feel like?"

I climb into bed with her. "I'm not sure. Maybe like sleep."

"Like in "Sleeping Beauty?""

"Yeah, kind of."

"Will he ever wake up?" she looks up at me with his eyes.

I wrap my hand in hers and snuggle in, caressing her hair. "No, he won't." I hold her close until her breath softens and she falls into the long length of a dream. "It's okay, I've got you, you're fine... you're fine."

Everything Was Good-bye

ABOUT THE BOOK

Set in lower mainland British Columbia, *Everything Was Good-bye* is a moving modern-day story about a young Indo-Canadian woman named Meena who's struggling to find her place in the world. Caught between the traditional values of her family and her desire to have the same freedom as other Canadian women, Meena is faced with difficult choices—and her decisions will lead to tragic consequences for everyone involved.

We first meet Meena as a seventeen-year-old girl in her last year of high school. Her family immigrated to Canada when she was still a baby, and soon after that her father was killed in a workplace accident, leaving her mother with the task of raising six daughters on her own. It is an onerous task not only because she must support the family, but she must also ensure that her daughters are all placed in acceptable arranged marriages. As the youngest daughter, Meena is expected to obey her mother and follow in her sisters' footsteps: "We dressed modestly, hiding our flesh, living somewhere deep inside our skins—chaste and quiet." But as a headstrong and rebellious teenager, Meena refuses to accept the role that has been assigned to her.

In school, Meena is an outcast—she doesn't fit in with any of the social groups—until she meets Liam, who seems to be the only one who accepts her for who she is. Her mother forbids her from seeing him for fear of ugly rumours spreading in the close-knit Punjabi community, but Meena recklessly disobeys. Upon graduation, Liam announces that he wants to run away to Toronto and asks Meena to come with him. Torn between her desire to be with him and her obligations to her family, she hesitates, and he disappears.

A few years down the road Meena is a young career woman still living at home with her mother. Facing increased pressure to accept an arranged marriage, she finally agrees to marry Sunny, a successful lawyer and the son of a prominent Indo-Canadian family. Neither Meena nor Sunny are truly happy, but both agree to the marriage in order to please their families. But when Liam reappears in Meena's life she must confront her true feelings. She is faced with the difficult choice of leading a life that fulfills her family's expectations or a life that fulfills her own.

Debut novelist Gurjinder Basran has created a world filled with fascinatingly complex characters in a powerful, uniquely Canadian story. Beautifully written and searingly honest, *Everything Was Good-bye* is a novel that explores the meaning of love, the pain of heartbreak, and the journey toward self-acceptance. ∎

Q. What inspired you to write *Everything Was Good-bye*? How much of the story is based on your personal experience?

The idea for *Everything Was Good-bye* grew out of some journaling and storytelling my sisters and I were doing around our own shared history. While writing vignettes about my childhood, I found myself fictionalizing details and reordering events, and by doing so the stories seemed to get to a truth that the facts did not expose. This is, of course, the wonderful thing about fiction—you can abandon the facts in favour of the truth. Because *Everything Was Good-bye* was imagined and informed by portions of my own life, Meena and I share some history. I grew up in a similar environment and endured many of the same struggles with identity and cultural expectations. However, the more I wrote about Meena, the more she took on a life of her own, a life that ended up being quite different from my own. ▪

Q. The beginning of the book takes place in the early 1990s. There are a number of scenes in which Meena and her family are subjected to discrimination and racism. Do you feel that the situation in British Columbia has changed at all? Are people more accepting of different cultures now than they were back then?

From the early 1970s and onward, Meena's family experiences racism in a variety of ways. They endure violence, vandalism of property, prejudicial attitudes, and racial taunts, but as times goes on the racism becomes less overt, partly because society has become more aware and partly because of the growing diversity in the Canadian population. I've come to believe that this is still the case. Racism is not as obvious as it was, but prejudicial attitudes are still prevalent and often displayed without malicious intentions. Even though we have a multicultural country, there is still little cultural understanding, and as such many people form generalizations which can be harmful and lead to the marginalization of ethnic communities. ▪

Q. The family bond is a major theme in this book. Do you think it's possible to ever escape the pressures and expectations of this bond?

I don't think you can escape the bond of family, nor do I think you should. Family can be your greatest source of strength and community, and even though there are expectations that come with those relationships, there are ways to navigate those expectations. A big part of that navigation comes with communication and a deep understanding of self. It is difficult to engage in meaningful and fulfilling relationships when no one is clear about their intentions or why they are behaving the way they are. This is the case with many families. They tend to take each other for granted and work in hierarchies that are unearned. ▪

Q. Which characters were you most drawn to? Was there a particular character whom you found challenging to write about?

When I started writing, Liam was one of the first characters to appear on the page. He was full of contradictions, and unlike the other characters in the book he was at ease with it in a way that suggested he was at peace with himself or had accepted his limitations. Meena on the other hand was difficult to write about. Since I was drawing on some of my own experiences to inform her life, I thought writing her would be easy, but it actually made it harder until I got to the place where I could dissociate myself and start thinking like her rather than thinking like me. ▪

Q. Some may view Sunny as the most unlikeable character in the story. How do you feel about him?

Sunny is a product of his environment in much the same way Meena is. He was raised with certain norms and expectations that cause him to behave the way he does. His life sets him up with a false sense of entitlement and hers sets her up with an unfair sense of loss. I have a good deal of compassion for Sunny; he could have been a far better man than he actually was, and I believe that if he'd been willing, he and Meena could have built a life together—but both of them were so caught in their own pasts that they couldn't move forward. In the end it's only because Sunny was raised with entitlement that he feels the need to control Meena, or that he feels justified in his anger at her fleeting happiness. ▪

5. Marriage plays a large role in the lives of many of the characters. What does the author reveal about each of the characters through these relationships?

6. Before they're married, Sunny admits to Meena that he still cares for his ex-girlfriend, Jasmine, and that his parents wanted to keep him away from her. In what ways do you think his feelings for Jasmine affected his feelings for Meena? Do you think he would have ever loved Meena?

7. When Meena learns that she is carrying Liam's child, she tries to hide the truth from Sunny. Could she have handled the situation better? What would you do in her position?

8. When Meena unexpectedly runs into Harj at the store, they agree to sit down for coffee. During this reunion, there are a number of awkward moments with many things left unsaid. Do you think Harj will ever reconcile with her mother? Is the bond between sisters unbreakable?

9. Do you believe that Meena will one day marry Kal? Discuss what reasons Meena might have to change her mind? What could be her reasons to continue their current relationship?